I0611656

SETH FERRANTI PRESENTS
PRISON STORIES
VOLUME 2: BANGIN' BEHIND BARS!

Gorilla Convict Publications (St. Louis)
www.gorillaconvict.com

Page 166 modified photograph (Freepik - Freepik.com), Page 170 modified photograph and cover elements under Creative Commons Attribution-Share Alike 3.0 Unported (livepict.com).

ISBN 978-0-9889760-8-5

PRISON STORIES ②

TABLE OF CONTENTS

COOKIES AND CREAM
Fucking and Beefing Over a Female Staff Member in the Bureau of Prisons

My dumb ass waited all the way until I got to my unit to remember that I had left my master betting sheet back down in the Education Department. It was 8:05 and the department didn't close until 8:45, actually it closed at 8:00 to all other inmates except for me and Billy, the two orderlies.

Fa'real, whether it would still be open or wasn't even the issue. My ass just didn't feel like shooting all the way back down the hill in the rain. But because it was Tuesday night and a lot of dough was riding on the NBA games, not going back never became an option. I needed to know exactly who was betting on what so I would know how much I'd won or lost.

I was the type of bookie who liked having niggas' stamps, macks, or cigarettes waiting on them when they came to collect the next morning, mainly because I had it like that. I wasn't one of those chump-ass bookies who had to go in hiding for a day or two until he bummed up enough to cover those betters who he knew would punish his ass, while spinning the betters he was keel with or felt less threatened by.

"Yo, Crown!" I called my celly as I remained just inside the foyer. I spotted him coming from the microwave room. "Do me a favor. Put this bag in the room." I handed him my little gym bag I often used as a book bag.

"I gotchu son." Crown took the bag and kept it moving.

I turned and mentally prepared myself to bolt out into the rain then jetted down the hill like Jack without Jill. There was no running on the compound but damn that. As long as there was rain pouring on the compound there was going to be running on the compound.

I quickly made it underneath an overhang that allowed me to go the rest of the way without getting wetter. Shaking off, I dipped into the education building and shot straight to the library department which was located in a tiny section in the back of the building's one level department. Trying to go unnoticed by the staff on duty, Mrs. Riley or my co-worker Billy, I rushed to the middle of three huge book racks and hurriedly retrieved the book I had stashed my sheet in.

It wasn't until after I had placed the book back into position that I noticed how dim and quiet the department was. I mean certain areas of the department were lit while the majority of it was damn near blacked out. I let my vision scan the joint and peeped that the lights to the three small classrooms were off. The only source of light came from that area or was coming from the bathroom's open door at the end of the short hall. In fact, with the exception of Mrs. Riley's lit office, the bathroom's light was the only light on.

Growing a bit curious, I damn near tippy-toed down the hall in the direction of the bathroom. As I passed each darkened classroom, I looked for signs of either Mrs. Riley or Billy but neither were present. I reached the empty bathroom. I hesitated a moment, puzzled.

Even if he had just shot to his unit I would've ran into him on my way down. Unless . . . unless he had taken the opposite way out? As far as Mrs. Riley's disappearance was concerned, I thought that she might've been using the bathroom located inside her office. But I then began thinking that maybe I should just get my ass out of there before she popped up, saw me and asked me to do something. On that I decided to bounce but not before I was compelled to open the janitor's closet that was a couple of feet away from the bathroom. Once I did I got the shock of my life and all my questions were answered.

Billy and Mrs. Riley were in the damn closet fucking like dogs in heat! The closet was sort of long and narrow. Mrs. Riley was bent over with her head facing the direction of the wall. That and the fact that her dress was parachuted over her head prevented her from even noticing that I was present. Billy noticed. He continued pumping while we momentarily locked stares. If his facial expression had a voice it would've said, "FALL BACK MUTHAFUCKA!"

I quickly closed the door just as quietly as I had opened it and stood right in front of it. Thoughts of Billy's hands mounted on either side of Mrs. Riley's pale white ass, continuously winded itself causing my dick to get hard. Word ta-my-flimsy mattress I had the mind of going straight Cuban and making a reentry. But only this time in a way that would draw.

My co-worker Billy always stayed until 8:45 but would dip out early for Mrs. Riley's attention. I began thinking that her knowing that I had busted them would prompt her to offer me a reward for my silence. And since she didn't have to pull to grant my freedom the only other service she could possibly provide would be sex. Evidently she was up for that sort of thing. I'd been down for eight years and pussy would've been the next best thing to freedom.

Trust me when I tell you I had no intentions on reporting them, please don't get that twisted. I was no snitch on my case and certainly wasn't about to become a jailhouse rat. However, I would've liked to hank on her to fear that I would report her and not catching her in the act would have certainly lessened that fear. Having explained that— you know what it is—I reconsidered. Deciding not to let such a grand opportunity slip through my fingertips, I marched back to the closet and snatched the door wide open.

"Damn, man. What's up?" Billy asked. He was heated because my rude interruption caused Mrs. Riley to straighten up which in turn left him standing stupidly with a hard, condom covered dick.

"Y'all tell me." I eyed Mrs. Riley's stunned expression. It was an odd frightened but calm look.

"Yo, get the fuck outta here, man," Billy said while stuffing his piece back in his unbuttoned khakis.

Billy was from Philly and had a nice size to him. I was from NY and about as big as him and didn't give a fuck about his bark. "I ain't going no fuckin place nigga." I duplicated his aggressive attitude.

"What the fuck you want then?"

I fixed a cold stare between he and Mrs. Riley and said, "I'm tryin' to go—"

"You can leave, Mr. Griffin," Mrs. Riley's dumb white ass interjected. "Please, can you keep this to yourself?"

The silly ho's response revealed that she had misinterpreted my statement. "I'm not leaving," I said like a dumb ass. "I'm tryin' ta go but first I want my head swung." I eyed Billy knowing he knew what the hell I was talking about.

"Fuck outta here, man. She ain't giving you no muthafuckin head." He stepped out of the closet.

"What, nigga!" We squared off.

"No, no stop!" Mrs. Riley knifed in between us, keeping us both at arm's length. The last thing she needed to happen was for us two strong muthafuckas to start rumbling up in that bitch. "You don't understand, Mr. Griffin. Billy and I are in love—"

"I understand all of that," I cut into her statement. "And I ain't tryin' to come between you two love birds. I just need a fix and I'm gone."

"Nah, nigga. You gone without a fix," said Billy, flexing.

"No please, Billy." Mrs. Riley subdued him. "Okay, listen Mr. Griffin. What exactly is it that you want?"

"I want some head," I reiterated before spelling it out. "You know. A b-l-o-w j-o-b." Silence momentarily fell between us as she appeared to be considering my demand. And I guess after weighing her options, she looked at Billy and dreadfully nodded in agreement.

"Nah! Fuck that shit!" Billy flipped.

"No, Billy." She turned her back to me and pressed her hands hard up against his well built physique. "Please, sweetie. Let me just do it and get it over with. I can't afford to lose my job and end up locked up myself."

Once again silence fell. She let her soft words penetrate Billy's anger then after a few seconds she cautiously let up off him and moved down the hall in the direction of the building's exit.

"You hot ass nigga," Billy spat with venom.

The nigga called me a snitch and my character was something I held deeply. Under any other circumstances I would've had to take it to Billy's ass right then and there. But because I so badly wanted my dick sucked by his snow bunny, I decided to harshly swallow that bitter pill. "My paperwork is in the unit. Where's yours?"

"Nigga, I don't gotta show you shit."

"Yeah. That's what the fuck I thought," I responded. Behind me, I heard the lock click as Mrs. Riley secured the door.

"Yeah, whatever. Fuck you."

"Nah. It's fuck wit me." I matched his steely stare.

"Let's go in here." Mrs. Riley opened the door to the third classroom which was furthest down the hall. It was a wise suggestion too because the spot allowed us to view the entrance without being discovered. "We have to hurry because it's already eight twenty," she stated to remind us that recall was at 8:45.

It had been so long for me I doubted if I even needed half that time.

I moved to the teacher's desk just inside the room and leaned my tail up against it. Wasting no time I anxiously pulled out and watched as Mrs. Riley bent down and began slickening my log with her mouth.

It felt so good I wanted to close my eyes. I didn't because I had to keep them glued on Billy who stood at the opened door directly behind Mrs. Riley. He was grilling me hard and if looks could kill my ass would've been upstairs on line not too far behind Rick James.

To let the nigga Billy know that I'm never scared, I placed my hand on top of Mrs. Riley's head and guided her motions. My actions caused Billy's glare to harden. I assumed it also sparked some type of challenge because after a second he turned up his lips as if to say that Mrs. Riley was his piece of ass. To further prove it, he whipped it back out and lifted her dress and slammed his meat inside of her pussy like it was a refrigerator.

"*Uhmmm*," she moaned as Billy began smashing it doggy-style. He was pumping hard and furious while grilling me.

I, on the other hand, displayed only a slight grin. Not totally in response to his screw face but because Mrs. Riley had suddenly begun doing a better job on my knob. Unbeknownst to Billy she was bullshittin' until he'd started fucking her. It was like he had untamed the freak in her.

"*Uhmmmmm*," she moaned again then momentarily removed my dick from her mouth. She continued to slowly jerk it though. The sensation caused my juices to team up like the Yankees. I could tell that the pipe Billy was laying was feeling good to her because she tilted her head back facing me with her eyes closed and mouth wide opened. Her continuous hand work caused me to gun her down with my warm release.

She smothered my dick with her hand, face and mouth and I glazed her like a honey bun. But my dick was so hard it wouldn't go down, even after I had shot the load. Mrs. Riley appeared to be loving it too. While Billy steadily rode her, she opened her eyes and locked gazes with me. She let a smile surface underneath my scattered cum. Then on some porn movie type shit, she spat on my dick placed it back in her mouth and tore my cock up like it was a Bomb Pop. She worked me as Billy worked her.

"*Unt . . . Unnt . . . Unnnt*," she grunted as she began to get off. I could tell because while continuously jerking my dick she tilted her head back and her O-face was obvious. "*Uhmmm*," she moaned, placing me back inside her mouth. Seconds later, I dumped my second load and because Billy had frozen up, I figured he had blown a gasket as well.

"REEECALLLLL! REECALLLL!" The announcement roared over the department's PA system, instantly snapping us back into the reality of our environment. Mrs. Riley shot to her office, Billy slid to the closet and returned with a wet mop, and I straightened out items on the desk.

"Here come Soulman," I whispered to Billy as I watched the CO entering the building. He was actually Officer Mooney, but because he was white and often did a poor job at acting white, the compound secretly called him Soulman.

"What's up dudes? Y'all ain't done with this shit yet?" Mooney approached us in his usually spirited manner.

"Big Mooney, what's up?" I fronted while Billy returned the mop in silence. I figured he was upset still so I continued rapping in an attempt to draw all of the attention. "What your Boston mob gonna do against them Knicks tonight?" I asked on our way down the hall.

"You already know. We 'bout to crush y'all muthafuckas."

"Stop it. Y'all ain't got nothing coming." I laughed.

"A'ight homes. I don't wanna come to work tomorrow night and find out you done checked into the hole because your team sold you out." He laughed motioning toward Mrs. Riley's office while Billy and I headed out the door.

"Imagine that," I shot back, then moved out behind a wordless Billy. He being mad was a no brainer, but so was me not giving a fuck. We walked off in opposite directions. It had stopped raining and I didn't have to run back to the unit. I took my time and walked back behind a group of niggas that were either in my unit or one of the ones before.

"Damn, man. I was looking for you," said Vending Machine. His name should describe him. He stood at the very end of the concrete walkway that led to my unit. "These are all late games," he explained, extending a betting ticket and what appeared to be a bunch of loose stamps.

"Why didn't you holla at Rob?" I asked, naming my runner.

"Rob be on some bullshit with me," he snapped. It was true. Rob was hot and on top of that he'd always try and place bets with loose stamps that were often raggedy.

I didn't like the nigga neither. But if I turned away all the hot betters I wouldn't have had a ticket. "Nah, Vending. You on some bullshit. I told you about trying to pass me off these dirty ass stamps," I said, sorting through the dozen or so stamps. "How many's here?"

"Fourteen."

After plucking out six filthy ones I extended them back to him. "Here, take these shits to that muthafuckin bookie down on your end."

"C'mon, man. I would have to change the ticket and everything," he whined, leaving me hanging.

"Let's bring it inside fellas. Recall's been announced!" My unit CO who stood just outside the unit yelled out to all the loitering inmates who were in front of my unit handling their last minute business.

Out of fear of the CO spotting Vending accepting the stamps, I quickly drew my hand back. "Keep 'em. I'll bring you six good ones in the morning," Vending said.

"Your fat ass betta have my shit," I warned as we parted ways.

"I gotchu man!" he yelled back.

Once I made it inside the unit, I rushed to my cell, grabbed my mug, and raced to the ice machine. I needed a cold drink to go with the tuna fish sandwich I had planned on eating during 9:00 count. I returned to my cell and instead of putting together just one, I punished two tuna sandwiches and a half bag of Doritos. By the time the count cleared my meal was a wrap.

I hit the shower then returned to my cell and stretched out across my bottom bunk. It was halftime at the Knicks/Boston game and my celly was in the TV room so I calmed myself chilling out until the third quarter chilled. Relaxed, I chilled all the way up until I heard the CO popping the doors at 5:20 Wednesday morning. And even then I just laid still on my bunk thinking how Mrs. Riley literally sucked the energy out of me. That pleasant memory brought a smirk to my face that would've lasted all morning had I not subsequently thought about Billy and his remark about me being a rat. That shit erased the smirk clean off my face and motivated me up and out of bed. While that was a pill I had previously swallowed, it sure wasn't one I could stomach. I had to go check that nigga Billy. And I had to go do it first thing that morning.

In an attempt not to wake my celly, I moved about the dark room as quietly as possible, getting myself together. Once I was khaki suited and booted up, I slid out of the room. I went to the slop sink in the janitor's closet at the end of the tier to wash my face and brush my teeth then bounced back to the room and put up my shit. I left a second time but in the opposite direction to the TV room and waited for the unit's doors to pop. We were last out of the eight units so I knew it would be a minute. I stood at the huge window shifting my focus between the TV and the compound. From my vantage point I could spot and recognize the niggas that were either on their way to or from the mess hall.

"Damn, kid. What you doing up so early?" my man and homie, Breeze asked the second he entered the TV room and spotted me.

Practically everyone that I fucked with knew I worked in the evenings and rarely went to breakfast. So Breeze's question wasn't as crazy as it sounded. "One of those nights, kid," I responded in a way that meant I couldn't sleep.

"I can't tell. I went by the room last night to check you and ya ass was knocked out cold." We both displayed a slight chuckle. "Knicks got they ass busted. Stephan didn't play though."

"Word," I dryly stated. I then glanced out the window and peeped four dudes standing at the halfway point of my unit's walkway. I curiously strained my vision until I was able to recognize Billy and at least one of the other dudes that I knew. He was Billy's homie named GQ.

"The door open?" Breeze asked when he saw how fast I was moving out.

"Nah. Not yet," I said and kept it moving out onto the tier.

I raced down the steps onto the first tier and straight to the janitor's closet. I already had one *blicka* on me that I had retrieved from my stash spot in the upstairs janitor's closet but I wanted another one. I rambled around the closet until I was able to get my hand on my other *blicka*. Unlike the twelve inch, pointy tip, fiberglass *blicka* I had nestled down the side of my right boot, my second joint was a fourteen inch piece of steel that was a little thicker than an ice pick with a handle made thick from gray electric tape. I tucked that *blicka* down my waist then shot back to the upstairs room.

"What up, kid. You a'ight?" Breeze asked. He'd instantly picked up on my urgent demeanor.

I looked out the window to be sure that they were still there and they were. "Yo, c'mere," I responded. Because there were a few other niggas in the TV room, I practically whispered in Breeze's ear that I might have beef with some Philly cats. I pointed to the dudes that were chilling in front of the unit. "I need you to hold me down."

Without verbally responding, Breeze hurried off just as I had done moments earlier. He quickly returned to the TV room's doorway and gestured for me to step out. "What up? We gonna take it right to them niggas or what?" Breeze was trained to go.

"Whatever," I responded as we moved down the tier. I wasn't the type of nigga that ran around trying to pull all the homies in my beefs. If I fucked with you and you were around when it popped off then of course I expected you to step up and hold me down because I'd done the same for you. In other words, Breeze's willingness to move with me fell nothing short of what real niggas do. He was that way.

No soon as we got downstairs the doors popped. We stepped outside the foyer and paused at the top of the walkway. "Ayo, BX," GQ called out to me the moment our visions locked. "Can I holla at you for a second?" His tone was in no way aggressive. He had broke away from Billy and the others, indicating he had just come to play mediator.

"Chill," I mumbled to Breeze then stepped off to the side.

"What up?" asked GQ in a no-nonsense manner. "Ayo, homie. Ain't no beef." GQ smiled in an attempt to persuade me to relax. GQ was a stand up dude out of Philly who didn't fuck with hot niggas. He was a pretty boy who was supposedly getting a lot of dough out in the world. The way he carried himself and the way all of his homies looked up to him quickly established his credibility as being 'that nigga' from Philly' And his being on the set with Billy allowed me to believe that Billy was actually no rat himself.

"So, what's up?" I kept the same tone while carefully eyeing Billy.

"Yo, you and Billy trippin' you know what I mean. And I'm just trying to dead this shit—"

"LAST CALL FOR THE MORNING MEAL! LAST CALL!" interrupted the PA system.

"Ayo, fellas go eat. I'll holla at you when You come back up, Billy," GQ sent them off with that.

"Ayo, I'm good," I turned and said to Breeze.

"What up, Breeze?" GQ threw in his acknowledgement.

"A'ight. What up, G?" Breeze said then slid back into the unit.

I figured it was to put his *blicka* away. On the strength that I was still dirty, I suggested to GQ that we keep it moving. We slowly circled the compound while he filled my ear up with information. It turned out that he'd known about Billy and Mrs. Riley. They had been fucking for months GQ explained. And he was the only homie that Billy had told. GQ also went on to inform me that Billy had told him what had happened the night earlier between the three of us. GQ wanted to know if I had told my New York homies.

'Nah, that ain't the type of shit you go around telling niggas," I assured him. "But yo, man. The nigga called me a rat." I still needed to see Billy about that.

"Yeah he told me that." GQ lowered his eyes. "I already straightened that naw'mean. I told Billy that I knew for a fact that you're a stand up dude. So yo on the strength of our little friendship I'm asking you to let that ride homie?"

It's been said that over 90% of federal inmates are snitches. And on first sight, it was common to assume that the next nigga was a rat. Taking that into consideration along with the circumstances that surrounded the situation at the time Billy labeled me a rat, then throwing in GQ's apology on Billy's behalf into the equation, allowed me to easily exercise a pass for the out-of-line remark. "You got that," I responded.

"That's what's up." We clapped five. "So now where you and Billy stand on the pink toe?" He referred to Mrs. Riley.

"It's like this, kid, I stumbled onto their shit. It ain't like I was spying on them or all up in their business. I caught a staff member dead to rights and now I got the press game on that bitch. Surely y'all don't expect me to just fallback. I mean, I understand Billy's position. But, son, you have to understand mine too . . ."

"Yeah, no doubt." GC mulled my explanation and silence fell between us before he continued. "See Billy's short. He got a couple of months left and I know he don't plan on fucking with that bitch when he touches down . . . he betta' not." GQ smirked. "Seriously though. You niggas gonna have to share the pie. And no disrespect but I gotta put this out there. Can you share the pie without telling your homies? Me and Billy kept his shit on the hush, that's why you never heard any rumors about it and you was right there with the muthafucka— naw'mean?"

And that is no bullshit. Plus I'd seen too many niggas in the same situation get trapped off for running their mouths so I didn't plan on telling a soul. "Yo, that ain't even in the talk. But what about Billy? At the end of the day he's the one that's gonna have to be willing to share the pie."

"I got Billy," said GC. "The important thing is seeing that Billy goes home and not get caught up in any shit. I got a lot of good things waiting on Billy. And they're way bigger than this shit here."

"Yo, kid. If you got Billy . . . then it's all good." I came to a stop in front of my unit.

"THE DINING HALL IS NOW CLOSED!" announced the PA

"A'ight then, homie."

"After you get with Billy tell him to come holla at me." I watched him acknowledge my request before he bounced. I couldn't apply credence to our agreement until Billy and I were face-to-face and I could feel his vibe.

On my way back into the unit I was held up by Rob, my ticket runner. He told me that we'd got rocked. Damn near half the compound had winning tickets. I was fucked up because up until that convo, I had forgotten all about being a bookie. It's amazing what good head after so long without could do to a nigga.

Because work call had been announced we couldn't really get into the depth of damage that was done. He had to roll out but I told him to make sure he got back with me at lunch time. When I got to my cell I immediately noticed two cheese-egg sandwiches. They sat in two separate plastic gloves on top of my metal desk. My celly Crown had already gone off to work and because he was knocked out when I left I figured Breeze might've copped the sandwiches for me while he was down in the mess hall. One thing for certain, whoever had left them sure did look out, because I was starving. I punished those shits with an ice cold orange juice my celly had in his cooler then fell back across my bunk. I wasn't stretched out for three minutes before there was a light knock at my cell's door. I looked up and saw Vending Machine's fat ass face plastered to the opposite side of the glass.

"What's up?" he asked after I gestured for him to open the door.

He knew better than to pass the door frame so he stood out on the tier, blocking the entire section.

"What the fuck you mean, 'what's up'? Where's my six stamps?" I remained laying down.

"I hit!" he stated then displayed a grin that looked like he had just gotten through eating two scoops of butter.

"What that got to do with my six stamps?" I was starting to feel like he was playing me.

"C'mon man. Stop bullshittin'," he cackled.

"Get ya fat ass outta here and close my door." I eyed his disappointed expression. "See Rob after the count fat ass muthafucka," I told him.

He walked off but didn't close the door. I got ready to jump up and kick him in his fat ass but Breeze appeared and that ended it.

"Damn that nigga smell like shit!" Breeze fanned his hand. He stood just inside the room.

I laughed at his twisted facial expression. "You left those egg joints?"

"Yeah," he said.

"Good lookin' out."

"No doubt, homie. Everything good?"

"Yeah, yeah, no doubt. Me and the nigga Billy had a few words yesterday but we straight." I needed to give Breeze some type of explanation then assure him that it was over. "Yo, there's that *Street Team* book right there on my locker. Take that *Don Diva* too. They got that baller Joe Black in there. And the Kevin Chiles article is hot."

"A'ight kool. Let me get up outta here before they lock the doors."

"Later." I got up and closed the door. Breeze probably thought my room needed some airing out time but it didn't. Vending Machine's funky ass odor was out on the tier but still lingering in Breeze's nose.

I fell asleep and didn't wake up until minutes before the 4:00 p.m. count. I'd usually go out on the rec move after count and get my workout on before I'd report for work at 5:30, but I elected to take the day off. When the doors popped after count I bounced to the mess hall then straight to work. Normally I'd arrive fifteen and sometimes thirty minutes late. Billy nor Mrs. Riley never seemed to mind though and it had become clear to me why.

The moment I stepped into the building I spotted her seated at her desk and on the phone. She had her focus glued to a piece of paper and didn't even notice my presence. I kept it moving on my way to my station in the library. Along the way I eyed Billy sitting at his station across from me in the leisure department. He was signing out CD players and movie videos and didn't notice me either.

After setting up shop, then taking care of the few inmates that were at my station and curious as to why Billy hadn't come and hollered at me, I stepped to him. I wasn't up for that silent treatment shit—that was for bitches. I'd rather know if a nigga was friend or foe.

"Yo, what's up?" I approached Billy's counter once he finished taking care of the last inmate in line. It was time to know if there was gonna be drama or what.

"Ain't shit up . . . and Imma tell you like this: I'm not gonna help you or get in your way. How you carry it, that's on you." The way he sounded I could tell that he was not cool with the arrangement and only willing to adopt it on the strength of what GQ had in store for him on the bricks. "And another thing. Don't get carried away."

"You mean that literally?" I asked sarcastically.

"Both," he answered with a cold stare.

I brushed the nigga's glare off and returned to my station. All that shit he talked about not helping me went in one ear and out the other. Hell, he didn't help me the first fucking time. In fact, the nigga tried his hardest to cock block. And to think, earlier I thought it would be cool if Billy and I could work together—you know—hold each other down. But being how the nigga came off—fuck'em—I'd be better off moving on my own.

"Mr. Griffin, I need to see you in my office." Mrs. Riley popped up at my station but I was so deep in thought I hadn't even seen her coming. She walked off before I could respond and all I could see was the sway of her ass. I shot a glance over at Billy who was mean mugging me. Paying it no mind, I trailed her into her office.

"Have a seat please." She gestured to the small sofa that sat off to the side of her desk. "How are you today?"

"I'm good," I said. From my position I could see Billy's ass sweating us.

"That's great. Now how about you and Billy? Are you two okay?"

"Yeah. Me and Billy straight."

"That's terrific. So you understand the seriousness of this situation?"

"Of course I do."

"Excellent. Because it's vital that you keep this to yourself. Billy and I love each other and—"

"Excuse me, Mrs. Riley," I interrupted before she could get started with all that bullshit. "I don't mean to cut you off but let me tell you my story. I haven't had pussy in eight years and I got eight years to go. I wanted some last night but Billy was already in it and I didn't want his sloppy seconds." I paused while eyeing her blank stare. "Now I know you and Billy are in love and all of that. And trust me I'm gonna protect y'all's big secret. But also I want you to know that one favor deserves another."

"Mr. Griffin, please don't do this. Billy and I planned on getting married and having kids when he's released in the next couple of months."

"Mrs. Riley, you're *already* married."

"My husband and I are separated and will be divorced by the time Billy's home. And we plan to wed soon after." She had a wistful look in her eyes, as if living in fantasy land.

I wanted to drop it down on her, remind her that she was a long time married with kids and no longer a young woman. But I reminded myself of my angle and measured my tone. "Y'all still can get married. But it would be fucked up if he got out just as you were getting locked up yourself." I had to get raw with her. There was no need to be cutting corners because she was clearly in love with Billy even if he wasn't in love with her. I was cool with that. But in order to protect their love, her job, and possibly her freedom, she was going to have to understand that her fairy tale ending rested in my hands.

"What favor do you want?" she responded briskly as if she got the picture.

"I want some pussy." I raised my tone. "I want some pussy tonight."

At ten minutes to eight that night, I watched as Mrs. Riley led Billy into her office. I figured that she was going to break the news to him that she was going to let me gut her out. Well she probably wasn't gonna put it to him in those exact words, but gutting her was my intention. They chatted for all of five minutes before Billy stormed out of her office.

I watched the sucka ass nigga return to his station, only to snatch up his gym bag. I wasn't worried about him doing anything dumb because with eight years to go, opposed to his two months, and possibly being put back on by GQ, he had way more to lose than I did.

Actually, his punk ass attitude nearly tickled me. I mean what the fuck was the nigga's problem? It wasn't like Mrs. Riley was a dime. She was a seven and a half and I tacked on two and a half points because her head game was official. I also added another point because we were locked up. As the time drags on even a worn out ho starts looking like a queen. In all reality she was a four and that's not even mentioning the bitch was on sitcom status—married with children.

The second Billy left the building, I slid over to his station and announced that it was time to return all the equipment. I'm usually not on no shit like that, but I had to straighten up his station, my station, and sweep the joint. Besides it was five minutes to eight anyway, so niggas couldn't beef.

I collected all the equipment then went back to my station and gathered all the newspapers and magazines everybody had left out. As I began to.sweep the place up I noticed Mrs. Riley locking the door, something she must've forgotten to do the previous night. I guess she vowed to stay on point. I was glad too. I didn't think she could handle too many muthafuckas pressing her.

She returned to her office while I swept the place in record time. Actually I'd broken plenty of records that night. Some of the equipment and shit I didn't even sign in. We'd ordinarily mop, but as you should know, this was no ordinary night. Besides, my dick was so hard I felt like I had three legs and made like a tripod around the room. I returned the broom then checked my bullshit and saw that it was only ten after 8:00. *Kool*, I thought. That gave me thirty minutes to work with—plenty of time to get a nut or two.

I stood by the janitor's closet a minute longer thinking that Mrs. Riley would be appearing any second and when she didn't, I peeped down the hall and spotted her at her desk still. "Mrs. Riley. Everything's all straight," I called to her through the open office door.

"You can go get a broom and mop bucket," she responded while jotting down information on some stationary. I'll be around to open the classroom in a moment."

Clean up time is done, bitch, I stood there thinking for a second, then quickly granted her request. Moments later and before I could get the half filled mop bucket out of the closet, she was making her way down the hall. She had on a long gray skirt and a matching buttoned up blouse. Now if I had to judge her based on ass and tits alone, she'd be a nine.

"Just leave that stuff sitting in the hall," she instructed as she opened the door to the last classroom.

I did as told and followed her into the dark classroom. She came to a complete stop at the same desk she blew me on and turned around with an extended condom in her hand. "Put this on," she ordered and eyed me as I did it. Her tone and attitude was supple. I sort of felt like I was about to bone an intelligent professional hooker.

Once she confirmed that the condom was actually on, she turned, faced the desk, and with her skirt pulled up on her back she bent over resting her hands on the desk. A tiny ray of light that seeped in from the hall allowed me to quickly examine her firm, bigger than average white girl's ass. I spread the cheeks and caught a clear view of her reddish-pink pussy. Because it looked good enough to eat, I used a finger from my right hand and slowly swiped at it one time.

"Don't worry," she said as she looked back over her right shoulder and saw me sniffing at my finger. "I take very good care of myself."

Most older women usually do and from the smell of it she was telling the truth. I might've been buggin', but her shit smelt like strawberries. In fact, her pussy smelt so sweet I stooped down and stuck my tongue in the muthafucka. I elected to try and put myself in a position to make her want to give me the pussy instead of having to continuously threaten her. I licked and sucked on her shit like it was the last of a mango.

"I . . . I thought you wanted to fuck me?" she was barely able to get the words out while riding the wave of my tongue.

"Oh, I'm gonna fuck you," I whispered in her ear and replaced my mouth with my hand. I stuck two fingers up her wet shit and finger fucked her while eyeing the huge clock on the hallway. It was 8:25 which allowed me twenty more minutes. "You like that?" I put my lips back to her ear. Though she refrained from answering, by the way she was grinding on my fingers, I could tell that she did. "What's up, baby? You ain't gonna talk to me?" I lightly tugged at her ear.

"I . . . I like it," she broke down and submissively answered.

"Can I fuck you now?"

"Yes . . . Oh, yes," she cooed.

I took my wood like dick and patted it three times on the very end of her back, just above the crack of her ass. I wasn't even sure if it was meant to enhance the pleasure. It was just a move I'd been longing to do. I'd gotten it from one of my DVD movies I'd sometimes secretly watch.

"*Oohhhh*," Mrs. Riley sighed when she felt my log creating space within her.

Her insides felt soft and warm. My hormones began to stir up like a quiet storm. With my hands on either ass cheek, I was digging her out like I was drilling for oil. Mere moments later, while it may have not been oil, Mrs. Riley's jerking and shivering let me know that I had struck fluids just as warm and rich. As she orgasmed, her pussy caused me to fill the condom up with rich warm fluids of my own.

I pulled out of her while eyeing the clock at the same time. It read 8:40 giving me just five minutes. It was going to be close but I knew I'd make it. I shot in the bathroom and Mrs. Riley disappeared down the hall. I carefully worked the rubber off and flushed it. Once it was gone, I mopped from the bathroom all the way back to the desk, like I was cleaning up the scene of a crime.

As "REEECALL! REEECALL!" sounded out from the tinny speaker I straightened out the desk, closed the door and was ready to go before Soulman showed up. Mrs. Riley spotted me waiting by the door then came out of her office. She kept her focus down at her keys, purposely I thought, until she reached the door and left without saying a word

In the three weeks that passed, I fucked Mrs. Riley three times. And if I had to judge her on the pussy and head game, she'd finally earn the ten. However, I had no choice but to label her the gift and the curse. You see, after the first time I fucked her, the next two times it damn near felt like she was fucking me. That was the gift of it all. But the curse was that since I've been smashing her my ticket business fell off, my weight lifting fell off, and my half ass friend status with Billy was dropped to full fledged foe status. It was all going down the drain with each flushed condom.

But fuck Billy anyway. He was the last of my concerns. And even the weight lifting was secondary. It was the near demise of my ticket business that had me sick. I mean ever since dealing with Mrs. Riley I hadn't been sweating the games or nothing. Fa'real all a nigga did was sleep while muthafuckas were banging my ticket out left and right My head was getting hit so much at one time I thought that Rob, my runner, was possibly scheming with Billy to take me down. I mean Rob was from Philly so it wasn't like my theory was farfetched. And word-ta-my flimsy mattress, if it wasn't for Breeze convincing me otherwise, no telling what I would've done to that nigga Rob—Billy's ass too.

All of that shit was out the window though. After wrapping shit up at work one night, while mopping I contemplated on how to step to Mrs. Riley and demand a new favor. It had nothing to do with sex. That was sewed up. I needed to make a major leap into a new hustle. My new demand would be to get some weed. I needed dough and if Mrs. Riley was going to continue sending Billy money slips, she would be in need of dough too. At least that's one way I'd thought about presenting it to her. Regardless of whether she needed dough or not, I needed it. And that alone became reason enough—fuck it.

It was Tuesday night, my night to fuck her. Over the past two weeks the only time Billy and I spoke was that one night we sorted out a little bullshit schedule. He had Mondays, Wednesdays and Fridays and I had Tuesdays and Thursdays. Fuck it, she was his first so I didn't mind falling short a day. Fair was fair, even in prison.

By the time I got through mopping, it was 8:15. I put everything away then marched into Mrs. Riley's office as if it was my cell. Our relationship had grown a little bit and I charged that to the ninja I had been putting on her and the last two Tuesday nights when I just talked with her, fucking her brain instead of her pussy. She still claimed to be in love with Billy though, which was good. I wasn't trying to make her love me. I just wanted to make her feel like she needed to do things for me as if she loved me.

"Would you like one of these doughnuts?" Mrs. Riley paused from typing on the computer to point at a large Dunkin' Donut box that sat on her desk.

I took three. Not because I wanted them but because they were from the street. Anything from outside tasted as good as a four star restaurant, even the day-old Dunkin' Donut she'd been setting out. I imagined Billy was getting hooked up too with pizzas, quarter pounders, deli sandwiches, and little shit like that. All of that shit was tasting so good, I sometimes felt while I was out in the free world when I took a fast food drive through for granted.

"Goodlookin," I said and it seemed to slightly tickle her. I knew why too. It goes back to that night she had given me a double cheeseburger from Wendy's and I said good looking and she thanked me as if I was complimenting her. When I explained that I meant the burger, we cracked up laughing. For the record though, she looked a'ight that night.

"How's your son?" She kept her focus on the computer screen.

"He's good. He had a basketball game tonight," I proudly stated.

"Really? That's terrific! How old is he again?"

"Seven."

"Wow! And he's already a little athlete, huh? How many points did he score tonight?"

"I don't know," I admitted. "I'm on phone restriction. The DHO took my phone privileges three and a half weeks ago."

"Why?" She paused and looked up from her work computer.

"For being down at rec without a rec pass."

"And what does that have to do with the phone?"

"Go figure?" I shrugged my shoulders.

"What a jerk." She resumed typing. "Would you like me to see what I can do about it?" Her thin fingers continued to drum on the keyboard.

Until she had asked, I didn't know why I hadn't pressed her for phone calls.

"Yeah, that's what's up."

She reached into a desk door and offered me her mobile phone. Take this and go in the bathroom. Without delay, I took the joint and slid into the bathroom. It had been awhile since I had used one, so it took me a minute to navigate the menus and buttons. Soon I was poppin' and called everyone I could think of: my seed and his mom, my ex-girl—had to curse her out because she appeared to be more concerned with how I called than the fact that I had called. I only rode that call for about eight minutes. I started to get open but checked the clock and saw that it was 8:25. I wondered if it was time to pop the question—or demand, more specifically. I deleted the call log and then stepped back into her office.

I peeped Mrs. Riley stooped over her desk sorting through paper-work paying me no mind. I noticed the camera icon on the phone and clicked it to open the app. Like a cinematographer I carefully positioned the view screen to capture the curves of her ass and keep her head out of view. I couldn't help but brag about my exploits to my boy Big Mack in the street.

GETTIN' IT — BX, I quickly texted along with a peach emoji. I had told GQ I wouldn't talk about what was going on but Mack was straight and I was confident that gossip wouldn't trickle back behind bars. I deleted the message and blocked his number so Mrs. Riley wouldn't find out.

"Thanks," I said as I handed her the phone.

"What happened to *good lookin*?" She said it funny as hell.

"Yeah, that too," I chuckled as I sat on the sofa. "Mrs. Riley, I need you to do something." I got serious, back into press mode. She knew it too because she froze and stared at me like I had suddenly turned into another person. "I need you to bring me in something."

"Wha . . . What is it?" she stammered.

"Some weed." I bluntly stated. One, because the clock was against me, and two, there was simply no other way to put it.

"Please tell me you're kidding?" her eyes instantly became glassy.

For a split second I almost wished I were. "No, I'm not kidding."

"I can't," she flat out cried.

"Yes you can, Mrs. Riley," I calmly replied as if I was trying to convince her that she could fly a plane that lost its captain.

"Didn't you say your husband was a big pot head?" I took her withdrawn silence as a yes. "So I know you know where to get it from. All I need is an ounce. I'm even gonna split the profits with you," I said with a devilish grin.

"REEECALLLL! REEEECALL!" called out the intercom letting me know my time was getting short.

"Please, Mrs. Riley. I need you to do me that favor," I said as I rose to my feet. "And if you don't tell Billy, I won't tell Billy." I said then stepped out of her office. Before I could reach the exit I spotted Soulman at the door.

"Yeah, dude! What I told ya ass?" Soulman shouted out to me. "Didn't I tell you them Celtics was gonna break your boys!" He was loud as hell. I was glad though. I knew he had alarmed Mrs. Riley to go in the bathroom and collect herself.

"You got that, but my boy didn't play," I made an excuse.

"I don't give a rat's ass about who didn't play. I told you y'all was gonna get that ass kicked. Didn't I?"

"Whatever. We got our asses kicked this time," I admitted.

"Yeah, now burn the road up," he said with a smug laugh and I bounced. "Let me see ya head get small!" he yelled as I grew distant.

"Go suck a fat man's dick, cracka," I replied under my breath. I laughed about that all the way up to the unit.

The next evening I showed up for work at 5:15. I was there fifteen minutes early for two reasons. One, I ain't gonna front, I was anxious as hell. After lying awake all night thinking about it, all sorts of crazy thoughts ran through my head. For instance, what if Mrs. Riley had gotten fed up and decided to set me up in trade for leniency? Or what if she'd gotten busted? Surely she would flip on me? I mean that's the type of shit that was rambling through my mind. The second reason I showed up early was because if indeed my angle had worked I wanted to pick up my weed before Billy came to work. I did not need that nigga peeping my move.

As soon as I arrived at the locked education door, Mrs. Riley appeared and unlocked it. She watched me enter, then quickly locked it and led me into her office. She nervously handed me a small brown paper bag, folded over, and sealed with so much duct tape, you think she was smuggling the Queen's jewels.

"See how easy that was?"

"Please, just put it away before Billy comes or someone else sees you."

"Don't worry. I got this." I crammed the bag down in my back pocket then covered it with my long shirt. At that point I erased all doubt of anything going wrong. "Trust me, Mrs. Riley. If anything goes sour you don't have to worry about your name coming up in anything."

"I hope and pray you're speaking the truth," she said as she escorted me out of her office.

"U.S. vs. Griffin, look it up." I invited her to visit my case for assurance. I was guilty of many things but being a rat was not one of them.

Before she could unlock the door to let me out, Billy along with a few other inmates arrived. It was common for either Billy or myself to be inside by the time anyone showed up so I wasn't too concerned with any of the other inmates becoming suspicious. Billy on the other hand seemed to be staring at us in a way that caused me to believe he'd suspected that something was up. Once the door was opened, instead of matching his glare like I'd normally do I fixed my focus past him and bounced through and around the group like a cop through traffic. I made it up and into my unit with ease and went straight to Breeze's cell.

"Where ya celly at?" I asked Breeze as I stepped into the room and closed the door behind me.

"I don't know. He might be down at the gym," Breeze responded from his top bunk. He was in a lying position and reading the *Street Team* book I had given him. "Yo, this book is good as hell!"

I already knew that and instead of commenting on it I got right to my intended issue. "Yo, check this out." I placed his shit sign in the door's small window then pulled out the bag.

"What is it?" He rested the book on his chest while taking the bag from my extended hand.

It took him a minute to unwrap it but as he started to get a whiff of the green he tore away the paper like it was Christmas morning. "Oh shit!" He popped up like toast and grinned. "This you?" he asked.

"That's *us*, fam." I matched his grin.

"Damn, kid. This shit looks like a whole ounce?" He said while dumping out the weed on top of the *Don Diva* magazine.

"It is, yo. How much dough we looking at?" I wondered out loud.

"This shit is about twenty-five hundred." Breeze quickly did the math in his head.

Twenty-four hundred dollar profit, I thought. "Can you handle it?" I asked, already knowing the answer.

He gave me a look to say I should already know his answer.

"A'ight, kool," I said.

"Yo, just play the tier while I bag some of this shit up," he instructed while ripping pages out of a notepad. I peeked out from behind the shit sign to make sure the coast was clear and once I saw that it was I stepped out onto the tier leaving his sign in his window. I shot four doors down to my room and snatched a chair and Nikki Turner's

Project Chick book off my locker then quickly returned and posted up along the wall next to Breeze's room. I had him in mind before I'd even chosen to demand the weed.

Breeze used to move crazy weed on the compound when his shorty was knocking the doors down and blessing him on the VI. At one time his name rang over the PA system every other weekend. Then all of a sudden it just came to an end. I wasn't sure exactly what had happened between him and his girl because I never asked. Shit simply happened and the green stopped coming.

That's what was also cool about our relationship. There weren't a bunch of unnecessary questions. I mean if I had rolled up on anybody else and flashed the weed folks would start questioning where I scored it. Simply telling Breeze the weed was mine was good enough—he didn't press me on the details.

"Ayo, BX!" Billy angrily called as he marched down the tier. And behind him was one of his homies, someone other than GQ. "What the fuck is up with you? What the fuck you trying to do, get me a new beef?"

"What the fuck is you talking about clown?" I stood up and sat the book on the chair. I could only guess that stupid ass Mrs. Riley had told him about the weed.

"You know what the fuck I'm talking about nigga." He lowered his tone so that only I could hear. "I told ya fuckin dumb ass not to get carried away—"

"Who the fuck you think you talking to?" I said, narrowing the distance between us.

"Ya bitch ass," he said just as Breeze opened the door.

And even if Breeze hadn't heard Billy's last comment we were still gonna have to get it on. I mean this nigga didn't seem to have a problem calling me out of my name. "I got'cha bitch ass, nigga. Let's go in the TV room."

Billy and his man marched behind me and in front of Breeze. I started to head to the upstairs TV room but with it being tuned to sports that it would be automatically crowded with prisoners catching the action.

"Why don't y'all take it down to rec?" Billy's man suggested

"Nah, we got McDiggins on right now." Everyone knew he was a CO that stayed in the office and on the phone. "We can get this shit on right in here." I came to a stop in front of the TV room where the news was on. I knew it wouldn't be but a few old heads in there because all the young cats either hung in other rooms watching videos on BET or making bets on basketball and football.

"Ayo, Billy. Man you too short for this bullshit," his man said once he realized it was really going down.

"Fuck this nigga. Imma knock his ass out." Billy was clearly fed up and not backing down.

Instead of riff-raffing with the nigga, I did the customary thing and moved to his man so that he could frisk me for any weapons while Breeze did the same to Billy. Once I was declared clean I backed into the TV room facing Billy who entered almost immediately after. There were three elderly black dudes and two old white cats in the room and I'd heard their chairs frantically screeching to the side as they instantly recognized what was going down.

"What are you two brothas doing?" One old man tried to intervene while at the time backing out of the way.

"Get the fuck out the way, pops," I said with my balled fists held high and adrenaline on blast.

Billy swung with a wild right hook that I ducked. I came right back up with an uppercut that was just as wild, I missed everything too. We were both clearly over anxious and a bit rusty. I was at least. Billy threw another punch, this time it was sort of a straight right jab that landed almost flush with my jaw. It stung and momentarily forced me to take a step back. I noticed he was going to try and aggressively follow up so I lunged a left jab as he stepped forward and caught him just above his right eye. I knew I had caught him good because my knuckles began to tingle.

My blow wasn't enough to stop Billy though. He came back with a whistling over hand that probably would've Roy Jonesed me had it connected. It missed real bad though, I was able to tag him with a short jab of my own. This one landed square on his left jaw, injecting a heavy dose of my punching power.

Billy crashed back into the wall but bounced right back up off it as if it were ropes. He shot back at me so fast I didn't have time to protect myself from his left hook that crushed onto the top of my head. It rocked me too, allowing him to follow up with a grab and attempted body slam. My strong hold around his neck is the only thing that prevented me from being slammed down onto the floor. Instead, we both went down together.

"Break that shit up. Niggas is coming!" I heard Breeze call out as our tumbling came to a halt up against the wall. "Grab ya man and Imma grab mine," Breeze continued.

With a lot of effort they were able to pry us apart and separate us so that we stood at opposite sides of the small room. "You a'ight nigga?" Breeze asked, pressing up on me like as if he was my trainer.

I was breathing so hard I could do nothing but respond with a nod.

"You bleeding kid. Take ya shirt off you got mad blood on it," Breeze said. He visually searched my body after I removed my blood stained shirt. "That's not you," he said before turning to Billy. "Ah, shit. Yo, go get a towel," Breeze instructed someone when he realized that the cut over Billy's right eye was bleeding profusely.

"Take your shirt off," Billy's man told him. He snatched the blood stained shirt and balled it up until he could produce a clean enough section of it to place over Billy's eye.

"Bring him to my room, homie," a guy from Philly suggested. Knowing that the important thing was now to try and keep either of us from getting locked up for fighting, they rushed off one way and Breeze and I rushed off the other.

We made it to my cell and our rowdy entrance caused my celly to jump clean off the top bunk. "Go get some ice," Breeze told him. "Run some cold water over your face. You got a big fuckin' knot on your forehead. I gotta go make sure the TV room's clean," Breeze spat out then jetted.

Within minutes everything seemed to be calming down. With the exception of the lingering nosey muthafuckas that were slowly pacing back and forth across the first tier it was hard to tell that something had popped off.

"Yo, that nigga's shit bleeding crazy," Breeze came back to my room informing me of Billy's condition. "He gotta go to medical and get that shit stitched up."

"Damn, you know they gonna lock 'em up," I said.

"I don't know. Maybe he can sneak in the gym and say one of the dumb bells fell on him?" Breeze began to reach for straws. While

Breeze's idea sounded good, the gym was just too far of a walk. And on top of that, not only the rec officers but COs stayed hanging out in the gym. To try and make it all the way to the gym and then around to the weight pile without being spotted by staff would've been highly difficult.

I worked to find a quick solution that would hold water. "You know what? We got a better chance of making it down to the library," I suggested.

"The library?" Breeze arched an eyebrow at me.

"Yeah, we can say that one of those big ass *Black Law* dictionaries fell off the shelf."

"You buggin'," Breeze said as he waved his hand at me. "Mrs. Riley ain't gonna fuck around and both you niggas are gonna get locked up."

From the outside looking in, Mrs. Riley did possess that type of attitude. You'd swore she hated inmates. At one time I thought that way too. But boy did I find out differently.

"Nah, we got Mrs. Riley," I said without him knowing the half of it.

"And what you gonna tell her about your knot?"

Even though it didn't matter, for argument sake, I suggested, "I'll just say some books fell on me too. Besides, once Billy goes into her office and says the book fell on him she's gonna send him to medical and that's a wrap."

"Yeah, but you know medical gonna call the lieutenant's office." Breeze continued to argue against my plan.

"So what? As long as Billy sticks to the story and doesn't admit to having a fight we're good." I spoke from close experience. My man Rolex once got lumped up and swore up and down it wasn't from a fight and beat the investigation. "Trust me, fam. It'll work."

I eyed his uncertain expression. Finally Breeze decided that it was the right play and went to drop the game on Billy. Soon after, the four of us were able to make it down to the library without me or Billy being recognized by any COs. Actually, luckily for us there were none out walking the compound.

I had my skully and baseball cap on which made it difficult for inmates to immediately spot my knot. Billy had a thick small piece of cloth taped over his eye covered by a skully and a cap worn low. One would've had to directly approach us in order to notice our bruises.

By the time we stepped into the building I spotted Roach over in the small typing area. He was an elderly white dude who was the jailhouse lawyer and also the library's weekend orderly. Whenever Billy and I both were gone he knew to automatically hold us down.

"Ayo, Roach. Good lookin' out!" I yelled out to him, letting him know that we were back.

"Sure thing." He never looked up from his typewriter.

I turned to Breeze and Billy's man and suggested that they break out so that Billy and I could handle it from there. They did and for the first time in nearly a month Billy and I saw eye-to-eye on a common goal— keeping our asses from getting locked up! We corrobated our stories one more time then walked into Mrs. Riley's office.

"Oh my god!" Mrs. Riley stood up with a hand over her mouth. She was instantly unraveled by our bruises that were revealed the second we removed our caps and skullies. "You two shouldn't have never fought." She figured it out at once. And because the bitch ran her mouth I didn't expect her not to.

"Mrs. Riley, you have to call medical," I said, gesturing to the rag Billy held pressed up against his eye. "He needs stitches."

"And tell them what?" Her concern thickened.

"Tell them that we told you a bunch of books fell from the top shelf," I said. It was a very questionable story but it was ours and we just had to stick to it. Plus, by her saying that we reported it opposed to her saying she'd actually seen it alleviated any problems for her when and if it came down to an investigation.

"But there's no mess over there," she countered.

"Don't worry about that. We're about to go over there and make that happen right now," I said.

"When you call you have to act like yourself," Billy added.

"Yeah. Do it like you don't believe our story," I threw in. I eyed the confused expression on her face then added, "Just trust us. The most that'll happen is we'll go to the hole for a fighting investigation."

Billy and I left her office and went over to my station and staged the accident. The noise of the crashing books drew the attention of several inmates, the exact attention we were aiming for. Before they could gather around Billy planted blood on the huge heavy *Black Law* dictionary then allowed the cut over his right eye to bleed. I, on the other hand, held a hand up to my forehead as if a book had hit me as well.

"You niggas a'ight?" asked the first inmates on the scene.

"Oh shit, Billy, you're bleeding." another gawker chimed in.

I turned to Billy and looked stunned. "Go tell Mrs. Riley to call medical. Me and Roach got this."

"You need to go to medical too," Roach studied my knot with a concerned look.

"Nah, I'm a'ight."

"No, son. I'm telling you. It's a bad swell. These damn books. I told Mrs. Riley that they were dangerous up there," he added. Roach was the perfect witness. "You two ought to file on these sons of bitches."

"Will you hook up the paperwork?" I fronted.

"Damn straight," he quipped, going along with our play.

"Bet. I'll see you when I get back from medical," I said, holding the lump on my head.

By the time I got to Mrs. Riley's office Billy had already been rushed off to medical. I started to tell her I needed to go also, but she hit me with some disturbing information first. She informed me that I was wanted at the lieutenant's office. "They just called me for you," she said with crazy fear in her voice.

I tried not to look concerned because I didn't want to scare her anymore than she already was. "Somebody probably dropped a note," I said, calmly. "Trust me Mrs. Riley, everything is cool."

On my way out of the building I told one of my homies to tell Breeze that I had to go to the office. I kept it moving until I pulled up on the two COs that were posted up in front of the lieutenant's office.

"Who are you?" one of the officers asked.

"Griffin."

"Go sit inside. The LT will be right with you."

I sat in the waiting area for about ten minutes before the next officer came out and gestured for me to follow him. He led me to the LT's door and informed him that I had arrived before he directed me to step in.

"What's up, man?" the LT lively stated. He was a white dude and a straight asshole. "Have a seat, Mr. Griffin." He nodded to the sofa that sat in front of his desk. His tone was urgent yet calm.

"What's up, LT?" I placidly responded while taking a seat.

"Wow. That's nice." The LT directed his comment about my knot to the CO who stood beside the large desk.

And just like the bootlicker that he was, I knew the CO was gonna add something slick. "I sure hope you got the license plates of that truck?" he said, smartly.

"So Mr. Griffin. How can I help you?" The LT fixed a wicked stare on me.

"How can you help me?" I asked, visually confused. *You called me down here cocksucker*, I thought but held my tongue. With this guy it was simply the beginning of a word play game he was about to try and put on me. It's a game where he would try and trick me into giving him enough evidence to stick a fighting shot on me. "Mrs. Riley said you wanted me?" I responded confused.

"Oh, I wanted you?" he and the CO eyed each other with silly looks as if they had no idea what I was talking about. "Why would I want you?"

It was a shame that niggas even got paid to do this shit, I thought and because I knew he was full of shit, I played just as dumb. "I must've misunderstood her. My bad." I rose to my feet, attempting to leave.

"No, no, no. Sit down." The LT's tone turned serious. "What the hell happened to you?" He pointed at my knot.

"Some books fell off the shelf in the library," I said and studied his slightly amused expression.

"Come on, Mr. Griffin. You got a better story than that?"

"Story? That's the only story."

"Yeah, well what if I told you I got another story?" he baited me.

"If it ain't the same as mine I'd say you got the wrong story," I said matter-of-factly.

"So those same books are the reason why inmate Cole is over at medical getting eight stitches?"

"Some people's heads are harder than others," I quipped.

"Well, my sources tell me that you and Billy had a big fight up in your unit."

"I'm sure they did. Maybe you need to get some new snitches?"

"What were you and Billy fighting over?" The LT ignored my last comment as he pressed me hard.

"There wasn't no fight. I told you the books fell on us."

The LT appeared to dwell on my last statement then turned to the CO and asked, "Is Cole still over at medical?"

"No, sir. He's out front," the CO said.

"Alright. Take this guy over to medical and when they're done with him give him a new home," said the LT, indicating the hole awaited me.

Right after leaving medical I was escorted to the hole. I could only imagine that Billy was going through the same bullshit interrogation as I did and hoped that he was handling it as well as I did.

A month and a half later, Billy and I were still in the hole pending a fighting investigation. Because we continuously stuck to our story they had no evidence to charge us with fighting. It didn't matter how many of his snitches saw and reported it. He had nothing unless a staff member witnessed it or we admitted to it. And because he had no such luck he decided to keep us locked down until Billy or I broke or until Billy went home.

I'd learned that piece of information from Mrs. Riley a week prior when she made her weekly rounds to the hole to drop off reading material for the inmates. Mrs. Riley's truth was also confirmed by my counselor four days later when he told me I'd be going back to the compound in about three weeks if nothing changed.

My counselor and I were jive kool and that was his way of telling me to stick with the story. I was going to do that anyway. I mean the longest the LT could've had held me for was ninety days and I already had half of that in. But my counselor's tip that I was going back to the pound produced a silver lining in a dark cloud. I waited patiently and plotted my return. Between my relationship with Mrs. Riley and my work with Breeze, the compound would be in for a crazy storm.

THE DOWN LOW WITH CO'S
Why Do Female Prison Guard Keep Having Sex with Inmates?

As incarceration numbers have topped out in recent years thanks to what looks like the beginning of the end of the war on drugs, women have gained a stronger foothold in the prison industry, getting jobs that—like so many others in America—have traditionally been dominated by men. But along with that progressive change has come a steady drip of lurid tales about sex between guards and inmates. The news routinely reports shocking stories of correctional officers that get busted getting down behind bars and getting charged with sexual contact with inmates, punishable by up to four years in prison.

We probably shouldn't be too shocked, though. There is no rule, regulation, or state of affairs a savvy prisoner cannot subvert. This has been proven many times over and is confirmed when you talk to long-time inmates.

"I love when I see a new, young, and naive female working in prison," says a convict we'll call Mack. He has spent the better part of the last 20 years in and out of state and federal prison. He's in his 40's, a born-and-bred criminal who is all about what others can do for him in the here and now. I met many people like Mack during my 21 years of incarceration—sharks who prey on the vulnerable, exploiting anyone who fits the bill to their own nefarious ends. Fans of HBO's *Oz* will recall that Ryan O'Reilly, the Machiavellian character played by Dean Winters—the guy in all those Allstate insurance TV spots—had sex with at least one guard to secure advantages inside.

"It doesn't even matter if she is pretty. I mean that helps, but all that matters is if she is game," Mack says. And by "game," Mack means being down with whatever he wants the guard in question to do—bring in contraband items like tobacco, cell phones, and drugs, or even have sex with him. It starts out with a little flirting at mail call, or asking a guard if her office needs cleaning. Then the prisoner can start asking for little favors like being allowed to eat early, or for the guard to look something up on the internet. But how do guards let themselves get involved with their charges?

"I believe that a lot of times the females that engage in this type of ethical suicide have major issues going on with themselves before they are even hired," explains Tamara, a former corrections officer who has moved into prison administration at a Midwestern facility. "A lot of them are single mothers who are looking to fill a void in their lives, whether it be not having a spouse, or a father figure on the outside." And convicts like Mack know how to play right into that.

"Shit, I can be their daddy, I can be their man, their boyfriend, best friend or whoever they need me to be," Mack says. "As long as they get me what I want I can be whatever and whoever they need me to be. It's all a game really, a tradeoff. I know nobody does nothing for free, and if I got to sex one of these broads down to get her to bring stuff in to me, then you know what time it is." With minimal training, some of these women are being thrown into the lion's den without the tools to succeed. And the hiring practices of prisons don't help the situation.

"A lot of people that choose to work in corrections really shouldn't be working in corrections and probably wouldn't be if every employer did psychological evaluations in addition to background checks," Tamara says. "Nowadays, it's all about what I [the guard] can get out of it." That feeds right into the convict's mentality of, What can you do for me right now. It's all about instant gratification. And like Mack says, it's a tradeoff.

"If she wants sex and attention for drugs and phones, that is a fair trade in my world," Mack says. "I am just trying to make some money because money equals power and in here, power is respect. I am trying to do the time, not let the time do me. And female diversions are nice, especially when they help me keep my rackets going." The correctional officer might see herself as the one in control of the situation because she is the one with the keys, but sometimes they're just getting played.

"I hate to say it, but a lot of correctional officers, male and female, have low self-esteem," Tamara says, which can lead to them befriending or starting relationships with inmates.

But female guards who get caught up in all this are paying a price. I saw numerous female guards lose their jobs and get walked out of the prison during my incarceration. A lot of this sort of thing is swept under the carpet by prison officials, leaving fellow guards to speculate about what exactly inspired the dalliance.

According to Tamara, the appeal is "a combination of getting away with something that is forbidden, the rush of being with someone as hardcore as an inmate, and the false sense of control that they think they have over the situation [but] not necessarily over the inmate. They may have lost all sense of control over every other aspect of their lives, and this form of relationship is something they think they have control over by not getting caught by their superiors or other inmates."

With better training, higher standards, and the proper psychological evaluations, these episodes might be prevented. And they should be stopped, because the only ones benefiting are the most manipulative portion of America's massive prison population.

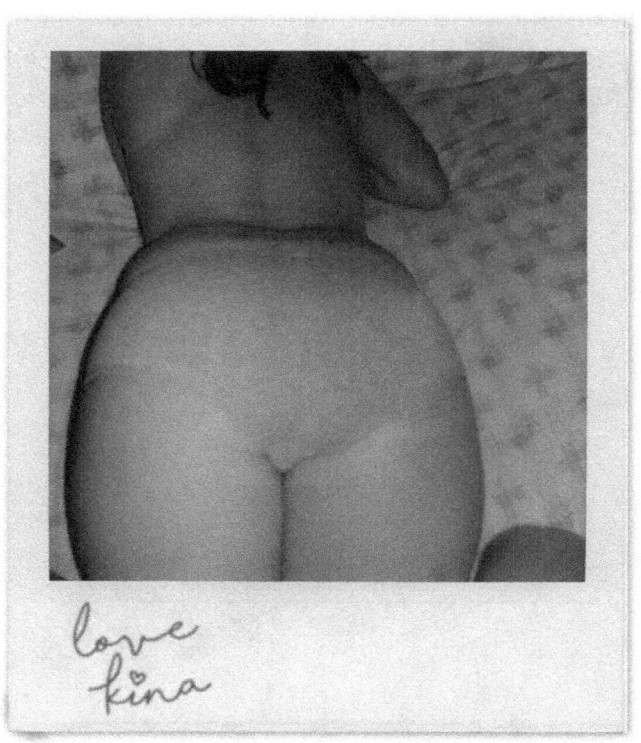

JOURNEY INTO HELL

Drugs, Love, and Survival
in a United States Penitentiary

"Hipster, you know I love you, kid."

"I love you too, bro," I say to Yaberz a six foot tall, cut up, tat'd up convict.

"You ready for this?"

"Do I really got a choice?"

"Guess not."

"Fuck it. Let's do it!"

With that I sit down in a chair, pillow behind my head, with my back against the wall.

"Alright, I'm going for the right eye first," he says with his fist pressed up against my eye. Gloves on, sizing me up. "One, two, three"—*WHACK!*

"Motherfucker!" I yelled.

"Dude, that's a good one. It'll bruise up for sure. Let's go to the left. One, two, three."—*CRACK!*

"Fuck!"

"Sorry, bro. That one sucked. I got to do it again."

"Alright, but get it this time." My head is spinning and my eyes try to focus.

"I could just break your nose and they'll both bruise up."

"Man, fuck that! Just do this shit!"

"One, two, three"—*SMACK!*—"Yeah, that's good. Now I got to get your eyebrow. One, two—"

"Fuck the counting. Just do it." I don't know if I got one more left in me.

"Alright"—*THWACK!*

"FUCK! You coulda gave me a fucking warning though!" I catch my balance and stand up straight.

"We're good, kid. Now get a razor and cut your lip."

So I get out a razor blade and slice my bottom lip.

"Motherfucker," I yell out.

"Don't be such a pussy. Cut that shit!" Yaberz orders.

"Fuck!" I yell again as I cut open a big gash and spit blood into the sink.

"I hope she's worth it, Hipster."

"You and me both, kid." I hold my hand up to my lip to stop the bleeding.

The girl he's talking about is Kina. A five foot nine, blond haired, brown eyed, tattooed, long legged, skinny wasted, perfectly breasted, tanned, Hawaiian beach goddess. She's a straight up rocker chick with purple streaks in her hair, who was down as fuck. I fell in love with her the first time I talked to her. The type of woman you'd kill for—or willingly get your ass kicked for!

Which brings me to the current situation. It's the reason I'm now getting pummeled by my best friend. Kina is also my celly's kid's mother! There are a lot of ways to misstep on the pound but fucking with a cell's baby momma is one of the biggest "no-no's" in the penitentiary.

Everything was going good for me. I was seven years into a 16 and a half year prison sentence for armed bank robbery and a shootout with the cops. I started out in a medium security prison, but quickly got tossed out and bumped up to the pen for selling cigarettes and weed. They sent me to what was pound-for-pound the most violent Federal Penitentiary in the United States. It was a joint where seeing someone getting stabbed was as common as getting a traffic ticket.

In the pen it's not pretty. You have to be on point at all times and be ready to pay the price given. Your knife is your MasterCard and it's like they say in the commercial, "You don't leave home without it."

In the pen everybody is in some sort of gang by necessity. Convicts group up and affiliate for protection. There is power in numbers, but still it's a terrible way to have to live. It's a place where human life means very little and any little thing can get you killed. Being a white kid with dreadlocks hanging down to your ass is like having a huge bullseye on your back! But this is the predicament I found myself in. In the pen that's how it goes.

"Attention compound, We'll be releasing the bus in 5 minutes," the loudspeaker blared out while I was in the corridor on my way out to the yard. They actually announce that we're coming out! It's so the whole prison population is there to see the action. To see if they know anyone. To see if they can point out and smash a rat, child molester, rapist or "check in artist." To see if someone from the wrong gang made it onto the yard, and to see if anyone from their gang or city came. In the pen it's prime entertainment.

Walking out the doors to a crowd of over a thousand people is pretty intimidating—even more so when every one of them has a mini sword stashed under their shirt! The commotion is loud as different groups call out for friends and enemies:

"Bloods"
"Crips"
"Chicago"
"New York"
"GD"
"Norteno"

The crowd parted as names were thrown out. Letting you know where your "people" were. It was like being on a Grateful Dead lot. Only these dudes are selling their gang or town instead of drugs.

As people made their way to their different gangs, I kept walking. Just trying to make it to my housing unit. Willing myself there! The other white guys that came with me got grabbed up and checked to see what gangs they were with. But I made it through. The dreads throwing off everyone. Dudes weren't sure who or what I was.

I make it to my unit and cell and there's my celly, Yaberz. He's sitting on his bunk covered in swastika tats, and the obligatory naked women, and skull prison tats up and down his body.

"What's up, kid," I say as I shake his hand. "They call me Hipster."

He jumped up and looked me up and down, not sure what to make of me. "You Black?"

"Nope."

He looked me up and down again. "Mixed?" he asked.

"Nope."

"Spanish?"

"No," I say and stifle a laugh. "I'm white."

"Half Puerto Rican?"

"Nope, all white." I get it all the time.

"You sure?" He arched an eyebrow, trying to figure me out still.

"Um . . . yeah."

"You're all white?"

"Yeah, dude. I'm a hippie kid."

"Alright, cool," he said and sat back on his bunk. "I was going to smash the shit outta you if you weren't." He seemed a bit disappointed.

That night I was informed of the finer points of penitentiary life. How to cut and sharpen knives. The best places to stab someone. Who to avoid and who to talk to. Who called the shots for the different groups. The real things you need to know in the pen!

The next day Yaberz took me around the compound. "Hey, this is Hipster. Don't let the dreads fool you, he's all white," he'd explain when he'd introduce me to people.

"Gotta let dudes know you're cool and not a *wigger*," he qualifiied it and went on to the next group.

"If you say so," I said.

"You don't want someone to stab you for thinking you're trying to be black."

"Fuck no, I don't." I wasn't trying to be stabbed for any reason.

"Then we gotta let everyone know that you're cool."

After a few weeks or so, everyone knew I was alright. They knew that my paperwork was good and that I was just doing my time. Keeping to myself. Plus, once I got into the band room and rocked the fuck out, it was solidified that I was in fact "cool". Never doubt the power of loud and aggressive music!

I had been playing in bands since I was a teen. The bass was my main instrument, but I could play guitar, drums and sing. I had played in several prison bands during my incarceration and had a knack for writing loud and fast, original punk rock songs. I was even profiled on *Vice* in an article about prison bands. It was my claim to fame.

I settled in and got into my routine: running, working out, playing music, practicing yoga and meditation (They didn't call me "Hipster" for nothing.) All I had to do was a year. Not get into trouble and I was back to a medium security prison. Which I of course didn't do! Hell, I even moved over to a program unit where it was filled with the lamest of the lames. I've never been into programming the whole time I've been down. I didn't believe in them. But I made the move just so I could stay out of the way and get out of "the slaughterhouse" as soon as possible.

Even that didn't work though. I told the head program coordinator to "fuck off", which apparently is frowned upon, and caused me to get a write up and an immediate "back to the ghetto you go" pass. But I didn't care. This was prison! Where you could score whatever you wanted at any time! Wine, weed, shine, cigarettes, heroin, coke, Big Macs, cell phones. Shit, for twenty dollars you could actually rent a porno DVD and for 30 minutes go into a cell with a TV and DVD player and get busy with it. But real pussy? That shit is as rare as a presidential pardon.

Prison is all about what you make of it. If you do your time, stay out of the way, and don't step on anyone's hustles, then you'll be all good. Aside from the racial spats that flare up every now and then, everything is pretty cool. There are checks and balances and politicking that keeps an uneasy peace among groups.

Really, the ones you have to watch out for are your friends. Often, it's your own kind you got to be wary of. Your own race will do you in. I had a solution for that—stay the fuck by myself. Besides Yaberz and the few people I played music with, there was no need. *Why set myself up for more people to stab me in the back while I'm not looking?* I thought.

After being there for about a year, I went through a couple different cellys before I got into a cell with my guitar player Brent, a chill dude from Vegas doing 15 years for cooking meth. Everything was going smooth. I'd drink every now and then, maybe a joint here and there, but for all intents and purposes I was clean and living healthy.

I'd wake up in the morning, meditate and practice yoga. Then go out and run five miles before coming inside and doing another workout. After lunch it was three hours in the band room. Back for count, then dinner. Then back up to rec to listen to CD's and write.

Because I was in charge of teaching all the recreation classes (yoga, spin, abs, etc.) I got to have my own CD player and CD's, which I took full advantage of. I had two good hustles, selling certificates for class (you getting credit for the class and never showing up) and selling homemade incense. Since there were so many winemakers trying to cover up the smell of their brewery, it was a good little money maker.

I got so comfortable that I didn't even have a knife! This is even after almost getting involved in two different race riots that thankfully got resolved before they popped off. I always figured I could throw my lock on a belt and beat someone's brains in if it came down to it. I saw too many people kill someone accidentally when they were just trying to stab them (there's no such thing as a fist fight in the pen) and go from a couple years to life. I was going home after all. No need to kill anyone, right?

The way I saw it was dope fiends, gang members, and degenerate gamblers were the ones that always needed to have cold steel on them. They were the ones always getting into shit. Hell, they were the ones wanting to get into some shit! Getting extorted only came about if you had money, was lame, and threw it around like you had it. Basically, you pinned a bullseye on yourself. There wasn't anyone getting raped either. That shit gets sensationalized by the media. There's plenty of gay dudes, gumps, and undercover fags. If you swung that way, there was someone willing to accommodate you. Since I was in none of their categories, I was cool.

So here I was, surviving life in the big house when a clean cut skinny white kid named Dom moved into the block. He was 31-years-old, looking like he was 16. Fresh with two life sentences plus forty years for smuggling weed and coke for the Mexican cartels. He'd never been in trouble a day in his life. He heard all the stories about the penitentiary (who hasn't), and was scared to death. Normally, I don't say anything to new dudes until I see what they're about first. Half the people that show up are either rats or check-ins from another spot. Either way, I'm not going to set myself up for failure. Like I said, it's your friends that get you. If you're friends with someone that turns out to be hot, well, it's on you to take care of it. If you don't, someone else will . . . and then take care of you next!

But with Dom, I made an exception. I had dudes take me under their wing when I came into the system when I had the same "deer in headlights" look as him. It was time for me to repay the favor in kind.

"What's up, kid? They call me Hipster."

"What's up? I'm Dom."

"Where you from?"

"Baltimore."

"No shit?! You're East Coast. You ride with me then. I'm from Pittsburgh."

We began talking. He told me about his case. All the drugs he was smuggling for the cartels and different places he lived. He told me how he was a "multi-millionaire" and a bunch of other shit. I had him come down to my cell so I could give him the welcome to prison starter pack: hygiene, food, sweats, coffee, all the essentials.

"You have a guitar in your cell?" He walked over to the guitar acting like he never believed they had music in prison.

"Fucking right! I'm the guitar teacher so they never take it either."

"Can I play it?"

"Go for it."

He started playing a couple different Led Zeppelin tunes decently.

"How long you been playing?" I asked him. "I can get you into the band room to jam with one of my bands if you want."

"Yeah, I might check it out. You think I can use your guitar tonight?"

"No problem, kid. Go for it."

He took it down to his cell with my boy Harley, a super ADHD tweaker from Texas. A good dude whose motor ran non-stop like his namesake bike.

By the time I made it down to his cell the next day before lunch, the word was out. Dom had money! Evidently he had been talking that multi-millionaire cartel shit to whomever he met. Having loot is not the best thing to be known for in the pen. Motherfuckers come out of the woodwork to try to get a piece one way or another!

It was nonstop action at his cell. Dudes coming by with weed, shine, tobacco, and heroin. Dom was buying it all! The kid spent seven grand the first month he was here!

I would pretty much keep my distance during the day. I had my routine down, working out and my bands. At nighttime I'd go down to his cell, smoke a joint and jam on some songs. My celly, Brent, had a guitar too, so we had two guitars to play on. With Harley tapping out a beat on the side of the bunk it was almost a band session.

I had to teach Dom how to play chords. He learned how to play Led Zeppelin . . . and that's it! So it was a tedious process. Especially with

Harley going a mile a minute with that mouth. But hey, I was stoned, so how could I not be cool with it!

We decided to put a band together. I put Dom on the bass and Harley on the drums. Both of them were pretty terrible so we went with the good and trusty three chord punk songs! Just crank everything up to 11 and let it rip! I've always been a huge believer in what you lack in skill you can make up with in aggression. As long as it's loud no one hears the imperfections. So once a week we'd go in and fuck around— high as hell of course!

Slowly Dom and Harley started getting into the smack. When the weed wasn't around, they'd go right for the next escape. The one thing that seems to never run out in the pen is dope. There's just too many junkies and too much money to be made off of it. It's by far the number one drug in prisons. Guaranteed to check your mind out of hell for a couple hours. Once you get into that cycle of escaping reality though, it's hard to get back to "normal" living.

I hadn't used any heroin in over three years at this point in my bid. I had a little run when I was in the medium security prison, but kicked the habit. I got more into yoga and meditation. Trying my best to keep my mind calm without the drugs. That's why I got into it in the first place. Sitting in the hole again, for a drinking write up. Telling myself there had to be another way. I was so depressed from getting all the time that I did, I was on a suicide trip for a while. Trying to kill myself the only way that I really knew how—drugs. I just didn't give a shit. But after about my third trip to the hole I thought, How can I be high, without the drugs?

The Hare Krishna's came to mind. Dancing around in their robes, chanting their chant, smiling the whole time. Then I thought of the Buddhist monks, dousing themselves in gasoline and setting themselves on fire. Sitting there serenely, not making a sound while their skin peeled off and their bones blackened. *Fuck*, I thought. *These guys HAVE to know the secret to life!*

I was so stable in not getting high that I would even shoot Harley up sometimes. I'd damn near shit my pants while I was doing it but I'd still hang strong. The weed and occasional drunken night was good enough for me. That all changed one day when I got the news. My brother had died of a drug overdose.

Andrew was way more than my little brother, he was my best friend. My partner in crime. He was three years younger than me and grew up doing everything I did. Which obviously turned into getting high as well. We'd get high together, sell dope together and always had each other's backs when the shit was flying. If I had told him I needed a bazooka smuggled in he'd say, "Oh, you fucking motherfucker!" and then make it happen! He was by far the most solid kid I've ever known.

The death of my brother just devastated me. I just didn't give a fuck anymore. I didn't want to think about it. That night while I was down at Dom's cell he said. "You want to do some dope?" and that was all I needed to hear.

"Fuck it. Why not?" I needed the escape.

I got the *binky*, threw the dope into the spoon, sucked it up, tied off, hit my main vein and I was back home again! There was no more sadness, no more depression, no more prison. I remembered why I fell in love with this drug in the first place. She takes away all your pain. When you're in prison, that's what your life is—pain. I was back doing what got me here in the first place. Back to doing the one thing that I knew would help support me through this life—heroin. Lou Reed wasn't lying when he sang the words, *Heroin, it's my life/It's my wife.*

Right around this time, Harley's old celly came back from court. Coincidentally the same day my celly left to go to a medium facility. So in some simple twist of fate Dom ended up coming down to live with me. I knew what I was getting into having Dom move in with me. It was like a 7-Eleven with all the hustlers coming and going. Dom staying up all night and sleeping all day. But I also knew it'd mean that I'd be getting high for free all day long! In the pen it's all a balance of trade offs.

In a lot of ways Dom was like me. White middle class kid who got into drugs at a young age. The only difference was he never got arrested till he was 31. I, on the other hand, had my first taste of the law at age 16. So I had no illusions about the justice system. They will fuck you. That's a fact. It's only a matter of how hard!

I'd always tried my best to keep Dom's spirits up. Telling him that he'd get back into court and get his case overturned. That or some laws would change and his time would get reduced. It's the pipe dream that all cons hang on to. Even the most hard are praying for that a miracle will happen and they'll be home sooner than later.

Dom would stay up all night and sleep all day, which in the penitentiary is not the smartest move. I'd still get up at 6:30 a.m. for breakfast. Then back to the cell for some yoga and meditation. Then off to run five miles before lunch. After that I'd go to band practice. By the time I'd get back Dom would just be crawling out of bed. Rolling up a cigarette at the desk.

"What's up?" he asked as he wiped the night from his eyes. "Not a whole lot. You just getting up?"

"Yep."

"What time you go to bed?"

"Pretty early. Around five."

"Damn, kid. What are you going to do if a riot pops off and you're lying in bed?"

"They're going to have to come in here, wake me up and stab me cause I'm not going out there." He offered me the needle slim rollie. "You want to hit this?"

"No. I'm cool."

"Ok, more for me."

After the cig, he'd roll up a joint and cut it into four pieces. Then with an empty toilet paper roll, he'd poke a hole and put one of the pieces in. Light it up and let it rip. Jailhouse steamroller. We also had a homemade bong for special occasions. Which was when he got a couple caps of weed.

The lid off a chap stick is considered a cap of weed. Sometimes it's packed in, most times it's not. That's how drugs are measured in prison. After you get your caps, you break it down into little weed papers. Which basically is something you brush on the floor out on the street. In prison it'll cost you ten dollars! Caps would go from anywhere between eight to fifteen books of stamps. Which in prison is your money. It'll get you anything from a piece of chicken to a piece of ass—at least a tattered, stained picture of one.

There were always a lot of drugs on the yard. If you knew the right people you could get quantities of whatever you wanted. The way Dom was, he didn't care. He'd buy five papers for 10 books. Instead of buying a cap for ten and getting way more. The way he explained it when I asked him was, "I've got more money then I know what to do with. So I don't give a shit."

And he damn sure didn't. He'd get nickel and dimed all day long. Just as quick as he'd buy books of stamps and count them, they'd be gone. There'd be nights where I'd be up late counting a couple hundred books of stamps. In the morning I'd go out and pay off all his debts on the compound while he slept the day away. I was still getting about $100 a month sent in from friends and family which along with the $50 I made teaching classes added with my hustling was more than enough money to live good. That is if you are not getting high.

I first tried to pull my own weight when Dom moved in. I paid for as much drugs as I could. Which, when you're trying to match a "multi-millionaire" just won't work out. I also started smoking cigarettes again too. With it costing five dollars for a tiny roll up. Well . . . it adds up quick.

At first I'd only smoke a cig after puffing on some weed or doing some dope. Seeing how that was about all the time, I was right back to where I was when I started my bid. Doing everything and anything I could to get my head out of prison. I also started to sleep in late. Another big *faux pas* in the pen. You never know what's going to pop off at any given moment, and you damn sure don't want to be in bed when it happens!

We'd stay up till around midnight playing music or chess. As soon as the doors locked for the night, it was party time! Dope in the spoon and a search for a functional vein. Sometimes I'd hit right away. Other times it could take a while. Being the dedicated junkie I am, I wouldn't give up until the dope was in its home—my vein!

"Where they at?" I'd ask.

"They're like ten cells down," Dom would respond on lookout.

"Ok, I almost got it."

"Dude, they're five cells down." He snapped his fingers rapidly to get my attention.

"Alright."

"Three away!" he said, panicking.

"Fuck!"

"Next door! Just put it down!"

"Fuck that! It's almost in!" I'd say as I'd turn my body away from the door. Belt tied around my arm, blood dripping down from missed attempts with a dull needle! After they'd go by I was free to stab away like a pin cushion.

After I'd finish, I'd clean out the rig and shoot up Dom. The kid had fresh veins and I could damn near throw the *binky* at like a dart from across the room and not miss. Then we'd smoke a cig, pull out the guitars and play some songs. About thirty minutes later we'd smoke some weed and break out the chess board for our ongoing battles. Smoke another cig or two and then I'd lay it down for bed. I'd still make sure that I'd hit my run and practice some yoga every day. Yeah, I was a junkie again. *But I can damn sure be a healthy junkie!* I thought.

My drummer ended up leaving under some bad circumstances, so all of a sudden Harley and Dom became my "good" band. We'd have practice almost every day. Getting as high as possible before we'd go, which wasn't the smartest thing. Dom and Harley's ability to memorize and play songs was terrible when they were stoned. Almost to the point of digression, so there was really no getting any better. Just trying to not get worse.

Dom used to hang pictures up of all his different chicks in thong panties. Telling whoever came into the cell different stories about the women as they stared at the pics. Harley and I would always ask Dom how he's cool with dudes looking at his chicks. He'd say, "I don't care if dudes look at my girl. I take it as a compliment that they think my girl is hot."

After staring at his girl Kina half naked for almost a year, meeting her for the first time was like running into one of the models out of *Maxim* magazine. My dad, sister, and some of her friends came down to see me the same time that Kina and Dom's two kids came to see him.

I didn't even notice her at first. I was in the visiting room waiting for my sister to get some food for me. I started humming a Beatles' song when I heard a soft female voice ask, "What's that?"

"I Wanna Hold Your Hand?" It came out as as question.

"Oh, do you know?" she replied.

I turned to see a sexy girl with her hair tied up behind her in a ponytail standing by a vending machine. It was no mistaking who she was as I'd stare at her pictures for hours. She was wearing a red sweatshirt, tight jeans, glasses and her hair tied up behind her in a ponytail. I could only see her in those tight little black lace panties. She was a perfect picture!

"No, I don't think Dom would like that." I laughed and brushed a dreadlock away from my face. "What's up, Kina?"

"Are you Dom's celly?" She smiled the warmest smile. "You gotta be. There can't be that many dreaded out hippies in this place."

"Yeah, I'm Hipster." She bent over to grab the soda out of the machine as my eyes followed. "Nice to meet you," I said practically talking to her ass. She had no idea how crazy it was driving me watching her bent over like that.

"Well I gotta get this to Dom," she said as she held up the soda can

Out of the corner of my eye I watched her walk away. It would normally feel dirty mugging a celly's girl like that—prison code is like bro code only with stabbings for violations—but I figured Dom wouldn't care. After all he was the one that had been passing around her photographs without even having the sense to get some stamps for it.

She turned around to look over her shoulder catching my drifting eyes. "It was nice to meet ya, kid," she said and then went over to Dom. He had a proud look in his eyes, feeling like a king amongst thieves that a dime piece like that was bringing him a Sprite. Lots of guys talked about that perfect 10 they had back in the streets, but she was here in soft pink flesh.

As I ate the flavorless microwave hamburger and caught up with my sister, I could only think about Kina. As my sister talked about her new job I wondered, *How'd Dom score a chick like that?* Maybe he wasn't lying about all that money either. Maybe he really was some big cartel shit. It was hard to believe he was that hard though as he got the short end of prison hustles daily.

That night I found it hard to sleep as our first meeting replayed over and over in my head. "Nice to meet ya, kid," was the best music I had ever heard. It almost sounded as if she liked me back, but it could have just been my fiending imagination. After thinking about Kina all night, I was ready to see her again and it couldn't wait until the next visiting day.

"Yo, kid. Can I see that picture of your girl?" I asked Dom back in our cell one early the next morning.

"You mean Kina?" he said sleepily from the bunk below. He fished the photographs from the stash spot under his thin mattress and handed them up to me.

I nonchalantly picked them up and flipped through them. I didn't want to be staring them up like I was ready to lotion up but even a split second was enough to cement the image in my mind. Even though he was below and out of sight I could feel his glazed eyes looking up at me.

"You're right, kid. She really is a 10," I said. "Don't be mad at me for thinking you were just talking shit and showing off pictures you bought from someone."

"I'm not mad," he said. "Did you see all them guys up in that visiting room staring at her. I'm not just talking about prisoners."

I started to hand the photographs back but Dom waved me off. "Keep em for a minute. There's one her friend. The one in the Corona bikini. I got to tell you stories about her but I need to get some more sleep."

I wasn't interested in the Corona bikini, however well formed. It was all black panties for me. I was ready to dive into them and forget about all the penitentiary bullshit when Harley barged into my cell with the latest non-scheduled interruption.

"Yo, you guys better get out here!" His eyes were wide.

"What's up, Harley?" I asked.

"There's like 90 DC's grouped up ready to kill us!"

"The fuck happened?" I said as I was putting my lock on a belt.

"Anthrax blew the power shining and now Tookie wants him to pay for his batch cause he can't shine it!"

"Goddammit! How many of us are out there?"

"Just the seven of us. But Sammy says all his homeboys are coming over as soon as the compound opens to eat, so we only got to hold them off till then."

"Well, motherfucker I guess we're going to get fucking slaughtered then!"

"Yeah, pretty much. Let's go!" Harley said resigned to his duty.

As we went out of the cell, Dom just shuffled off his bunk, looked out the door to see everything and sat down to roll a cigarette.

Outside Sammy, the shot caller for our block, was in the middle of a heated discussion with Buck, the shot caller for the DC Blacks. Trying his best to hold back the attack while we waited for reinforcements.

The five of us stood behind him as I kept glancing back at our bunk hoping Dom would be coming out. Three different groups of about 30 Blacks in each, stood in different spots. All of them around us armed to the teeth with makeshift weapons. Everyone was waiting for the first strike to happen and then all hell to break loose. Just when the tension couldn't get any thicker, they opened the compound for a move.

Then came about 20 white dudes thinking they were going to get some spaghetti and walking straight into madness. In the pen you never know when you'll be called to action. As soon as everyone came in, and the numbers were a little more even, it got even more tense. The Blacks thinking we sent some signals out to get everyone over here. And the whites getting ready to get slaughtered. We were still outnumbered four to one.

"Damn, Hipster. What the fuck is going on?" a long haired, bearded tweaker named Monk asked me.

"Some bullshit. Fucking happy you guys are here now!"

"So we can get killed with you huh?" he joked.

"Sammy's been talking to Buck for a minute now, so hopefully it'll all get squashed."

"Shit, I didn't even bring my knife. I don't think any of us did. We were just coming for some 'sketti."

"Fuck, all I got is a fucking lock on a belt right now," I said.

After a little bit more of a discussion, Sammy and Buck gave each other a fist bump and we all knew a deal was worked out. Which ended up being the whites shining Tookie's wine for free. That was cool with all of us. Hell, it's a lot better than getting your brains beat in.

Harley and I walked back into the cell to see Dom sitting there, smoking a rollie and strumming the guitar.

"So what happened?" he said, not looking up.

"It got squashed."

"Where the fuck were you at?" Harley demanded.

"I knew nothing was going to happen, so I stayed in here. Everybody always talks that race riot shit but it always gets squashed."

"Yeah, and what if it did?" Harley asked.

"They'd have to come in here and get me." Dom swung around his guitar like a club and laughed. That was the first sign that Dom wasn't about doing anything when the time came.

This fear was proved true over the whole *Jackass* thing. We were sitting in front of the "white" TV. All seven of us, when we started to see some action below.

"No. This is bullshit!" howled a dude named Poo-Poo to a couple of other DC Blacks. It was his actual name and he wore that shit proudly.

"Poo-Poo, it's their TV, they can put on whatever they want," one stocky DC Black shouted back to him.

"Fuck, that ain't no white TV, it's a movie TV!"

"So what are they supposed to watch then?"

"They can watch whatever is on the non-movie TV's!" Poo-Poo yelled back so everybody could hear him. Which immediately drew the attention of everyone in the unit.

"What the hell is that dude talking about?" Justin asked me.

"I have no fucking clue." I shrugged my shoulders.

In prison any number of things could set a dude like Poo-Poo off. It was only later that I'd get all the details of how it jumped off. What was going on was Poo-Poo was drunk and didn't want to watch what we were watching—*Jackass*.

James, who at this point was our de facto shot caller, went over to see what was going on. We listened, waiting for the silence that would mean the issue was squashed. All we heard was Poo-Poo yelling, "That's the movie TV and they got it on some *Jackass* shit. It ain't even the *Jackass* movie."

"No, this is the white TV," explained James back to Poo-Poo. "We watch a lot of movies, but we can watch whatever the hell we want." He had to raise his voice to be heard over Poo-Poo's protests.

Some more DC Blacks came over to where they were talking. Then more started to group up around the ends of the block.

"Look, Poo-Poo," James said pointing at different TV's. "DC entertainment television. Spanish entertainment television. Black entertainment television. Sports, which means black entertainment television.

White entertainment television. You can watch whatever you want on your TV's. On ours if you don't like what's on roll out."

"Yeah, Poo-Poo, they got to have something to watch," a Mexican Mafia Chicano jumped in.

"What? Why the fuck you getting in this?" Poo-Poo snapped back now bringing the Mexicans into the situation. They grouped up right away as they always did.

"This is starting to look pretty fucking bad bro," I said to Justin.

"Yeah, I'm going to get my lock too." He already had his knife on him. Shit, everyone already had their knives. You just didn't go without one for this exact reason.

It was about this time Dom came creeping out of the cell. "What's going on?" he asked. "Shit woke me up."

"It's getting ready to go down. They're trying to take our TV," I said. "You better go throw my lock on a belt."

"Um . . . yeah," he mumbled, then slithered up the stairs and started talking to some Blacks.

As the five of us were standing behind James, hands in our pockets holding our knives, TJ said to me, "What the fuck is Dom doing?"

"I don't know."

"We're down here about to get killed and he's up there kicking it with them?!"

"I told that kid the deal."

We then saw Dom slide into a Black cell. Trying his best to not be seen. "That motherfucker just went into Stone's cell!" TJ shook his head.

"If it doesn't go down here, then I'm going to get that fucker afterwards," Jason chimed in.

"I'll deal with him," I said. "But let's stay focused on this shit right now."

The inner group of James, Poo-Poo, and some other Blacks and Mexicans started to calm down a bit. There weren't so many animated hand movements going on anymore. Poo-Poo started to chill somewhat while his people were talking to him and letting him know he was in the obvious wrong. After a couple of long minutes James and Poo-Poo dapped fists and James came back over to us.

"So . . . what happened?" Jason asked.

"That drunk fuck almost caused a riot," James explained.

"What's the outcome?"

"That's our TV. I wasn't going to give in to that dude."

"So it's over?" I eased up.

"Yeah, we're good. Let me holla at you for a minute, Hipster," James said, pulling me to the side.

"What's up, James?"

"You seen your celly?"

"Yeah, I saw him." Fuck. Everybody saw him.

"Let him know if that shit happens again he's fucking done!"

"I got you, man," I said. "He's just scared and don't know no better."

"Well, now he will, and I'll get him personally if it happens again."

"It won't, man. I'll make sure he knows the deal."

"Fucking *Jackass*," James cursed under his breath as he stomped away. "I don't even watch that stupid shit."

Back in the cell later I told Dom what was up.

Dom didn't seem to care. "He'd just be doing me a favor if he got me," he said as he flipped through a car magazine.

This is the type of shit I had to deal with on a daily basis. In the pen everything is life or death. There's no time to become complacent in what you're doing or with your surroundings.

Dom continued his mission to spend as much fucking money as he could. He didn't care that he was getting nickel and dimed like crazy. Just like he said, "I've got more money than I know what to do with."

I knew a couple dudes that were making moves bringing in different shit. I told him he'd be better off just spending money upfront and buying a quantity of something, rather than get pieced out. I'd paper it up and sell it on the compound. He'd make his money back and we'd get high for free.

A New York dude named Face came over to the cell and we worked out a deal to get an ounce of weed for fifteen hundred. As soon as the money hit, we'd get the ounce. I'd make sixty caps and sell them for 10 books a piece. The $1,500 would turn into three grand in about two weeks and we'd be off to the races.

The problem we ran into was another New York dude named Mustafa stepped to Dom about some heroin. He'd give up three grams for a thousand dollars. Which really wasn't too much of a deal. Yeah, you'd make two grand off that thousand, but you're dealing with a different crowd of people—junkies!

Dom was on and off the phone like crazy. Calling Kina, her mom, his mom, and everyone else he knew to try and come up with the cash. I'd ask him what the problem was and he'd say they were all holding his money and being tight with it. I ended up having to be the middleman between the two of them. Dom wouldn't leave the cell and Mustafa did not want to come into our block.

Every day it was the same thing. Dom would tell me, "It'll get done tomorrow." While Mustafa wanted to know what the fuck was taking so long.

After three weeks Dom finally got $750 sent out. It was well short of the agreed upon thousand. Dom said to just give him two and a half grams, while Mustafa wanted the rest of the money before he gave up the dope. It was a goddamn clusterfuck and I was stuck in the middle.

I had to call my boy Mark for help. I did time with him when I first got locked up. He was a real good dude who got five years for an ecstasy charge. We made some weed moves together in my first spot. He knew how things were in prison. He also knew that if I called him asking for some money that I really needed it.

I told him I'd be able to pay him back in a couple days. After getting the dope, I'd easily be able to do it. Dom also told me that he'd have Kina send him three hundred back the following day. He explained that she just wasn't able to get to it right then.

Mark, knowing how I am, went out in a snowstorm to catch a bus to send it Western Union. "If you really need it, I got you kid," Mark said on his way out the door to make it happen. After getting off the phone with Mark, I ran out to catch Mustafa to tell him whatw was up and get the dope.

"Shit, you're too late now," he said.

"What?"

"It's gone," he reiterated.

"The fuck you mean it's gone? You got the money now."

"But it took you over a month. All the grams are gone. It's just in papers now."

"I don't want no fucking papers. I want what we agreed on."

"Listen, there'll be more grams in a week or so. You're just going to have to wait till then."

"Man, fuck that. I'm not leaving without my shit," I said aggressively.

"Hipster, it's all good. You're going to get them. If Dom would've sent the money when he said he was, you'd already have it. You know how this shit works. Dudes aren't going to sit on some shit and wait for someone. They're selling it first come first serve."

"Man, fuck that. You can send my money back is what we're going to do."

"Alright look, I'll get you four papers for right now just to tide you over. When the grams hit you're locked in for the three."

"No, I'm cool. Send the money."

"Here, go give these to Dom and tell him what I said." Mustafa pressed the papers into my hand. "If he wants the money back then I'll do it. It's his money anyways."

"I'll go talk to him and see what he says. But be ready to send that money in the morning," I said and stormed out of the cell to go back to my unit and Dom.

"Yo, man. This motherfucker doesn't have the grams," I explained to Dom as I entered the cell.

"Why not?" He looked up from the book he was reading on his bunk.

"Because it took too long for the money."

"So you didn't get anything?" The disappointment was clear in his voice.

"No, he gave me four fucking papers and told me to tell you the grams will be here in a couple weeks."

"Get out the rig," Dom said, jumping out of his bed with a new found energy.

"I told that motherfucker to send the money back," I said, going to the stash spot to pull out the *binky*. "He said to ask you what you want to do since most of it's yours."

"Fuck it," said Dom as he rolled up his sleeve. "He might as well just hold onto it until the dope hits."

"What? Fuck that," I said. "Who knows when it's even going to hit, and I have to pay Mark back."

"I'll get the money sent to him."

"When's that going to happen?"

"I'll call my old partner. He used to run all of my businesses and has a lot of my money." Dom opened up the papers and dumped them on a plastic spoon.

"Why didn't you call him before so I didn't have to call Mark?"

"I didn't want to get him involved with anything. The feds might still indict more people and they don't know about him."

"Dude," I said, glaring at Dom. "Call that motherfucker so you can pay these fucking bills."

"Alright. I'll call him tomorrow," Dom said and drew up half the dope into the rig. "Hit me."

It took Dom about a week to get a hold of the guy. In that time frame he managed to rack up almost $600 worth of bills to some dudes. One of them was the shot caller for the DC Blacks named Chuck. I had to cosign on that to get the stamps. Which meant that I had to pay for it if Dom didn't.

Another dude was named Alex, an independent Mexican who used to be a body builder. Independent meant he didn't run with the gangs. He hung with the other independents that weren't in the gangs.

I was cool with both Alex and Chuck. That's why they gave me the shit up front. It's something that I've never done in prison. You don't want to get shit for someone else, unless they give you the money to get it. You never know what could happen. If things fuck up you're stuck with a nightmare debt.

The next day, Dom came back to the cell with a smile on his face. "Ok. I got a hold of him and he's going to send money," he said.

"Thank God." A wave of relief passed over me.

"He's going to send twenty-five hundred."

"Good deal. I'll be able to pay Mark and everyone else."

"It's an income tax return for my businesses," he explained. "But I need to send it to your sister so she can cash it and send out the money."

"Why don't you just send it to Kina?"

"She might steal it."

"What about your mom?"

"No, she'll tell me I need to budget it."

"I mean—fuck—I guess I can have my sister do it," I said reluctantly.

After my brother died, my mom told me to never get my sister involved in anything. I was breaking another one of my rules. Getting my family involved in prison shit.

"But all the bills to Mark, Chuck and Alex are getting paid off first."

"Yeah, sure. Do you think you can get some more papers from Alex?" asked Dom.

"Dude." I could not believe this guy.

"The money's on its way. All I have to do is give him your sister's address."

"Man, alright. But he better get it there quick," I said and went to find Alex and score some more dope.

Weeks went by and there were still no grams of dope . . . and no money. Every day consisted of the same thing. I was either running over to Mustafa's unit to see what was up or I was running around trying to calm dudes down that Dom owed. Either way it was stressful. The whole time I was doing this, Dom just laid around in the cell like everything was all good.

Mustafa would just keep telling me the same bullshit, "It's coming, man, you just have to be patient."

With Alex, Chuck and a bunch of other dudes he owed I'd have to tell them the same thing. "He's waiting on a chunk of cash. It should be any day now," I eplained. You can really only tell dudes this so many times before they really start to get in their feelings.

"Yo, Hipster, what the fuck is up with your boy?" Chuck asked me in the unit.

"Just waiting, dude," I explained for what seemed to be the hundredth time.

"I'm starting to feel some type of way about this shit." Chuck shook his head. "He don't come say shit to me about what's going on or nothin.'"

"Yeah, he just lays around in bed all day and stays up all night."

"Hipster, tell him that I'm not playin.' I want my motherfuckin' money."

"Alright, man. I've been telling him, but I'll go get on him again and let you know."

"This is bad business, Hipster."

"I know, bro. I'll take care of it."

I went back into the cell and woke Dom up. He was sound asleep at 5:30 p.m.

"Yo, you got to get a hold of whomever and get this money out to Chuck."

"I'll call in a couple hours."

"Man, fuck that. You need to go call now."

"Okay," he said, not even pulling the covers from over his face.

"Yo, I'm fucking serious. Chuck just pulled me up and was pissed. He wants his money or there's going to be problems.

"Alright, I'll go call," he mumbled from under the covers.

"Dude, fucking do it."

"Ok," he said, turning over to face the wall.

"Man, I'm going up to the band room. I'll be back at recall. You got to have something lined up for when I get back so I can tell Chuck." I grabbed my bag and got ready to move for indoor rec. "Get the fuck outta bed and do it," I say stressed on my way out of the cell.

Around seven o'clock Sammy came busting into the band room. "Yo, Hipster, let's go, they just locked Dom up!"

"What?" I said stopping in the middle of a song as the distortion faded into the background.

"They just came and grabbed him off the phone."

"For what?"

"I don't fucking know," said Sammy. "He was someone else's phone though."

"Yeah, but that doesn't mean shit here," I said.

"Well, he's going to the hole."

"What?" It didn't make sense. "Dude you can stab a motherfucker and not go to the hole here."

"No shit. That's why this seems sketchy."

"What do you mean?"

"You think he pulled a check-in move?" Sammy asked.

"Man, that kid got two life sentences. He's not gonna pull no fucking stunt." To check in would mean being ostracized for the rest of his prison life. He would never be able to walk mainline again without fear of his life.

"He owes out a lot of money and dudes are pretty nervous."

"Let's go to the lieutenant's office and see what the fuck's up," I said as I put my guitar away.

Sammy and I headed to the lieutenant's office but they wouldn't tell us shit. All they said is that he was going to the SHU for an investigation. We tried to find out for what, but they wouldn't let anything slip. Whatever was going down they weren't going to talk about it.

"Man, fuck these bitches, Hipster," said Sammy in front of the COs. "Let's get the fuck outta here."

On the walk back to the block we put together what we'd say to dudes on the compound. With all the money he owed, motherfuckers were going to be pissed. We just had to say it was over some bullshit and he'd be back out in a couple days. Then we had to pray to God that it'd come true.

It was like a wave of madness when we came in the block. All types of dudes were coming at me wanted to know what was up. They rattled off the different amounts of money he allegedly owed them and wanting to know when they were going to get paid. The only thing I could tell them was what Sammy and I agreed on. Dom didn't check in. Everything is all good. As soon as he got out in a couple days they'd all get paid.

There was a DC dude named Foxy that Dom owed almost six hundred bucks too. He'd piece Dom out papers of weed, cigarettes, dope, anything he could get and turn around to make money off Dom.

Foxy came into my cell talking shit about this and that. Puffing up his chest about wanting to get paid. He said he knew about the Mustafa deal and he'd take half of that.

"Alright," I said to Foxy. "We'll go over there and you tell him that half of that money is yours and you want it."

"Fuck him," Foxy said puffing out his chest. "Let's go right now."

"Fuck it. I could use the other half to pay off his debts. Let's go."

As soon as we got over to Mustafa's cell, Foxy's tone changed right up. He wasn't on any of his raw-raw shit. When Mustafa told him politely to go fuck himself, that the deal was with Dom and Foxy wasn't gonna get shit, he just put his head down and walked away.

"What happened, dude?" I said goading Foxy on the walk back. "I thought you were going to get that shit."

"Man, he's right. That's between him and Dom. But trust and believe I'm gonna get my muthafuckin money."

"Whatever, bro," I said, breaking off to head back to my cell.

Dom gave me Kina's number a bunch of times to give to other dudes to call her for money. I'd always get on him about it. You don't give out your people's number to just anybody in prison. You never know what the fuck they'd do with it. Dom didn't care. He gave me her number to call if he ran out of minutes or something ever happened. I'd say that going to the hole and the massive bill he had to pay, that was falling on me, counted as good of a reason as any to ring her up.

That first time I called Kina was exhilarating. I was only calling to tell her that Dom was in the hole and that she had to send the money that Dom owed out to everybody. I had a debt to cover of his myself and I was getting ready to lose my fucking mind having to deal with all the motherfuckers pressing me over his debt. Really, at that point though, dialing Kina's number was like being back in junior high school all over again. Calling a girl with your heart beating so fast and your hands sweating like you are on some trucker crank.

As soon as the call went through I heard "Caress Me Down" by Sublime playing in the background. It happened to be one of my favorite songs by the band. It was easy to convince myself that it had to be fate.

Once the message played through with all the options, to accept, decline, or block out permanently I waited until she pressed five to accept.

"Hello," came the sexiest voice I've ever heard in my life.

"Hey, Kina. This is the Hipster. How you doing?"

"I'm cool. Just putting the kids to bed. What's up?"

"Well . . . the Dom is *no mas*."

"What happened?"

"They came and got him for using someone else's phone. They put him in the hole for investigation about sending money."

"How long do you think he'll be in there?"

"I hope not that long. We're going to try and post his bail tomorrow."

"You can do that?"

"That's the beauty of the pen."

"How much will it cost?"

"I don't have to pay any money. Just let the cops know he'll be ok if they let him out."

"Well . . . will he?" Kina's voice shook.

"He'll be alright. He's just got some bills he's got to take care of. That's why I'm calling." Hey, I wasn't going to tell her I've been thinking about her non-stop since seeing her four months ago.

"Yeah, he told me he needed $500 a couple days ago, but I only have like $200. I was going to use it to come down and see him though."

"Well, fuck it. Use it to come down and see him."

"But if he's in the hole, will I get to see him?"

"Yeah, it'll be behind glass. But you'll get to see him. I'm sure he'd like that more and it'll get him out of his cell."

"What if they don't let me in?" It was her first time dealing with the pen too and I tried to ease her worries.

"Don't worry, you'll get in. Don't stress about that. Everything's going to be all good. Hopefully he'll get out tomorrow and can call you."

"If he doesn't, can you call me back and let me know what's going on?"

Hearing that sent a jolt throughout my whole body. I instantly prayed for Dom to spend another day in the hole so I could hear that sweet voice again.

"Yeah, no problem. Either way one of us will get a hold of you. Have a goodnight and don't stress. Ok?"

"Alright. Thanks, Hipster."

I went straight back into my cell, looked at pics of Kina that Dom had left under his mattress and was out of my head in love.

Dom didn't get out of the hole the next day. It took more than a week before he got out. Over a week of motherfuckers that Dom owed money to pressing me for the cash. I was really only on the hook for $200 though for going out and getting stamps for him, and the dude let me know it was on me when he gave it to me.

"Hey, Hipster. You came and got those from me. So I'm not trying to hear anything other than when I'm getting my money," demanded Buck, the stocky 40-year-old DC Black shot caller.

"Yeah, I know, bro. I'm going to make some calls and get it done." Which I did. I had to call all of my friends and raise the funds. Fifty from one, thirty from another, sixty from another, until I got the full two hundred.

I damn sure wasn't paying the other dudes Dom owed. That was on them, and Dom, for getting all those fronts. But they damn sure tried. Texas Syndicate, Bloods, Aryan Brotherhood. All of them came to my cell with the same story.

"Hey, Hipster. We need our money."

"Ok, what do you want me to do about it?"

"Have your people do something."

"Man, I don't owe you nothing. You didn't give me shit!"

"Yeah, but you were doing the shit with him."

"Whatever Dom did with the shit is on him. And I didn't do all that shit. So you're just gonna have to wait like everybody else till he gets out."

The only thing that was getting me through this shit was talking to Kina. I'd call her to quickly update her on the situation. Then we'd talk, about whatever, for the rest of the 15 minutes.

Hearing her voice, hearing her laugh would get me right out of prison. No matter the shit going on with the yard. For those 15 minutes, I was free. When the phone would beep, signaling that I had a minute left and she'd tell me to call back, was better than a shot of dope. I'd have butterflies in my stomach while I waited in line to call. When she'd answer, I'd have the same feeling as the rush of seeing dope going into my body. I had once thought there was a way to get high without drugs. I found it with Kina.

Sometimes it felt like we were just chatting, sometimes it felt like more. I never tried to make a move. I kept it cool. But it seemed like she might be warming up to me. I did little to discourage it. I had come to rely on those phone calls and wanted nothing to jeopardize my fix.

Meanwhile, being in the hole did little to slow Dom down. He still managed to rack up a bill in there. As I was going back into my block, after scoring some wine for my birthday, I heard a pounding on the window of the hole.

"What's up?" I said, looking into the window. "Hipster, Dom's supposed to send me $200. He said for you to call Kina and get her to send it!" demanded a twenty something, tat'd out Mexican Mafia kid.

"What the fuck?"

"She's got my info, you just got to find out when she's going to do it."

"I'll try," I said as I went back inside to celebrate turning thirty in fucking prison.

Back inside my block I got nice and trashed. The way you're supposed to do it in prison for your birthday. Can't let the swine hold you back. Live your life how you normally would and I'd normally get blitzed on my birthday. And just like on the street, you're going to run out of booze. When that happens, you gotta go on a beer run. That doesn't change in prison. So as soon as they opened up the compound for 10 minutes for people to go to where they needed to go, I made a break to go score some more booze in another block. As soon as I came out of my block, the window beating started.

"Motherfucker," I cursed under my breath as I went over to the window. "Dude, I didn't talk to her yet. I'll let you know."

"Hey, homie, we really need it. So make sure you call."

"Alright, bro. I gotta run. I'll let you know." I turned and started to run across the compound. After all, I only had 10 minutes to get it, and then get back. I only made it about 10 feet before I got nailed with the spotlight.

"Stop running!" commanded a voice over the tower loudspeaker.

I slowed down to a speed walk as I made my way through the yard— the spotlight chasing me as I zig-zagged through people. I could hear over walkie talkies from the CO's that I passed for calls to stop me. So when I made it over to the unit at the end of the yard, and with four waiting cops, I turned around and threw up my hands for them to pat me down.

Since I didn't have anything on me, I thought they'd just let me go. Hell, half the time they'll let you go even if you do have something. So when they made me walk up to the lieutenant's office, complete with a two man escort, I started to protest. "The fuck is up with this shit?!"

"They radioed and said to stop you and take you up to the lieutenant's office," replied the CO.

"Man, I didn't do shhhhhhit!" I slurred.

"I don't know what's going on. That's just what they told me."

When I made it to the lieutenant's office, I did my best to stay as far back from the lieutenant as possible. No need for him to catch a whiff of the prison shine.

"What were you doing by the windows?" he pressed me.

"What windows?"

"The windows for the SHU. Why were you there?"

"Some motherfucker was beating on it. I went to see what was up."

"Which was?"

"I don't fucking know. I couldn't hear him."

"You're not allowed over there."

"Mmmm . . . ok."

"Put him in the tank," snapped the fat balding lieutenant to one of his underlings.

They took me to the drunk tank, which already housed two extremely intoxicated Indians waiting to sober up. They didn't put you in the hole for being drunk. Just made you sober up enough to blow lower than a .08 and then let you go back to your unit, with a write up of course. I wasn't in the tank to sober up, which I obviously needed. I was there so that they could go inspect the windows of the SHU to see if I smashed or cut a hole in one. Because how the hell else are they going to get all their drugs if someone didn't? Which I obviously didn't do. But after they checked my bag and smelled my empty wine jug, I was officially a member of the drunken fools club.

When I blew a 1.5 on the breathalyzer the cop chuckled and said, "Yep, you're going to be here for a little bit."

After a couple hours, I managed to blow low enough to get back to my block and my cell. Spending most of my party and buzz at the station. Again, it was just like having a birthday on the street.

Dom finally got out to the SHU a couple days later. It was time to get the situation fixed and fast.

"Dude, you know what the fuck I've been having to deal with out there?" I grilled him.

"Man, I wasn't trying to go to the hole." Dom brushed me off and sat down to play the guitar.

"I had to call every motherfucker I know to get the cash to pay Buck!"

"Ok," he said, fingering a cord.

"And motherfuckers were coming out of the woodwork trying to get me to pay them money you owe!"

"Alright." He began plucking the strings.

"You going to pay 'em or what?

"Yeah, sure." He worked the G string tuning knob and plucked the string again. I could tell he put it way out of tune but it didn't register with him.

"Then get it done. These motherfuckers are pissed."

"What's up with Mustafa?" he asked.

"Man, that dude isn't about shit. I tried to get the motherfucker to come off the money, but he kept saying shit about waiting on the cop. I even took Foxy over there. Told him that Mustafa owed you a grand and he could get paid from him."

"What happened?"

"Foxy was talking all that rah-rah shit about he's going to make him pay the money. And as soon as Foxy goes in the cell Mustafa tells him he's not giving him shit and to kick rocks."

"No shit." Dom strummed an off-tune chord.

"Yeah, and big bad Foxy just said ok and left."

Now Foxy was about six foot, cut up kid from DC. He had almost 10 years on a life sentence. He walked around like he was the baddest motherfucker on earth. But when it comes time to put that work in only a couple real dudes are about it. All Foxy wanted to do was fuck around with the fags. But that's how most of them dudes are.

"I'm going to tell Mustafa I'm done waiting and to give me my money back," Dom said and sat the guitar down.

"Shit, it's about fucking time. He's only had it for two fucking months! We'll go over on the next move with some knives. If he doesn't pay we'll gut the motherfucker," I suggested.

"Nah . . . I'll just go over and talk to him by myself."

Which he did, and of course came back with nothing but a shrug. Dom simply told me Mustafa was going to give him some more time to get everything together. Eventually Dom did manage to pay everyone off that he owed, all the while building up more debt with everyone else.

Putting up with Dom's bullshit was only tolerable before when I could look forward to calling Kina. With him out of the hole, I had no reason to call her. I was moody. I was irritable. It was like I was going through withdrawals. That was until the day that I received an unexpected letter from Kina.

"Hey Hipster," it began in pink ink. "I missed talking to you and decided I'd just write you." She went on to talk about the usual. The kids. Her job. The beach.

Before long we were talking about the future — our future. Kina knew Dom was going to be locked up forever and had only been maintaining contact for the sake of their mutual children. Any love between them had cooled before his trial and incarceration.

I wrote back and forth a bit before we began talking on the phone again. In between I'd reread the letters that I kept safe in my locker. I had them ordered by date which made me wonder when I found them unsorted one day.

Only Dom had that kind of access and I suspected that he had broken into my locker. I couldn't prove it but his sudden iciness toward me spoke volumes.

It was another blazing hot summer day in the swamp that was made even more uncomfortable being in the cell with Dom. No words were spoken again. I had to believe he knew . . . well he knew about everything. Things between Kina and I had gone from casual to comfortable to damn cozy. We were even calling each other baby.

I left early in the morning to go out and run. When I came back inside Dom was out of bed and already gone. It was a rare break from the tension trapped inside such a suffocating cell. I pulled out my guitar and played some songs. Just getting my head out of prison for a bit. Then I went and called Kina.

"Hey, baby." I said.

"Hey. You alright?"

"Yeah, why?"

"Dom called earlier and said that he's going to do something today to save your life."

"The fuck does that mean?"

"I don't know. But he said he could get you killed for what you did."

"For what I did? That motherfucker is breaking into my locker. And he can get me for what I did?! What a little fucker."

"Just be careful, ok?" Kina sounded concerned. "Don't worry. I've been down a while. I know how to handle myself. I'll call you later."

I hung up and went back to my cell. Trying to figure out what he was up to. I'd seen him talking to different dudes. But I didn't think he'd put our business out there. I know I wouldn't. At lunch I let Yaberz know what was going on.

"I told you to smash him!" Yaberz said after finishing off his sandwich.

"I know but I didn't want to do that." "Just be careful, kid. I'll catch up with you later."

I went to commissary to get some supplies. Since I wasn't having to cover debts for Dom with the little bit of money I was getting I was finally stocking up my locker. When I got back it was almost time for the yard to close for the afternoon count. That's when the CO came and got me. Once again, telling me I had to go to the lieutenant's office.

"For what?" I asked. "I don't know, but they've been calling for you for almost an hour," he explained.

"Fuck, alright." I said as I went out the door.

I wasn't on the hot list for drugs anymore. So I knew it wasn't a piss test. I could only figure that it was for either using a cellphone, or it was for Dom.

Walking up the sidewalk, I looked for Yaberz. You don't ever go up to the lieutenant's office by yourself! If you don't have a witness to confirm what you were there for, then you are setting yourself up to be labeled a rat. With the lieutenant it wasn't going to be a social visit. I couldn't find Yaberz anywhere. So I grabbed a young kid from Texas named Shorty off of the handball courts.

"Yo, they called me to the lieutenant's office. I need you to come up with me. This is either for a phone shot or it's for my celly."

"Why would it be for your celly?" Shorty asked.

"Just some shit going on. No biggie."

Standing in front of the lieutenant's office, waiting for them to come out and get us, I spotted Dom walking out of the psychology office.

"Isn't that your celly right there?" Shorty pointed at Dom.

"Yeah, that's him," I said as Dom looked over at Shorty pointing at him and us talking.

Dom walked about 50 yards towards our housing unit. Then he turned around and started walking back to the psych office.

"Well . . . here comes your celly again."

"Yep." I was wondering what the fuck he was up to when they called us into the office.

"Who's this?" the lieutenant asked, pointing at Shorty.

"That's my witness. You know I can't come up here without one."

"Yeah, you're right. I know how it goes."

"What's going on? I got a shot or something?"

"No, nothing like that. You got a note dropped on you saying you owe a lot of money on the compound and your life is in danger."

"What?" I laughed as I said it. Immediately I knew what Dom did. Looking over at Shorty I rolled my eyes and cursed under my breath.

"Look, I don't know where you're getting your information from, but I don't owe any money on the compound. Not even a stamp! So whatever you're hearing is bullshit. There isn't any problems, and there isn't going to be any problems with me here."

After I said it, the lieutenant's phone rang and he held up his finger to indicate he needed a minute. I could hear him talking.

"Yeah . . . I called him up here . . . He said there's no problem . . . I'm sending him back to his unit . . . Yeah, alright." He hung up and then told me to go ahead and go back to my block.

"That rat motherfucker," I said as soon as we walked outside.

"What was that about?" Shorty asked.

"My rat ass fucking celly tried to snitch me off the compound."

"Why would he do that?"

I saw Yaberz across the way. "Yaberz!" I called out and we walked towards each other. "Hey, Hipster. What's up?"

"Fucking rat ass Dom told these fucks I owe money and I'm going to get killed!"

"What the fuck?"

"Yeah, they called me up to the lieutenant's to tell me I had a note dropped on me."

"That's fucked up."

"No shit! I'm going to smash this fucker at count."

"Dude, you can't."

"What? Why the fuck not?"

"Because you can't prove it was him."

"What? Of course it was him. Shit, we saw him come out of

psychology, walk towards the block, look over at us and see Shorty pointing at him. Then he turned around 20 feet later and went back into psych. That's on top of all this shit."

"Yeah, I know. But without proof you look like the bad guy."

"That's fucked up." I shook my head.

"That's how it is."

"So what am I supposed to do?"

"Just go back to the cell and act like nothing happened."

"Are you fucking serious?"

"Yeah, I'll talk to Shorty and make sure he doesn't say anything. But don't do shit. Come see me after chow and we'll figure out our next move."

"Alright. It isn't going to be easy, but I won't do shit. Catch up with you later." We did a bro hug and left.

I went back inside the unit fuming. I couldn't believe that a dude with two life sentences, who didn't rat on the street, would come to prison and start snitching.

"That motherfucker tried to rat me off the compound," I told Kina the next time we got a phone call.

"What? What happened?" She sounded confused.

I told her everything that happened. Kina was quiet as she tried to understand it all. She sighed and said, "That doesn't surprise me."

"It doesn't?"

"No, he's a weasel like that. Listen, when I come see you, there's a lot of things that I'll tell you that will change what you think. Because he's obviously told you a lot of bullshit."

"Oh, yeah," I murmured

"Yeah."

"Alright, listen, it's time to lock in. I'll call you later."

After I got off the phone a couple different dudes that he owed money to came asking where he was. They also said how they saw him walk towards the building and then turn around and walk back to the office buildings.

"Yeah, I don't know where he is," I said knowing damn well what he just did. "I'll let him know you were looking for him."

I still thought that he was going to come back, up until they locked the doors and he was nowhere to be found. Then when the CO brought a bag for me to pack up his stuff, I knew he wasn't coming back.

When the doors unlocked I went into damage control. I immediately went to James. The shot caller for the unit and now over the whole midwest crew of dudes. James has been down for well over 20 years and was doing multiple life sentences. He had two murders since he's been down and was one away from the death sentence.

"Hey, James," I said. "Look Dom owes a bunch of money on the pound and told dudes that my sister was getting money for him. There isn't any money there and I know these dudes are going to press me."

"Yeah, I know, Hipster. I know all about Kina, the money, everything."

"What?" I said dumbfounded.

"Dom's been trying to get you hit for weeks now."

"What?" The surprises kept coming.

"He came to us and said you stole Kina's info out of his locker and have been calling her. That and he had money sent to your sister and you won't give it to him."

"That's fucking bullshit," I cursed loudly. "Dude, he gave me Kina's number to call her for money! And my sister has been waiting on this money for like four months now."

"I believe you. I told him when he came to us that I see how you walk around here doing your time, and how he does his time. That we'll get both of you in the cell together and find out the real story. By this time another dude named Joe, from the midwest car, who Dom started shooting dope with recently came up, mean mugging me.

"You feel good now you piece of shit," he said a foot away from my face.

"Who the fuck are you talking to?!" I snapped back.

His eyes narrowed. "Yeah, I know what the fuck you did to Dom."

"He's telling me what happened right now Joe. And it's just like I told you I thought it was," James jumped to my defense.

"Well, where's Dom at now?" asked Joe.

"In the hole," I explained. "All I know is I got called up to the lieutenant's office cause a note got dropped on me. Dom came out of the psych office while I was up there waiting and he saw me and Shorty. Then he turned around and went back inside. Now he's in the hole, you figure it out."

"Joe, go see if the cop will tell you what happened," said James.

After Joe left James laid it on me, "Now we're not the only people Dom went to about hitting you. He went to the DC car to get you too."

"Motherfucker!"

"But they obviously couldn't get you cause of the race thing. Now you gotta ask yourself who else he went to."

"No shit."

"I can control my guys. But you never know who might come at you."

"What a fucking bastard!" I yelled.

"No other race is going to jump on you. If they tried, I got your back, which means my guys got your back."

"Thanks, man."

James started laughing and said, "So how the hell did it all start?"

I broke it all down to him and he just laughed the whole time. "Well good for you. I told my guys that it's not like you can steal a girl from someone. If she wants to leave a motherfucker, that's what she's going to do."

"No, I didn't steal her from him." It wasn't like that.

"Listen, as long as you're up front with me about everything then I got your back."

Joe came back and said that the CO didn't know what he got locked up for. That if Dom checked in, then fuck him. He told me to pack up all his stuff and not steal anything.

"He'll get all his shit. I'm no fucking thief."

"Hell, you stole his fucking wife, motherfucker," Joe interjected as he walked out of the cell.

That night after chow, I tracked down Yaberz to tell him everything. "Dude, Dom's in the hole," I explained to him. "I talked to James and he said he's known about all this shit for weeks."

"No shit?"

"Yeah, and he said Dom tried to get me hit."

"Man, I fucking told you."

"I know; I know. How many people you think he told?"

"Does it really matter? The ones he told will just tell everyone else."

"Prison is worse than a fucking old folk's home," I muttered.

"You're just going to have to fall back for a while. No coming out to run, no soccer . . . Hell, don't even watch TV anymore."

"What?"

"I'm telling you, until something else happens here, you're going to be in the spotlight."

"Fuck that shit. I'll go crazy stuck in the cell!"

"It's better than getting fucked off," said Yaberz.

"Yeah, I guess. But—"

"But nothing. Look on the bright side at least you got the girl."

My mind drifted to Kina. And I felt a bit better.

"I'm going to go see how bad it is," said Yaberz. "Hipster, go walk around or something. Clear your mind."

While I was out walking around, doing my usual incense and certificate hustling, I could feel the animosity. *Maybe it's just in my head,* I told myself while getting the cold shoulder from dudes. The more the night wore on, the more uneasy I became. It was the first time in my almost seven years that I didn't feel safe. I was almost in a couple different race riots, "political" infighting with different groups of whites, but that wasn't the same. Now it was like I had a target on me. When Yaberz came back around, it wasn't soon enough.

"So what's up?"

"It's pretty bad, kid," Yaberz said, looking down at the ground.

"How bad?"

"It's all over the yard."

"Fuck!"

"The ones that don't know will know by morning."

"Fuck, what do you think is going to happen?"

"I can't really say." Yaberz shrugged.

"I mean—fuck—do I need a knife?" My mind started racing.

"Since you said something, yeah get a blade. I just didn't want to scare you."

"Well fuck, man I don't have one right now."

"Here take mine." Yaberz pulled out a bone crusher from under his shirt. "Go inside and stay in your cell. And stay on point. I'll come over after breakfast tomorrow and we'll figure out what to do."

"Thanks, bro."

"Don't leave your cell," Yaberz stressed to me as he walked away.

"Yeah, I got you," I called back as I crept my way through the yard back to my cell. Keeping my head down, but eyes up, scanning the prison for any immediate threat. My grip tightened on the hidden knife.

As soon as I got inside, I called Kina. She was my escape from the madness.

"Hey, baby," I said.

"Why didn't you call me back?" Her soft voice soothed the tension even if her question was urgent.

"Well . . ." I paused, took a breath and then I told her the whole story.

"Oh, my god, Hipster, I didn't think he'd go that far with it!"

"Yep, told dudes I stole his wife and money!"

"But we're not even together like that! I'm just his kids' mother . . . and the only one who didn't get arrested in his case."

"I know."

"That's because he never gave me shit. I paid my own rent, car, bills—everything."

"Yeah, but they don't know that!"

"Well, I'll write a letter to whomever and tell them," she said sincerely.

"I don't quite think that's going to work." I laughed as I said it even if I was thankful she was willing to step in like that. Her letters had started the problem so there was no need to escalate it further.

"What's going to happen?"

"I don't know. I just know it's really bad right now. I'll know more tomorrow," I said.

"Ok, call me in the morning."

"You know I will." I paused, racking my brain to see if there was anything left to say in the ticking seconds. I settled for "I love you" not believing the words the situation had dragged out of my mouth. Fuck it. I did.

"I love you too," she instantly responded. Facing death to have a woman's love was at least something.

I went back to my cell and stayed posted up. Sitting in my chair, with my back against the wall. Knife wrapped around my hand. The lights were turned off so I could see out, but any would be assailants wouldn't be able to see me. After the doors locked for the night, I could kind of relax a bit. Give myself a chance to absorb what had all transpired. I hung up some pictures that Kina sent to me. Why not? I thought. It's not like everybody didn't already know. I'd stare at her pictures and I'd hear what my best friend Bruce said to me after I told him the deal. "This is going to end bad," I mumbled his prophetic words to myself.

But I'd feel . . . hope, looking at this beautiful woman. I had really found the woman of my dreams and whatever I had to go through to be with her was worth it. Instead of getting out of prison and selling drugs, I now thought about how great it would be to just work a normal job. Hell, I'd work a fryer at McDonald's if it meant I got to fall asleep and wake up with Kina in my arms. I really and truly loved her with all my heart and soul. All I have to do, I thought, is make it out alive.

There really was no sleeping that night, the knife stayed wrapped around my wrist. I only had moments of drifting off, only to hear a noise and pop out of my reality escape. There was no way I was going to be sleeping when the doors unlocked. So when I heard the keys hit the lock it was like the ringing of the bell for round one. I made it a point to stay under my blanket, window covered and lights off. *I'll fool them*, I told myself. *They'll come thinking it'll be an easy hit. Then I'll spring at them like a wolverine.* I played out the scenario over and over in my mind like an action movie.

Breakfast came and went, then work call, and finally the yard was open. I kept waiting for Yaberz to come over and tell me something—anything—that would make this all disappear. Eight came, then nine, and still no Yaberz. I'd get up and peek out my window, seeing Yaberz going around to different groups. He was doing his normal politicking. It was usually to see and find out the latest news. Today it just so happened that I was that news. When he finally came in at ten and peeked in my window, all he could see was an outline of me under the covers.

"Damn, Hipster," he said to me as he walked in the darkened cell. "What are you fucking crazy?"

"Probably," I said as I launched out of the bed ready for battle.

"Fuck. at least you're in the right frame of mind." Yaberz laughed and cut the tension.

"I've been like this all fucking morning waiting on you." I tucked the knife away.

"Been out politicking."

"Yeah, I saw you. So what's up?"

"Well, everyone's talking about it."

"What are they saying?"

"That you stole his wife's info out of his locker and started writing her."

"What? Come on, man. You know—"

"And that he sent your sister money and you stole it."

"Dude, that's bullshit. Did you tell them the deal?"

"I'm just trying to see where everyone stands right now. They all know you're my boy and aren't going to tell me too much if I defend you."

"Well, what do you think?"

"I think if it was my old lady one of us would be leaving on a stretcher. But you did tell him what was going on, so it's not like you stole her or anything."

"Exactly, he had me calling her!"

"I don't agree with it, but you're my boy and I love you. So, I got your back."

"So now what?" I asked as I sat back down on the bunk.

"Just keep as low of a profile as you can right now. Let me talk to some more dudes and see what they think and where it's gonna go."

"Alright, kid, but hurry up. I'm fucking losing my mind over this."

Yaberz smiled at me as he walked out and said, "Cheer up, Hipster. At least you got the girl."

I didn't even go to lunch that day. I'd call Kina every couple of hours to let her know I was ok. That and to remind myself why this was all worth it. Instead of going to dinner, I met up with Bruce down at the rec center and played music. That and to just shoot the shit.

Bruce was the type of kid I would hang with on the street. He didn't have the prison mentality. Talking to him was like talking to a "normal" person. He was someone whose opinion I'd always take to heart. He'd never be on the "go stab him in the neck" mentality. But more on the "how the fuck can you get out of this in one piece?" mindset.

"Yep, you were right," I said. "It turned out bad."

"Yeah, I heard," said Bruce. The news really had spread that fast.

"Dom went to James and Foxy to try to get me hit."

"Of course, he's a weasel like that."

"And he tried to rat me off the pound."

"What else was he going to do? If he couldn't get dudes to hit you, he damn sure wasn't going to do it himself."

"I didn't expect him to do that," I said.

"You always got to plan for the worst, Hipster. At least it's all out right now, so you don't have to hide from it."

"Yeah. I just got to hide from the motherfuckers on the pound that are making it their business."

"Something will happen and you'll be old news. You'll be alright," he said as he picked up a guitar. "Let's play some music; it'll make you feel better."

Bruce clicked on the distortion pedal and smiled as the electric hum filled the space. The music took me away for the hour that we got to play. I was actually kind of feeling alright about everything. Maybe Bruce was right. That mindset crumbled quick as soon as we walked outside in fact and the devil was waiting for me. The Aryan mafia's second-in-command Shady, the aforementioned devil, was waiting on me with Foxy.

Shady was in his mid-twenties and had been doing time almost his whole life. He was skinny with long black hair. Patched up with the AM when he was 16 and had a lot of rank in the gang. We used to live on the same block and all got high together. When Dom went to the SHU the first time I asked Shady to give me the money he owed Dom so I could pay off some of his bills but he told me he didn't have anything and then was out buying dope that night. I stopped fucking with him after that. There's nothing worse than a junkie. Especially one that doesn't take care of their bills.

Foxy and Shady were real close. To the point of hugging each other around the compound and kicking it in each other's cells with the windows blocked for hours at a time. A lot of questionable shit that if he wasn't an AM would have got him into a lot of shit. Kicking it that way with a known fag, who was a different race. But that was the double standard those dudes are on.

"What's up, Hipster?" Shady asked mockingly. "Feeling good about yourself?"

"Yeah, I am." I showed no fear.

"Let's take a walk," he urged me.

As we walked over towards the track, Bruce went to track down Yaberz for me.

"So, Hipster. You put Dom in the SHU?" Shady asked.

"Fuck, no. That motherfucker went up to psychology and ratted on me. Said I owe money on the yard and I was going to get killed."

"Oh, yeah. Who went up to the lieutenant's office with you?"

"Shorty did! Your homeboy was my witness," I explained.

This threw Shady off for a second. He didn't know that I covered my ass with one of his own people. There was no way he could dispute what went on.

"I'll ask him," said Shady, as if not believing me.

"Ok, you do that." I laughed out loud.

"You even feel like a piece of shit for stealing Kina?" asked Shady.

"First of all, she wasn't his girl. He might have told you she was, but she wasn't. That motherfucker hasn't told the truth about anything since he's been here. And second, he had me calling her. Just like he gives her number out to all these other motherfuckers that he owes money."

"Speaking of money, you stole his money."

"No, I've been waiting on money from him for over four months now. There ain't shit."

"Well, he owes Foxy $1,250. And you're going to pay it."

"No, I'm not paying shit. Cause there isn't any money."

"You lying, Hipster. Dom told me you got it," Foxy chimed in. He had been standing on the sidelines eyeing the situation.

"I don't care what the fuck he told you. There isn't shit."

"Foxy's going to get paid, Hipster," Shady said.

"With what? I don't have any money. I don't owe him shit, and for all I know he's making it up."

"You know he owed me money!" Foxy yelled out like a bitch.

"Yeah, but I don't know how much."

"I got everything written down."

"Ok, but you could just be making up numbers."

"Listen, motherfucka, I'm going to get my money." It was easy for Foxy to get lippy with his man Shady acting as a human shield.

"Well, then you better go to the hole and try to get it out of Dom cause you ain't getting shit from me."

"What?" Foxy yelled and moved towards me.

Shady stepped in front of him to keep him back. It didn't matter how close they were. It was a strictly "hands off" policy with other races.

"You got $2,400 coming right?" asked Shady.

"No, $2,100 is supposed to be coming, but it's been months."

"Well, when it gets there, Foxy gets his $1,200."

"No, Alex gets $750, Speedy gets $600, and my boy gets $250. That only leaves $500." I already had it portioned out according to Dom's instructions.

"No, Foxy gets his $1,200. Whatever's left everyone else gets."

"Huh? Fuck no. Dom and I talked about this in the cell. That's what I know he owes. And I cosigned on it. So they're getting paid."

"How do we know he owes that?" Shady asked.

"Shit, ask Foxy. He knows Dom owes them."

"I know, but he owes me too," Foxy said defensively.

"Yeah, but he's owed them for months. And he's owed my boy for 8 months! So they're all getting paid what I know he owes."

"Well, everybody is going to have to get less so Foxy gets his," Shady demanded.

"So what do you want me to do? Go tell them dudes that I know he owes you and we agreed to pay you this money but the AM want me to pay a bill to Foxy that I don't know about?"

"I don't care what you tell them," Shady said. "That's how it's gonna be."

"Then what? Then we're cool?"

"I didn't say we're cool. You'll just have done what we told you to do and we won't stab you right now." Shady started laughing maniacally.

I slid my hand into my bag and grabbed my knife that I'd kept stashed since this all began. I was thinking about just putting an end to it right then. But I knew if I stabbed him right there I'd lose my chance of going to a medium facility, but more importantly. I wouldn't get to see Kina.

Was this new love already making me soft? I wondered.

"Look, if this money comes then we'll work something out," I said. "But Dom's lied about so much shit that I doubt there ever was any money coming."

"Well, for your sake you better hope that money gets there quick, cause Foxy better get paid this week." Shady and Foxy strutted away.

"What the fuck was that about?" Yaberz asked as he and Bruce came up to me. They were at a distance watching what was going down the whole time, making sure that I didn't get jumped.

"That motherfucker said I got to pay Foxy," I explained.

"You told him you don't have any money right?" Bruce asked.

"Yeah, I told him. He didn't give a fuck. Said I better have his money by this week."

"How much is it?" Yaberz asked.

"Twelve hundred!"

"Dom rang up $1,200 to Foxy?" Bruce asked.

"Shit, he did that in like two weeks," I said adding it up.

"Fuck, can you cover it?" Yaberz asked.

"Can I cover it? Hell no!"

"So what do you wanna do?" Yaberz wondered.

"Shit! I don't fucking know."

"You're two months from going to a medium right?" Bruce asked.

"Yeah." I shook my head in dismay.

"I told you this was going to turn out bad," Bruce said.

"I know; I know. But we're a little bit past that now."

"When's Kina coming to see you?" Yaberz asked.

"Next weekend."

"So you got to make it to that at least," Yaberz said.

"Especially after going through this bullshit," Bruce chimed in.

"No shit." All this trouble had to be worth something.

"At least you'll get some tongue action," Yaberz teased.

"Fuckin' right," I said back as we walked around the track in silence for a minute.

"Man, I should just get this visit and have you jump me when I come out," I suggested to Yaberz.

Yaberz hesitated, weighing his next words. "I didn't want to say it. But that's probably your best bet," he said.

"I'd only have to sit back in the hole for a couple months before I go to an FCI."

"It'd be a lot better coming from just me than a bunch of other dudes."

"Well, no shit."

"You'd get to see Kina, know if you really care about her or not, and then be done with having to deal with this drama," Bruce said.

"And you'd get some tongue action!" Yaberz chimed in, laughing.

"Will you get sent to the gang program if you get me?" I asked Yaberz who was always getting into trouble for something.

"They said one more write up and I'm gone," he admitted.

"Man, I don't want to get you fucked up like that," I said.

"You're solid, Hipster. It'd be worth it to me to get you outta this mess."

"I love you, bro." We hugged over it.

"You just hook me up with one of her friends!" Yaberz said back.

"So this is what you really want to do?" Bruce asked.

"Fuck, it doesn't really seem like I got too much of a choice."

"How about you go back and think about it? You still got a couple days before you got to decide," Bruce said, always the voice of reason.

"You're right. I'll think on it. Call Kina and see what she thinks."

"Watch what you say over the phone," Yaberz reminded me.

"Dude, I know all about what not to say on the phone."

"Alright, I'll see you guys tomorrow," Yaberz said as he ran off.

"Man, it really sucks it's got to end like this," Bruce said to me as he hugged me and then walked away.

I figured with Yaberz getting ready to lay down some damage I'd better touch base with home. I never knew when I'd get whisked off to the hole for my protection. I called my sister and filled her in on what was going down.

"All over some fucking money," I mumbled. "I knew better than to trust Dom."

"That's here!" my sister said.

"What is?" I asked.

"The money. It's here."

"No shit!" That was a surprise.

"It's only for $2,000 though."

"Fuck it. It's better than nothing."

"So, what do you want me to do with it?"

"Cash it! I'll call you back."

I ran out to go find Yaberz, I wanted him to know what was up before I told anyone else. "Yo, kid. That money finally made it," I said.

"It did?" He was as shocked as I was.

"Yeah, I guess he told the truth about one thing," I said.

"So what are you trying to do?"

"Pay off the motherfuckers that I know he owes."

"What about Foxy?" asked Yaberz.

"I don't know that he owes him that much. I know that he owes him. But that dude could just be making up a number. For real, I'd rather just give it to Kina. She needs it more than Foxy does."

"So what, you going to pay everyone but Foxy and have me jump you after the visit?"

"I don't know. What do you think?"

"I can talk to Joey and see if you pay everything what will happen."

Joey was the captain of the yard for the Aryan Mafia. Whatever he said was law. Since the AM's controlled the yard nobody went against him.

"Yeah, see what he says. I only got a couple months till I can get a transfer. It'd be nice to not have to do that in the hole."

"Alright. I'm going to see him tonight so I'll let you know in the morning."

"Cool, I'll see you then."

"Hey, Hipster. Don't get caught slipping." Yaberz pointed his finger at me to remind me of the seriousness of the situation.

Things were looking better, but I was still swimming with the sharks in the deep end. "I'm way ahead of you on that, kid."

Back inside the block I went to tell Alex the good news. He was finally going to get paid. He'd been waiting for almost six months to get his money from Dom.

Alex was a good dude. A short and stocky Mexican who used to be a bodybuilder. I knew that I could trust him not to say anything about the money. As long as he got his money he couldn't care less.

"What's up, Alex?" I said smiling.

"What's up, Hipster? What are you smiling about?" He wiped the sweat from his brow.

"Same reason you're about to be happy."

"Why's that?"

"Cause that money got to my sister," I said as I gave him a pound.

"Man, that's good news. I really need it now too."

"Well, you got it, dude. Just don't say nothing about it. These motherfuckers are crawling outta the woodwork trying to get money."

"Yeah, I heard about Foxy and the AM's. You're going to be alright?"

"I got Yaberz working on it right now. I just wanted you to know that you're straight."

"Thanks, Hipster. I appreciate it." He dapped me again.

"No problem, bro. I'll catch up with you in a bit."

I went and called Kina. Told her all the news. About what I was planning and what all was going on. When I told her I was thinking about just giving her the money so she could do what she wanted with it, she told me how much she could use it. But her main thing was for me to be safe and smart. Do what I needed to do to make it out of all this in one piece. She thought a friend might move in and help with her bills and she'd be okay.

At the end of all our conversations, she'd tell me she loved me and blow me a kiss. It would always remind me that the whole thing was worth it. Then hang up, put my hand in my pocket to grab my knife, and crept back into my cell. Always weary for who was coming towards me.

Yaberz saw me the next day and told me about what Joey said. If I paid Foxy and everyone else that I'd be ok.

"Man, I don't got enough to pay everyone what I know he owes and still pay Foxy."

"He said you got to take care of Foxy and what's left pay everyone else," Yaberz explained.

"Did you tell him I know how much he owes out? And that we agreed to pay those dudes with the money I got sent to my sister. That and I don't know what he really owes Foxy."

"Dude, he don't care. You know Foxy is Shady's little fuck buddy."

"So, who am I supposed to short?"

"I don't know, kid. Just pay what you think dudes should get."

"What the fuck?"

"There's one more thing."

"Yeah, what's that?" In prison there's always one more thing.

"He said I got to fuck you up as you punishment for getting with the girl."

"What? I'm independent! I don't fall under the gang's bullshit."

"Look, I'll just give you a couple black eyes, cut your lip and he'll be happy. That and everyone else will fall back cause they'll see you got fucked up over it."

"Man . . . and then this shit is done?"

"Yeah, then you just lay low till you roll out to an FCI."

"Fuck it. Why not?" What choice did I have?

"That means no more running out here or soccer. None of that shit. You just stay in the unit," instructed Yaberz.

"Dude, I'm not fucking doing that."

"You got to stay out of the way. Let motherfuckers forget about you."

"I'll go fucking crazy stuck inside all day."

"Listen, you could still come out. I'm just saying the smart thing to do is to stay outta dudes' sight."

"Man, I'll fall back, but not that far."

"Alright, think about it though," he stressed.

"Alright. I'll let you know who's all going to get what, and when you get to beat me ass!"

"That's right. That ass is mine," Yaberz said with a smile.

I knew that I was going to pay Alex all his money. He deserved it after waiting for over six months. Plus the only reason that he really gave shit to Dom was cause I told him the kid was good for it. I wouldn't be able to pay my boy back, but I also knew he wouldn't stab the shit out of me if I didn't! Which left one other dude, Speedy. A Latin King who Dom owed for a while too. He was only going to be able to get half his money. Which I knew he wasn't going to be happy with.

"Hey, Speedy. Look, the AM's said I got to pay Foxy."

"Ok," Speedy said. A six foot cock diesel Latin King soldier. "So that means I can only pay you $250."

"What the fuck, Hipster? I'm supposed to get $600 of that money."

"Dude, I know. I told them that. But they don't give a shit. You know Foxy is Shady's little butt boy."

"Fuck that shit." Speedy stomped his foot on the asphalt.

"I know, it's fucked up. But there isn't shit I can do about it. If I don't pay him then it's my ass. You know they run the yard."

So I'm the only one getting fucked, huh?"

"Dude, I can't even pay back my boy and Dom's owed him for six fucking months."

"Shit, he's owed me for five months!"

"Yeah, but the whole reason I got this sent to me was to pay him back."

"Fuck this. I'll step to Joey and tell him what's up.

"Go ahead. I hope he does say to pay you instead. I fucking hate that fucking Foxy. But I'm telling you I already tried. He isn't having it."

"Fuck," cursed Speedy. The disappointment registered on his face. "Just pay me the $250 and I'll get the rest when Dom gets out."

"Dude, I don't think Dom's getting out."

"Why not? Cause you dropped a slip on him so that you could steal his old lady?" Speedy jabbed.

"What?" It shouldn't have shocked me that Speedy heard the story.

"Yeah, I know all about it," he snipped. "Everybody knows."

"Oh, yeah . . . hold on," I said as I went to find James,who told me if I have any problems to get him.

"What's the problem?" James asked.

"Speedy thinks I dropped a slip on Dom to get Kina and the money."

"Naw, I didn't say all that," Speedy backtracked. "Yeah, you did. You said I dropped a slip to steal his old lady."

"That's just what I heard."

"Listen, I went and asked the SIS what's up with Dom and he said that Dom did some dirty shit and he won't be coming back out," James said.

"Alright man. I'm just trying to get my money."

"So are a lot of other dudes too," I reiterated.

"At least you're getting some of it. Most of these dudes that he owes aren't getting shit," James said.

"Alright, Hipster. Just get me the $250 and we're good."

"Cool, just give me the info and I'll get it out."

We all turned to walk separate ways. I thanked James for having my back.

"I told you. I don't think you did anything wrong," he said. "Nobody is going to jump you in here."

"Yeah, that doesn't really help me on the yard though."

"Listen, if you feel it's going to pop off out there. Come get me. My guys have to roll if I jump in for you."

For the next couple days things were calm. I knew nobody was going to get me—at least till the money got paid. The gang and their nut swingers had their orders. It didn't stop them from talking shit to me everywhere I went. It wasn't uncommon to get a "fucking piece of shit" or a "scumbag" from dudes. But honestly, when I'd get on the phone and talk to Kina it'd all just drift into the background. The fact that she was coming to see me that weekend made it really all go away.

The plan was to send everyone their money on the night before the visit. I'd go up and see her, then come back and get a strategic beating. Hopefully, after that something else would take the front page away from me and I could sail away to a medium facility in a few months. Sounded good, right? But in prison, just like in life, nothing happens how you plan it.

"I can't get the money for a week!" my sister told me.

"The fuck do you mean you can't get the money for a week?" I yelled dumbfounded into the phone.

"It's going to take a week to clear," she explained.

"Dude, I don't have a week! It's gotta be on Saturday or I'm fucked!"

"Well, I don't know what to tell you. It's not going to happen."

"Fuck . . . Fuck . . . Fuck," I stuttered into the phone.

"Just go tell whoever that it's going to be a week."

"Yeah, that's not going to work. I'm barely hanging on by a string right now."

"Then go tell the CO's that you need to go to protective custody."

"Fuck no! That's never an option," I said.

"Well, what are you going to do?"

"Shit, I have no idea. I'll call you back."

I went to my cell to try and dream up some type of a miracle. I already knew if I didn't pay at the end of the week that I was fair game. They'd think I was trying to keep the money and I'd be hit. All the work that

Yaberz put in would go out the window. I'd be a pin cushion for sure! *What the fuck am I going to do?* was all that I kept thinking to myself.

I went out to call Kina. Lose myself for those 15 minutes of bliss. Take away the drama for just a short time. Basically get my sweet fix.

"Hey, baby," I said.

"Hipster, I just talked to you sister."

"Shit's so fucked up," I said.

"I'm going to pay everything with my rent and bills money. Then she's going to pay me back," explained Kina.

"No shit?"

"Yeah, but you've got to make sure she pays me back. If she doesn't then I'm screwed."

"Babe, you're awesome."

"It is half my fault that you're in this to begin with. So, it's the least I can do. Plus, I'm dying to see you and I know I can't until this gets taken care of."

"Fuckin' A. So, I'll be seeing you on Sunday for sure then?" I said. All those days of staring at her picture and it was actually happening.

"Yeah, baby!"

"I love you," I said.

"I love you too."

I never got tired of hearing that. "Alright, kid . . . it's all set up," I told Yaberz out on the yard.

"Everyone's getting paid?" he asked.

"Well, my boy isn't. Speedy isn't getting all of his money, but everyone else is."

"Ok, this is what we'll do. Get all the confirmation numbers but don't tell anyone. After your visit on Sunday, I'll come over before dinner, get the numbers, kick your ass, and you're good," Yaberz said as he slapped my hand.

"Yeah, buddy," I said with a smile. It was strange to be so happy to get a beat down.

The day of the visit was fucking intense. Visiting Kina for the first time was mind numbing. I wondered if we'd connect even more or if it would all fizzle. Then I had to face the fact that I was about to get my ass kicked no matter how calculated it would be right after the VI. I'd been in a couple fights in my life, but never willingly let someone beat me up. It was all getting real surreal.

I woke up early and did a little meditation to clear my mind. Then I smoked a joint. Visits from anyone were like a combination of Christmas, my birthday and the Fourth of July all rolled into one. With it being a smoking hot woman that I was crazily in love was kind of like a porno too.

I sat and waited, thinking they'd call me any minute. It was 8 a.m. and I was sure that she'd be the first one. After twenty minutes I went and got a cigarette. Something for the nerves, I reasoned. Twenty more minutes go by and nothing. I started to get paranoid. *Maybe she changed her mind? Maybe they wouldn't let her in?* I didn't know what to think.

I pulled my guitar down and played some songs. Anything to keep my mind from racing. It was 9 a.m. and still nothing. I strummed some more chords and sang a song. fast, catchy tune about waiting for a girl. *Where are you, right now? Where are you . . . right now?* I went through this song for almost twenty minutes. *Where the fuck are you?*

Just when I was going to try the phone to see what was up, the CO came to my cell to let me know I had a visitor.

"Fuck yeah!" I said and jumped up out of my chair. I grabbed my water bottle and walked out of the cell. My plan was to play it off as a drug test to everyone out on the yard. No eye contact, no hello's. Just shoot straight for the front of the prison. I was going to get the visit no matter what!

What happened afterward was totally different. I made it up to the visiting room with no consequences and was greeted by the CO on duty.

"She's here to see you?" the CO said to me as he stripped me out to go to the visit. He had already got an eyeful of her.

"Yep." I grinned like the cat that caught the canary.

"Doesn't she come see another guy too?" he asked, puzzled.

"Yeah, she used to," I said back while putting my khakis back on.

"Um . . . I don't even want to know." I could see the wheels turning in his head about what was going to happen with this.

"I know her from the Phish tour."

"I said I don't even want to know." He opened the door for me to go and embrace the woman that had changed my life in prison profoundly.

As I exited I saw her. She was breathtaking. The sight of Kina and the energy between us as I walked towards her was amazing. It was the longest and shortest twenty feet of my life. There were no words spoken when I reached her. We kissed intensely and passionately. All my worries melted as we became one right there, surrounded by walls and gun towers. All the hostility and violence evaporated for that eternally short minute. The visiting room was my nirvana. I couldn't get stabbed or harassed. Instead, I got to stare into beautiful brown eyes, feel the touch of the woman of my dreams, and it felt like I was free.

I felt like a fifth grader. Just so excited to hold my girlfriend's hand. To hear her sexy voice, to smell her perfume. I had never felt so alive in prison as I did in those few hours. Nothing mattered. Nothing. I could have gotten killed when the visit was over and would have been happy. She was everything I knew she would be and more.

She got me a soda out of the vending machine. I told her about everything that was going on. There was really only so much you could say over the prison phone without getting yourself jammed up. So when she found out just how serious it was, she couldn't believe it.

"But me and Dom weren't even together," she said, clutching my hand.

"Yeah, they don't give a fuck." I told her.

"Why do they even care?"

"Because they have nothing better to do."

"Can I write a letter to someone to tell them what's up?"

"No . . . It doesn't work that way." I laughed as I rubbed her thigh

She was wearing jeans that were ripped on the knees, and touching her bare skin was incredible. I started to talk dirty to her as we sat next to each other. Making her blush as she kissed me on the cheek.

"So, what's some of the bullshit that Dom's said to you?" she asked.

"Well . . . what's up with this money he says you have?"

"That motherfucker didn't leave me with shit. He spent all the money he made on his other girls. That's the reason why I didn't get in trouble. I work, I pay my own bills and I bought my own car. We had no connection other than the kids."

"He said his kids will never want for anything."

"Shit, the only thing the kids have are a watch and a ring that I kept, and he wants me to pawn that to send him money."

"Keep that for the kids," I said.

"He said he has to pay protection to the whites, blacks, and Mexicans.

"What?"

"He'll say if I don't send money then he's going to have to suck big nigger dick!"

"Are you serious?"

"And that he has to get raped to go to the law library."

"Baby, do you think if I had to get raped to go to the law library that I'd go?"

"No."

"Let alone tell someone about it." Dom was unbelievable.

"He just knows what to say to me and his parents so we give him money."

"That's fucked up."

"I've pawned everything he had to send him money. What's it for?"

"Dope, cigarettes, weed," I said.

"He's taking from his kids for that?"

"I thought you knew that?"

"Hell no! I thought it was for protection."

"What about the picture of the girl in the Corona bathing suit—"

"My cousin?" she cut in.

"That's what I thought." I clapped my hands.

"What about her?"

"He said it's your friend and you have threesomes all the time."

"My eighteen-year-old cousin?" Her nose wrinkled.

"And that if you were tired or whatever that he'd just fuck her and you were cool with it."

"Really? Do you think I'm like that?"

"Well, no. That's why I was asking," I said. "So, I can't do any of that with you?" I teased her.

"Fuck no," she said and slapped my arm playfully.

"I don't want any other girls. Just you."

Kina smiled and looked down, blushing. Her hand tightened around mine. "I love you, baby."

"I love you too, Kina."

The day went on like that until visiting hours were over and the guard made the announcement to make it official.

"Visiting hours are over. Say your goodbyes. All inmates to the walls and all guests come up front," the guard called out from the desk.

We looked deeply into each other's eyes and squeezed our hands together. The visit was like magic. It reinforced that we were meant to be together. That everything I was going through was worth it. We stood and kissed. It was as electric as the first kiss we shared six hours earlier. Her body pressed against mine. We really were one person, one soul. Nothing would be able to stop us from being together.

"Here we go," I smiled.

"I love you, baby," Kina said.

"Time to go get my ass kicked."

"Don't say that."

"It's all good, baby. That's how it's got to be."

"Call me as soon as you get out from count."

"I will *mi amore.*"

We kissed one more quick passionate kiss and reluctantly let go of each other. I couldn't take my eyes off of Kina as she swayed out of the visiting room. I was beyond addicted to her. But for now it was back to the slaughterhouse to await my fate. I knew Yaberz would be waiting for me.

"How was it?" Yaberz said to me when I stepped back onto the compound. He made sure to wait for me to come out, not wanting anyone to jump me for seeing her.

"Dude, it was fucking bad ass." I couldn't hide my elation.

"You get some tongue action?"

"Of course," I said as I let out a smirk.

"You fucking dog!" Yaberz punched me on the shoulder

"And it was fan-fucking-tastic."

"So, you ready for this?"

"Kid, I'm ready for anything." I gripped his shoulder.

"Alright. As soon as they call the move before chow, I'm going to shoot over to your block and fuck you up." Yaberz smiled as he gave me a pound and took off back to his unit.

Once I got back into the unit I went and found James. I wanted to let him know what was going on since he stood up for me.

"I just saw Kina," I said to him as we bumped knuckles.

"Oh, yeah?" he said as he pulled off his headphones.

"Fuck yeah. It was awesome!"

"I saw you walking up there with your water bottle. I thought that you had a piss test."

"That was the idea," I said with a grin.

"Good for you, man. What'd she have to say?"

"Dude, a bunch of shit. Pretty much everything Dom said was a lie."

"I fucking knew it. I told dudes that he doesn't have money like that."

"Yeah, well . . . what do you think about it?"

"About seeing her?" he asked.

"Yeah."

"Man, fuck these dudes. They're just jealous that it isn't them. You know where I stand."

"I know. I just wanted you to know what was up."

"You're fine with me and my car. It's Joey and the AM's you got to worry about."

"Alright, bro. I'll see you later," I said to him as I headed back to my cell, smiling. I knew that Yaberz and I had a plan to take care of the AM situation. One little ass kicking and I'd be able to ride out my last months before transferring out of that hell.

As soon as count cleared and they let us out of our cells they called the move. Because of all the murders and stabbings that had made our prison so famous, they started to keep each yard locked with a fence. It was a futile attempt at trying to keep the yards and inmates separated for better control. They figured that if a riot jumped off then only the inmates in that yard would have to be dealt with. An absurd assumption because as soon as anything jumped off, it would be go time in the whole prison.

I saw Yaberz coming from his unit. He already had his gloves on to soften the blows for both of us. He lived for shit like this. He stepped up to the gate and cracked his knuckles.

"As soon as they pop the fence we got to get this done," Yaberz urgently said to me from his side of the barbed wire fence.

"Let's get it done," I said.

"No, I talked to Joey and he wants me to wait till after dinner and bring Shady with me to do it!"

"What? That's going to fuck up everything."

"No, shit. That's why I'm going to do it right now."

"You're going to get into some shit for going against his orders."

"Fuck him. You're my brother, kid. Whatever happens, happens."

"Why did he change it up?"

"He wants to make sure all the confirmation numbers for the money are good and Shady wants to fuck you up," Yaberz stated.

"Fuck that dude!"

"I know, but that's his second in command. And you know he's the one behind all of this."

"Yeah, I know. But after you get me he can't touch me."

"That's right," Yaberz smiled and gave me a pound through the fence. "Now let's get this shit open so I can kick that ass."

"All inmates on the yard must report to indoor recreation." The speaker blasted out of the gun tower above us.

"What the fuck is this shit?" Yaberz yelled at the CO's standing by the gates.

"We can't let you guys go to other units right now. You all have to go to rec," explained a short balding CO in his mid-thirties.

"How about you go fuck yourself," Yaberz said back.

"It's not up to me. This is coming from the lieutenant."

"How about he can fuck himself too," Yaberz said to the CO as they opened the gate and we walked towards indoor recreation.

"Fuck, dude. This is fucked," I said to Yaberz as we went inside.

"Yeah, I shoulda fucked that cop up."

"No, dammit! I'm talking about the plan."

"We gotta act fast or it's all going to go to shit," Yaberz said, snapping back to reality.

"Fuck it. I'm cool with this cop. I'm going to tell him to let us out."

"Alright, let's ask." We walked into the recreational staff's office. The CO was sitting at the computer doing a lot of nothing.

"Hey, Cervena. I need a favor."

"What's that, Hipster?" he asked. All the CO's knew me from my dreads and knew that I didn't cause any problems.

"I need you to let us out to get back to my unit," I said.

"What? I can't let you out till after chow."

"I heard, but it's an emergency."

"What's up?"

"Listen. I never ask for anything and I never will again."

"What's going on?" He said looking from me to Yaberz, who was still wearing his gloves on a hot summer afternoon.

"It just has to happen," I stated firmly and he knew I was serious.

"Alright," he said.

The CO's were used to responding to all types of assaults and I was sure he knew that's what was going to happen. But I was also sure that he knew whatever was about to go down was something that had to go down.

"Thank fucking god," I whispered a little too loud under my breath.

"What?" the guard asked.

"Nothing," I said.

"If anyone asks, it wasn't me that let you out," he said as he escorted us to the door.

"Of course not," I said.

"Try not to kill anyone either," he said as we walked outside.

"We'll try," I said back over my shoulder as we headed to my unit to proceed with kicking my ass.

We covered the window so nobody could see what was going down. I had to look like I got fucked up. Yaberz had the reputation as someone not to fuck with, so punch placement was crucial for the both of us!

"Dude, you'll hit me where you're shooting for right?" I asked.

"This is what I do, Hipster!" Yaberz jabbed into the air and danced from foot-to-foot like a prize fighter. "You play music. I fight!"

"Alright."

"I was thinking that the best way to do it is to sit down, straight against the wall and put a pillow behind your head. It'll cushion the blows a little bit."

"So it won't hurt as bad?" I asked hopefully.

"Oh, no." Yaberz winked. "It's gonna hurt."

I moved my blue plastic chair to the far wall of my cell, grabbing my pillow in the process. Sitting down I looked at the side of my gray locker.

"Hold up," I said as I jumped out of the chair.

"What, you pussing out already?"

"No, just got to get a reminder," I said as I pulled out a picture of Kina and her kids.

The picture was of all of them at the beach with their arms around each other smiling. On the back was written, "Can't wait till you're here." It was my favorite picture of her and the kids. The family that I'd be coming home to.

I taped the picture to the side of the locker and transported myself on the beach with them. Closing my eyes, I could hear their laughs. Smell the ocean. Feel the sand under my feet. Taste her lips. It was a dream come true.

"Alright," I said as I opened my eyes, smiling.

"Damn, I've never seen anyone smiling before I kicked their ass."

"Yeah, well you never kicked the Hipster's ass before." We slapped hands and gave each other a quick bro hug.

"Hipster, you know I love you, kid."

"I love you too, bro."

"You ready for this?"

"Do I really got a choice?"

"Guess not."

"Fuck it. Let's do it." I sat down in the chair, placed the pillow behind my head as I stared at my future.

"Alright, I'm going for the right eye first. One, Two, Three . . ."

We finished a couple minutes before chow was done. Just barely leaving me enough time to clean up before they opened up the compound to let all the inmates converge on the yard.

"Let's smoke that joint before they call the move," Yaberz suggested while he looked out of the now uncovered window.

"Good idea. I pulled out a paper of weed and started to roll it up.

"Attention 10 minute move is now open," the PA blared from the housing unit speakers.

"Fuck, man," I cursed. "We're not going to have time to puff."

"Fuck it, I'll just stay in here and leave later."

"I'll get a couple of cigs and some more weed."

"That's why I love you, Hipster."

We both saw Shady come walking past my outer window that faced the prison yard.

"There's that motherfucker Shady," I said as I finished rolling the joint.

"Yeah, but he can't do shit now."

"Yaberz!" Shady yelled into the unit.

"Dammit, let me go talk to him," said Yaberz. "Don't spark that shit until I get back,"

Yaberz ran outside real quick to let Shady know he already got me and in doing so disobeyed an order. I could see the conversation happening from my window. Yaberz handed Shady the slip of paper with all the Western Union confirmation numbers. Shady throwing up his hands, which I was sure was from Yaberz telling him it was already done, and then Shady storming off.

"What'd he say?" I asked Yaberz as he came back into my cell.

"Well, he wasn't happy, that's for sure."

"What's he doing?"

"He's going to give Joey the confirmation numbers and tell him I got you."

"What did you tell him?"

"That you gave me the numbers and I beat the shit out of you."

"Did he ask you why you didn't wait for him?"

"I told him that you told me about the visit with Kina and I just got too pissed and couldn't wait."

"He buy it?"

"I think so. I told him you were rolling a joint and that's when I got you."

"What'd he say about you coming back in here?"

"I told him you knew you had it coming and that I'm trying to smoke that fucking joint." Yaberz sat down on the bunk as I started to light the joint with some batteries and wire.

"Yaberz!" another AM named Ritchie came yelling from the door at the front of the unit.

"Shit, now what?" Yaberz got up and looked out the door. "What's up?"

"Get out here!" Ritchy yelled.

"I'm trying to cheef," said Yaberz, annoyed.

"Get out here now," the AM demanded.

"Dammit," cursed Yaberz.

"You in trouble?" I asked.

"Probably, but whatever. You're my brother and I'll do anything for you." Yaberz took a quick hit of the joint and handed it back to me.

"Thanks, kid," I said.

"Just stay in the cell and don't come out till I get you in the morning," Yaberz ordered as he looked at my face to inspect the damage.

"Is it bad enough?"

"I hope you're a bruiser. Don't put ice on it!" he said as he ran out of the cell to another scream of his name from Ritchy.

I puffed on the joint and stared at the picture of Kina and the kids. It was really everything that I had ever wanted. To get out to a beautiful woman and two great kids. Living down by the beach and having a job to come out to. Kina worked for her mother who had a growing business doing weddings on the beach.

I would be leaving fifteen years of violence, madness and chaos to go to a peaceful community where I'd get paid to be on the beach all day with the woman I love. No having to ask, "Do you want fries with that?" A total fresh start after surviving the worst nightmare of my life. Feeling at peace from the thoughts of my future (and the weed) I jumped when I heard a knock on my door.

"You alright?" James said as he came into my cell and inspected my face.

"Yeah, I'm cool."

"Those motherfuckers!"

"Yeah, they had Yaberz get me."

"I know. It's all over the yard." Prison is like high school. Once something happens everyone knows about it immediately.

"He got me while I was sitting at my desk too!" I said. "Joey told him I needed to be punished."

"For what? You're not a gang member. You're independent. You don't fall under them."

"No shit."

"These motherfuckers are out of control." James was from the midwest, the second biggest car on the compound. They'd been beefing with the AM's for a while now and he hated Joey.

"You're telling me."

"So what, they waited for you to pay Foxy and then jumped you?"

"Yep." I shrugged my shoulders.

"That's cause they know you roll by yourself. They wouldn't do that shit if you were *clicked* up."

"Nothing I can do now."

"Fuck, If you want we'll go out there and book that motherfucker in the morning!" James made a stabbing motion. It was tempting but I was still holding to my exit plan

"Fuck it. Yaberz said it's done with. I got dealt with and it's over."

"You believe him?" James arched his eyebrow.

"Yeah."

"Look what he just did to you." James wasn't buying it. He knew things in prison always smoldered. He knew how the AB's worked.

"That's cause they made him."

"What happens when they make him get you again?"

"I just gotta lay low. In three months I'll get transferred to a medium and be done with all this shit."

"Fuck, you're a better man than me," James said looking at my swollen eyes. "Cause I'd kill a motherfucker if they did that to me."

In the pen you didn't take a loss. If someone got out on you, you got them back in whatever way you had to. But James didn't know what really went down. Or that me and Yaberz had a plan in case that order came down to get me again. All he saw was that I got jumped by a gang. James also knew that I was going home. It might have been in eight years, but to someone doing multiple life sentences that was the same as eight days.

"At least it doesn't look that bad. If you change your mind let me know. I got your back," said James, slapping me on the shoulder.

"Thanks, man." I said as I gave him a pound before he left.

I went out to go call Kina doing my best to shield my face from watching eyes. Not everyone knew what happened yet, and I wasn't really trying to advertise it yet either.

"*What's up, beautiful?*" I sang into the phone.

"What took you so long to call?"

"Well . . . I was busy getting my ass kicked!"

"How bad is it?"

"Really not that bad."

"Good, I don't want your face all fucked up."

"What, you think I'm hot or something?" I teased.

"Just a little," Kina teased back.

"How far from home are you?"

"Just a couple hours."

"What'd you think about me?"

"I think I'm coming back as soon as I can!"

"Oh, yeah?"

"Yeah, my birthday is in a couple weeks and I'm going to tell my mom for my present to give me money to come back up."

"Damn, baby, that'd be awesome," I said.

"I know. I miss you already."

"Shit, I doubt it's as much as I'm missing you."

"I bet it's more!" she said.

"I bet you didn't just get beat up while you were staring at my picture."

"Ok, you win."

"That's what I thought."

I laughed into the phone. "I'll call you in the morning after I see my boy, but everything should be all good now," I told her.

"I hope so. I can't believe all the shit you're going through cause of this."

"Me neither. But you know what? You're worth it, baby. I love you."

"I love you too, baby. *Mwah.*"

"*Mwah.*"

We got started blowing kisses to each other when we'd get off the phone. It was silly but it was the closest semblance to a real relationship that you could have in a place like this. And I lived, literally, for those air kisses.

After I got off the phone I went to see Alex to make sure he got his money. He knew that I got jumped on after my visit. He didn't know the whole extent of how it was going down. He was really just grateful that he got his money.

"What's up, Hipster?" He waved me into his cell.

"You got that cheddar?" I asked.

"Yeah, thanks, man."

"No problem. I told them dudes that you were getting all your money."

"I appreciate it," said Alex.

"Shit, you waited for like six months."

"I'm just glad I got it and it's over."

"So, what you think?" I asked as I outlined my face.

"It doesn't look that bad."

"Don't say that. It's got to look like I got fucked up."

"Why's Joey even give a shit?" He leaned close to check me out.

"Cause he's a scumbag and thinks he's king shit."

"That just doesn't make any sense. I'm an independent Mexican and it'd be like *La Eme* telling me what I can do."

"Yeah, the yards all fucked up for white dudes here."

"I mean, if it was my girl, I'd of fucked you up bad. But you were honest about it with him the whole time. So they can't say shit. It was between the two of you."

"Dude, I'm not even getting into all the shit she told me about him."

"Oh, yeah, he's full of shit, huh?" Alex said.

"You have no idea."

"I knew he didn't have money like that. If he did he'd of never strung me along."

"Yeah, but at least I got you taken care of. Now I gotta go show off this shit to all the white dudes tomorrow," I said pointing at my face.

"If you want, I can hit you a couple times and really make it look bad." Alex offered.

I looked at his muscled arms and declined. "Nah . . . I'm cool." We both laughed. "Once was enough. Tough shit If Joey doesn't think it's good enough."

"Well, good luck, Hipster," Alex said as I left to go to my cell.

I laid down for the night once they locked the doors at 10 p.m. It was the only time I felt safe. I hung pictures of Kina above my bed and stared at them while I laid on the bottom bunk. Dreaming of a better life after all of this was behind me. Before I fell asleep, I slipped the loop on my knife around my wrist. A habit that I'd started since all of this turned crazy. It wasn't the best way to have to sleep, but for me it became a necessity. I hoped for sweet dreams for now. I hoped everything would be good in the morning.

I woke up promptly at 5:30 a.m. every morning. The doors wouldn't unlock until 5:45, but I'd make sure I was up and ready. Washing my face, using the toilet, and drinking some coffee before everyone got up and moving on the block. I was still in a single cell, so life was a bit easier on me. As soon as the doors unlocked, I jumped back into bed.

My cell was completely dark since I covered the outside window so no light would come in. The blankets were pulled up to just below my eyes. My knife tight in my hand, the shoelace string, attached to the bottom of the knife was wrapped around my wrist. You did this so you wouldn't drop your knife while you were stabbing someone. With all the blood pouring out from the wound it'd make your sharpened steel slick. You also did it so that if you were getting rocked your piece wouldn't get taken.

My whole thinking was that if they came to get me they'd see me in bed and think I was an easy hit. But I'd get them. Spring up out of bed just before they got in striking distance. Throw my blanket at them like a net and make an example out of the closest one. They were going to come at least two deep. More than likely three. I'd have a better chance of Obama pardoning me then I would have winning that battle.

My hope was to savagely attack the closest one and that the others would back off. It was really just a human reaction. They'd either back away in shock, like wild antelope do when lions are ripping the larynx out of one of their own, or ... they'd come at me even harder. Since they came to stab me anyway, they'd just be completing their mission, down a man.

Laying there, replaying what I'd do if they did come, I'd also think about Kina. Thinking about if all this was worth it. Actually planning to use a sharpened piece of a metal bleacher to stab someone. I'd never even had a knife in my eight years in prison. Now I was ready to plunge one through the jugular of the first man that came into my cell. What was even more crazy was that if I had to do it all over again, I would. That's how crazy I was for Kina.

Yarberz' head popped into my cell window around 9 a.m.. He had to smash his face up to the glass to see if I was in there or not. Then he came in.

"Hipster, what are you crazy?!" he said. "You're still in fucking bed!"

"Fuck no," I said as I launched up, knife in hand. "Just laying a trap for the first motherfucker that comes in."

"Whoa! What, you trying to get revenge for me kickin' that ass?" He laughed as he turned on the light and inspected his work.

"How's it coloring up?"

I showed him my face and he shook his head.

"Not good," he sighed. "Joey wanted you to look worse than Tattoo!"

Tattoo was an Aryan who literally got the shit stomped out of him a couple months earlier and looked like he got hit by a Mack truck. He was eating baby food for a year.

"I'm swollen up," I protested looking at myself in the mirror.

"You're puffy but you're not black and blue."

He got closer to look at me. "Dammit, I knew I should've broke your nose!"

"Shit, you want to get me again?"

"No, it's too late. I'm just going to tell him you're not a bruiser."

"Are you sure? I want to make sure this is enough. I'm not trying to go through this again."

"No, it's cool. I'll deal with whatever he's got to say." "I don't want you to get into any shit."

"Listen, I do this shit, Hipster. This isn't what you're about. If they want to discipline me for going against their orders or not getting you bad enough, I'm cool with that. You're my bro and I'd do anything for you."

"Thanks, Yaberz."

"Just go show off your face to the compound today so they all know you got disciplined and then lay low until you can get a transfer."

"Got you."

"Remember, if your girls got a friend, tell her to hook me up."

We laughed and hugged before he rolled out.

Feeling good about my prospects, I went to call Kina. With her in mind the beating was already a fading memory. The pain was gone.

"Every day I love her just a little bit more, a little bit more. Every day I love her just a little bit more, and she loves me the same," I sang into the phone.

"I love you, baby." Kina cooed.

"Everyday I love her a little bit more," I sang. "Good morning."

I started singing to Kina to wake her up in the morning. She was the first girl that I'd ever sung to. I played in bands and sang in front of people for years. But to just sing without any music was terrifying to me. It also showed just how comfortable I was with her. Standing in a prison unit, filled with every type of criminal there was and singing a love song to a girl that everyone thought I stole from my celly wasn't the easiest thing to do. Still, I'd have my back on the wall so I could watch to see if someone was going to come at me. I'd also keep my hand in my pocket as I talked.

My friend gave me a holster for my knife. It was attached to a belt that I'd keep on under my pants. Basically it was an old western six shooter type of belt—only prison style. I had a hole cut in the side of my pocket so my hand could be on my knife handle for quick draw action. I couldn't allow myself to slip up for one second. Dudes in prison will always watch your routine, looking for the best time to hit you. I had to let them see that there would never be a good time. I was always ready.

"It's late, baby. Why didn't you wake me up earlier?"

"I had to wait till I saw my boy before I could move around."

"What did he say?"

"To go show myself off."

"And then everyone will chill out?" Kina asked hopefully.

"If all goes well."

"I still can't believe all of this."

"Me either. But I'll tell you this, it's all worth it for you, baby."

"I promise when you come home I'm going to make all this up to you."

"It's not your fault," I said.

"If we never hooked up you wouldn't be going through all this."

"Well . . . no, but—"

"So it's at least half my fault," Kina interrupted me.

"Only for being so damn sexy," I flirted.

"You're not going to regret it when you come home."

"I know I'm not. And I'm not right now either. But what I am going to do is go show off the beat down I got for my hottie."

"Ok, go show it off and call me when you get back."

"Alright, baby. I love you."

"I love you too."

"*Mwah.*"

"*Mwah.*"

I skipped lunch. Although it was a perfect place to advertise Yaberz' knuckle work to the looky-lou convicts, it was also packed with prison administration. I didn't really feel the urge to show the warden and his cronies my new look. The only appropriate place to show off my damaged face would be my home away from home. The band room.

"Yaberz did that to you?" Sergio said, shocked. Sergio knew Yaberz and he knew that Yaberz and I were like family.

"Joey made him get me," I explained.

"What a piece of shit."

"It coulda been worse," I said, holding back really happened.

"When did he get you?"

"Right after I got back from the visit."

"Damn, right after you saw the girl?"

"Yeah, he got me while I was sitting at my desk," I sighed. "I was rolling a joint."

"That's fucked up, homes." Sergio shook his head.

"He said it was my punishment for getting with her."

"Man, you don't even roll with those dudes. They ain't got no authority to discipline you."

"No shit. But whatever. Yaberz said it's done with now and I can chill."

Sergio nodded. "If Yaberz said it then you're good."

"Yeah, just trying to coast to an FCI here in a few months."

"Come on, you can coast through some fucking songs now. Hopefully Yaberz didn't shake up your ability to jam."

We played some of the songs I'd been teaching him. Nirvana, Weezer, Blink 182—all stuff that was easy to play with a driving beat. It was almost like I was out of prison for a bit. That was until they called the 2 p.m. move which allowed inmates to come and go.

I saw the whole AM squad pile into rec. They were about twenty deep. All of them weren't patched up. Some were prospects. Others were just nut huggers that did whatever they said.

"There's Joey and all them," Sergio told me. "I see 'em. They came up to see how I look."

"They aren't going to come in here. I'll tell you that!"

"No, they're just going to stand out there and gawk for a bit. They aren't going to come in here and fuck with your band time. They know better than that."

"Well, fuck 'em. Give 'em a show then."

"Why not?" I said. "Let's play the Rage song."

We launched into "Killing In The Name Of" by Rage Against the Machine. We'd been working on it for weeks and Sergio had it pretty close. As soon as I hit the first bar I threw off my sunglasses and started jamming.

The AM's crowded the window that looked into the room. Trying to see the work that Yaberz put in on me. The problem was that I had my dreads flying everywhere while I was jumping around! During the parts that I was singing I'd half face the wall, only allowing them to see my left side. I did all of this on purpose. I had to show it off but I'd do it on my own terms while letting them know how I felt about it.

At the end of the song the lyrics go, *fuck you I won't do what you tell me.* It's screamed with reckless abandon until you can't scream anymore. When I reached that point of the song, I turned and faced the window. With my eyes closed I yelled and let out everything inside. All the tension, all the stress, all the shit that these motherfuckers put me through came out of my body at that moment. And when I hit the last note and the song was over, I opened my eyes and stared at all of them. Giving them the show that they wanted. Giving them the show they wanted—my way!

"That's what I'm talking about, Hipster!" Sergio screamed over the fading reverb.

I just smiled as I watched Joey and his crew walk away. We played some more songs for the next hour until they recalled the yard for the afternoon count. Every few minutes one or two of his cronies would come up to the window and look at me. They'd laugh and slap hands before walking away. It didn't really bother me though. I got my point across. I also was the one that had Kina.

I was supposed to lay low. Only leave my unit for chow and the band room. Yaberz said to leave running and soccer alone. Out of sight, out of mind. But I couldn't do that. Being cooped up inside would drive me crazy. I'd spend almost my whole day away from the unit. That's how I did my time. It would be like being on house arrest—in prison.

I figured I would just have to be extra vigilant with my movements. Make sure that I didn't do the same thing over again. One day I'd run in the morning. The next I'd run at night. Every afternoon I was in the band room, so I couldn't help that. But I knew they wouldn't try to get me there if they were going to get me. The metal detector was a big deterrent. Another thing was they'd want the compound to see it happen.

The first reason for that was it sent a message to everyone that they ran shit. That if others didn't fall in line under them that this was what could happen to you. The second reason was that I wouldn't be able to come back on the yard. When something happened out in the open like that it got you labeled as a "victim" to the administration. Meaning if you came back out on the yard, you'd get it again. We called it "getting voted off the island", and it happened every day.

I knew that they'd have to get me on the walk up to rec, or when I was out running and playing soccer. It wouldn't happen at chow because you ate with your own unit. My unit was composed of Midwest dudes who fell under James. I still bought a little plastic knife that I could take through the metal detectors. Nothing serious. More of a "get back" piece. Meaning, "get the fuck back from me" knife. Something you would use to hold off your aggressors until the cops came.

The metal knife I had for the yard I kept in my bag. The CO's never checked my bag and when I'd go through the metal detector I'd throw it on the table next to the turnstile. Then I'd grab it after going through and be into rec. When I'd walk I would have my bag slung over my shoulder down at waist level. My hand would be inside the gray net bag grasping my piece. As soon as I got to where I was going I'd pull out the knife and put it into my belt holster under my pants. There'd be no slipping.

Running was a bit different. I made an elastic bandage that would go around my thigh. The tube off of a toilet paper roll was used as a sheath to cover my blade. It would still poke into me and was pretty awkward, but it's what needed to be done.

Soccer on the other hand left me vulnerable and naked. I tried playing with my bandage and got hit with the ball and cut my leg. I knew they wouldn't run out on the field and get me either. My whole team consisted of Texas Syndicate and Mexican Mafia dudes. It'd be a big show of disrespect to them if the AM's interrupted a game. I had to leave my knife in my bag during the game. After it was done I'd throw my bag over my shoulder and resume the clutch on my equalizer.

I also ended up buying a bone crusher. It was about twelve inches of sheer terror. I called it my Rambo knife. With grooves cut into the side for added carnage when you pulled it out of your victim. Because if you're going through the trouble of stabbing someone, why not pull out their guts while you're doing it.

I didn't really need the extra piece. But once you get locked into a serious knife collection and you see something like that you buy it. Better off you have a weapon of that caliber than someone else. Especially, if that someone else is coming at you. This was my unit piece. It was too big to fit into my holster, so I just kept it in my pocket. Anytime I'd walk I would have to hold my pocket because of how much it moved. When I had my Rambo knife I felt pretty certain that if I had to pull it out whoever was coming at me would think twice—quick!

It was always a quick cycle. Go to chow, grab my little dagger. Come right back and throw on my bag and head out to indoor rec. As soon as I'd make it inside, put my piece in its holster. Back in the bag to go back to the unit. As soon as I hit the unit, trade it for my Rambo knife. When the doors locked at night I could settle in for a bit till went to bed. Before I'd fall asleep, I'd slip my Rambo knife around my wrist till I woke up. And then I'd start the cycle all over again. An extremely stressful life to live, but one that ended with me living on the beach with my long legged Hawaiian hottie.

I slammed my final shot of heroin a year to the day of my brother's death. A fitting tribute, I felt for my best friend and a hopeful launch towards a new clean life with Kina. I had my year run of shooting dope. My brother's death was an unbearable blow to me. The years clean that I had were literally shot out the door. I coped the only way I knew how to with heroin.

With Kina, I needed to set an example. For her and for myself. I knew that you can't have a relationship with two women at the same time. One of those being dope. That's not to say I was a choir boy though. I was going through the most violently threatening ordeal of my life. I turned to what most "recovering" junkies turn towards in their newfound sobriety—alcohol.

Drinking wine and shine a couple times a week probably wasn't the smartest thing to do when a disastrously premature ending to your life was hanging in the air. But then again, wasn't that the time you needed it the most? The fact that I played music with two of the best brewers on the compound may have also factored into my inebriation.

One of them was Brian. He was the king of making shine. Every two days he'd come down with a batch. So, every two days I'd inevitably get drunk with him while playing death metal on the drums.

Jamie was the other one. He'd take his time brewing up his concoction. "I will not pull my wine before its time," he always said. Which apparently was every four days because that was how often I'd drink with him and Sergio as we'd play classic rock songs. I wasn't much of a classic rock type of guy, but for some free wine I'd play about anything.

Sergio and I would also go in on a gallon of prison hooch and drink it before a game every now and then. Just a little something to wet our whistles before going out and running for an hour in the oppressive Louisiana heat. Obviously we'd play like shit, but we had a lot of fun doing it.

After a month or so things started to settle back down for me. I was still out getting seen by everyone, but I was starting to become old news. It was easy to fall into the back of people's minds when they were seeing unscrupulous violence every day. Although Shady made it his life's mission to not let people forget.

Any time I would walk past him and the AM's I'd always get some smart comment about "stealing another man's wife" or "being a piece of shit." I'd just let all that slide right off me. It was like what James said, "They're only mad cause they couldn't get with her." I found it easy to take the insults from some dudes whose future entailed being a dishwasher at some greasy spoon that hired cons.

The people that knew me knew the real story, and that was all that mattered. I had already gotten my "discipline" for getting with her, so as far as I was concerned they could say whatever they wanted. That was until I saw Kina again and was seated right next to Shady and his girl-friend. Sometimes you just can't live it down no matter your intentions.

Almost a month had passed before I had the opporutnity to see Kina agan. I was filled with an exhilarating desire. To kiss her soft lips and touch her for hours while we sat next to each other in the majestic vis-iting room. It was the one place where I knew unequivocally I would remain unscathed. I was secure for those six hours to be me. Free for six hours to gaze into the captivating brown eyes of the woman of my dreams and tell her how much I cherished her.

Even with everything that had transpired on account of our rela-tionship, there was nothing in the world that would change the longing that I had for Kina. The sun rose and set with impassioned thoughts of our life together. When I wasn't talking to her on the phone, I was writing her. In between all that I'd stare at her pictures and plan our life together after I came home.

Seeing her again amidst all the insanity of what was now my everyday existence in prison was the equivalent of the Super Bowl, Christmas, and the Fourth of July all rolled into one. Walking into the visiting room to the sight of my ravishing girlfriend was like being released from prison. Then I noticed that Shady and his girlfriend were sitting in the space next to Kina. Which immediately crushed all my sense of unassailability.

"Look at this motherfucker," I heard Shady say as I wrapped Kina in my arms and gave her an intensely passionate kiss. Her lips and warm body were like heaven to me. Not even my biggest enemy was going to spoil our embrace. I copped a quick feel of Kina's tight firm ass as we sat down. It was the type of booty that you want to grab and never let go. The type of ass that women die for and I could get killed over. Kina poked it back at me as she smiled and sat down. She knew that I drooled over her heart shaped ass all day long.

"That's all yours, baby," she whispered into my ear.

"Damn, right," I said as I put my hand on her thigh and stole anoth-er quick kiss from her while the CO's weren't looking.

"I can't believe they made me sit next to them," Kina said as she looked in Shady's direction. She knew him from visiting Dom.

"How'd that happen?" I acted cool, as if I'd just noticed them.

"We came in at the same time."

"Fuck 'em. Let's not let them spoil our visit."

"Baby, I love you," Kina said to me as she held my hand on her thigh.

"I love you too," I replied.

I proceeded to tell her about everything that had happened since I saw her last. You could only say so much over the prison phone. She knew what had been happening but to get full details shocked her.

"Are you sure you still want to be with me?" she asked innocently.

"More than anything in this world." I had reached the point of no return long ago. I was all in and doubled down.

You get three warnings from the CO's for "excessive contact" before your visit is terminated. Kina and I would space ours out. We couldn't keep our hands off each other. I'd slide my hand in between her thighs. Slowly creeping it up every fifteen minutes or so, telling her all the things I wanted to do to her. Whenever the CO's wouldn't be looking she'd lean in and give me a kiss.

The physical contact after eight years in prison was incredible. Especially, with such a breathtaking woman that I also adored made it even more unbelievable.

"I'm going to marry you," I whispered to Kina.

"Are you proposing to me?"

"Maybe."

"Yes, I'll marry you," Kina said back and gave me a quick kiss, which drew the CO over for our first warning.

Shady pointed and chortled. Him and his girlfriend would give us dirty looks during the visit, making little snide comments that we could hear to try to ruin our oasis. But it didn't work. Kina and I were passionately in love and now getting married.

My life was in imminent danger all day yet I'd never been happier. She was everything that I'd ever wanted in life, and I found her in the belly of the beast. All I had to do was make it out alive. The day was bliss despite Shady being there and it ended all too soon. I was on cloud nine though as I left.

"Yo, kid, I'm getting married!" I said to Yaberz as I stepped out onto the compound after the visit. Even though Joey told him to stay away from me, Yaberz still made sure that I was safe. He wasn't going to let me get blindsided right after a visit. It was the one time that I'd be completely vulnerable without my knives.

"What?" He took a step back and clapped his hands.

"I asked her to marry me and she said yes."

"Damn, Hipster, you don't fuck around do you?"

"I'd die for the girl."

"Shit, you just might!" Yaberz said laughing.

"Man, fuck you," I said as I slapped his hand and gave him a hug.

"Congratulations, kid."

"Thanks, bro."

"So you had a good visit then huh?"

"Fuck, yeah, other than Shady mad dogging us and talking shit."

Yaberz nodded. "I found out last night that he was going. I didn't want to tell you and stress you out."

"This motherfucker was sitting right next to us talking shit."

"I kinda figured he'd be an asshole."

"Dude, it's fucked up. It's some seriously disrespectful shit."

"There's nothing you can do about it. You know damn well that you got nothing coming on this compound. Especially from the AM's."

"Yeah, I got nothing coming. But disrespecting my girl on a visit is a serious violation."

"Hipster," Yaberz sighed. "You just need to fall back and get off this compound."

"I did fall back."

He rolled his eyes. "You're out here every day running around and playing soccer."

"Dude, but I have to do that."

"You're going out on visits."

"Come on. There's no way I'm giving that up."

"All I'm saying is dudes are pissed about this." He threw up his arms.

"Fuck em. I already got jumped over it."

Yaberz was silent for a moment. "Listen, they took a vote on you."

"About what?"

"To either kill you, stab you, fuck you up, or let you be."

"I thought you getting me was enough?"

"Joey wasn't happy about it. Said I didn't get you good enough. I told him you weren't a bruiser, that's why it didn't look bad. He didn't care."

"What happened with the vote?"

"A couple dudes voted for stabbing, more for fucking you up—"

"Who voted for that?" I asked cutting him off.

"It doesn't matter. You already know who wants to get you."

"Fucking Joey and Shady. I should just stick one of those mother-fuckers and get shipped."

"Man, you'd get shipped to another pen far away from Kina and you'd still have to deal with dudes that show up from here that roll with them. You only got a couple months left so just chill."

"Who else voted in this shit?"

"I'm not even going to say cause it's going to have you looking at them all fucked up. All I'm going to say is that Mouse stuck up for you and that's why you're still here."

Mouse was the captain of the yard for another gang. He was an old school convict who'd been down for over twenty years and had a lot of respect in the system. Even though his gang was less in numbers, when he talked dudes listened. I'd only spoken with him a couple times over the two years I'd been here but apparently I left a good impression for him to stand up for me.

"Mouse backed me?" I asked.

"Yeah, it doesn't mean he's got your back. He just told them he doesn't think you should get fucked up over it."

"What'd you vote?"

"I voted to bust that ass up." Yaberz smiled.

"That's what I thought," I said and playfully pushed him away.

"Shit, you better get inside before I get that ass right now. I know you don't got a piece right now."

"Yeah, yeah . . . it won't be so easy the next time," I said as we slapped hands and headed back to our units for count.

That night I went outside to talk with my boy Bruce. I wanted to tell him about the marriage and the vote. When I saw him to tell him the news he already had something that he wanted to talk with me about. Bruce was one of the few people that I made plans with for when we got out. We wrote a lot of music together and had plans to play together after prison. He had a lot of ideas about doing different things with music and technology that he wanted us to do together.

Bruce got a sixteen year prison sentence when he was eighteen. He came straight to the most violent penitentiary in the system to do his time. What would have killed a normal kid, Bruce turned into a positive. He earned his bachelor's degree while inside and had never been in trouble. I really respected whatever Bruce had to say.

"You know, I hope you and Kina do get married and have a great life together after all of this," Bruce said.

"You and me both. Especially after all the shit I'm going through."

"Listen, I've got this plan for us to get big when we're out. I know that we can do it. I'm going to put everything I've got in me to make it happen."

"Yeah, I know."

"And I want you there with me."

"I'm going to be there."

"Yeah, but you've got to actually make it, to get there."

"Dude, I'm going to make it."

"I'm not even talking about these dudes. I'm talking about the drugs and drinking too."

"I don't even get high anymore."

"Right now you don't. But you've got to stay that way."

"I'm planning on it."

"I hope you do. But you're drinking like crazy too."

"I know, but it's mostly free, so why not?"

"Well, one because they're taking votes on whether to kill you or not and you need to be on point. Second, how you live in here is how you're going to live on the street."

"And?"

"And I can't put all this energy into making this happen for us and you being an addict," Bruce leveled with me.

"Dude. . . ."

"No, just hear me out. You've got a lot of talent, but it's not going go get you anywhere but back in here if you're getting fucked up."

"I know."

"I'm not trying to harp on you. I just care a lot about you. You're better than this shit and it hurts me to see you going downhill so fast."

"Yeah, things have gotten pretty crazy."

"I know you care a lot about Kina, but I told you when you first told me about it that these things always end up bad."

"I didn't think it was going to get like this though."

"Me either. I also know how losing your brother sent you over the edge and I don't want to see you lose it if you and Kina don't work out."

"We'll be ok."

"I truly hope you are. I'm just asking you this, do you trust me?"

"Of course," I said.

"And you believe me when I say that I'm going to make my vision a reality."

"Yeah." Bruce had a way of talking that made you believe he could make anything happen.

"And I want you to be there to make it happen with me. It's not going to be easy, but if we can do this, then we can do anything."

He could have told me he wanted us to become astronauts and go to the moon and I'd be convinced it was possible.

"Fucking right!" I said.

"I need you to slow down on the drinking and keep off the dope."

"Even when it's free?" I said laughing.

"I'm serious, kid. Do you want this or not?"

"Yeah, I do."

"Then slow it down," Bruce stressed.

"Alright, man, I will."

"I'm only saying this because I care," he said and gave me a hug.

"I know. I feel you, bro. I will. Now let's go watch this soccer game."

I thought a lot about what Bruce said when I went back inside that night. He was right. Even though I wasn't getting high anymore, I was still living crazy with the booze. Being an addict is what got me into prison, now was the time to really grow up and become a man. That was just what I did. I stopped drinking and started focusing on what I needed most. To get the fuck outta the pen alive.

I only had two more months to go before I could get a transfer to a medium security prison. Once I got that everything would be gravy. No more sleeping with knives and peeping out my window to see where all the white dudes were before I'd go outside. Compared to where I was, a medium prison was like kindergarten. The only reason you'd need a knife is to cut a petrified piece of toast at morning chow.

I did everything that I could to stay out of sight. Instead of going outside to run, I'd go to rec and ride the stationary bike. I'd skip the chow hall, and instead eat oatmeal or soup in my unit. I still talked to some people on my block, but mostly stayed in my cell and wrote to Kina. She was the lifeline that kept me sane.

We're only allotted three hundred minutes a month on our phone. I'd go through that in a week. So I bought other dudes' phone minutes. I was going through almost twelve hundred minutes a month and that still wasn't enough. I was an addict for love.

The half hour wait before I could call back and hear her sultry voice was like an eternity. I was like a super junkie on the street. Strung out to the max on speedballs. When I'd wake up I would be caked with sweat. Shivering with cold sweats till I got my fix. That was nothing compared to how hooked I was with Kina.

There were eight years left in my sentence. An eternity to some people. To me it was like eight days away. Always talking to Kina about what we're going to do when I get home. We'd have a kid and a dog. Get a house and have a beautiful family. It was almost like it was right there in front of me. A mirage oasis. Only I wasn't lost in the desert, I was trapped in a federal penitentiary in the sweltering swamps of Louisiana.

Even staying out of sight as much as possible, I was still a target for different dudes. I'd always check the yard before I moved anywhere. If there were a lot of white guys outside that usually meant someone was getting voted off the island. Since I was one of the highest on that list, that meant I stayed inside.

I'd sit with my back to the wall facing the door, with two knives in my hands. I still had to walk to rec every day. I'd always hear someone from Joey's crew talk shit. "I wish that motherfucker would try to write my wife," or "There's that piece of shit right there." I also still went out to play soccer. I wasn't going to leave my team high and dry in the middle of the season. Although I should have.

Superdude was another AM that just wouldn't let things blow over. He'd always have something to say when I walked past. He also played soccer on another team. Whenever I played against his team, Joey and the AM's would come to the games. They'd stand on the sidelines and talk shit. They also stayed there to watch as Superdude would throw elbows or tackle me anytime I had the ball.

They'd all laugh and cheer as I'd get hacked down and Superdude would throw his arms up like he was Rocky knocking out Ivan Drago. He knew there was nothing I could do, and nothing that my team would do against him. If I jumped up swinging on him, I'd get rushed by ten AM's. My team was all Mexican gangbangers. If they did something it would start a race riot.

So I'd let them get their little rocks off, knowing that this was the best their lives were ever going to get. I on the other hand had the life of my dreams waiting on me. During the fifteen minute phone calls with Kina I was free. It was during those in-between times that life became alarmingly difficult.

"Hey Hipster, what's up?" a drunken Joe asked as he came into my cell.

Joe was a skinny thirty year old from the midwest. I knew as soon as he came in that there was going to be problems. Right before Dom went to the hole he befriended Joe. Shooting dope and smoking cigarettes with him. It was all in an attempt to get Joe to come after me. He told him how I, "stole his money, wife and kids and wanted me fucked up." It didn't work because James was Joe's shot caller and wouldn't let it happen. But it wasn't for a lack of trying.

"What's up, Joe? You been sipping on some of grandpa's ol' cough syrup again?" I said, trying to ease the tension.

"Yeah, I'm fucked up. I drank a bottle of *ssshhhine,*" Joe slurred as he sat down and looked around my cell and saw pictures of Kina hanging up. "You know, Hipster . . . you're a real piece of shit."

"Oh, yeah, is that right?"

"You don't think you're a piece of shit?"

"Yeah, I'm a piece of shit Joe," I said in an attempt to diffuse things.

"At least you're admitting it."

"Yep," I said as I saw my transfer disappearing before my eyes.

"You should just kill yourself," he continued to dog on me.

"Really?"

"Just do yourself a favor and hang it up."

"You think so?"

"Yeah, I think so you piece of shit."

"I'll think about that. Right now though I'm going to use the phone."

"You're going to call that bitch," he called out to me.

"That's right, I'm going to call my girl."

"That ain't your girl. That's Dom's girl!" Joe hollered.

I turned back around to face him. "If that's what you want to think."

"What's that mean?"

"That means don't believe everything you heard."

"I know what Dom told me."

"And Dom is full of shit."

"But you're a piece of shit," he drunkenly repeated.

"Right, and now I'm going to bounce."

"I just wanted to let you know you're a piece of shit," he said again like a broken record. He snickered to himself as he stumbled out.

Later on after I talked to Kina, I sat down next to James to watch some TV. Joe came stumbling up and sat down next to James.

"Man, what's up with you?" James said to Joe.

"What? You told on me?" Joe said as he stared at me.

"Told on you about what?" James asked him.

"He didn't say anything?" Joe asked.

"Nope," I said.

"Now I want to know what's up," James said, eyeing Joe.

"I told him he's a piece of shit for what he did," said Joe.

"Didn't I tell you to mind your own business?" James said sternly.

"Yeah, I just—"

"You just almost got fucked up is what happened," James said, cutting Joe off.

"By who? Him?" Joe said sarcastically.

"He'd fuck you up. Then I'd fuck you up for not minding your business," said James.

"I was just playing around," Joe said backtracking.

"Keep playing around and see what happens."

"Alright, *mmman*," Joe slurred and stumbled away with his tail squarely between his legs.

"If he does something like that again you have my permission to fuck him up."

"Alright, James."

"I told all my guys to leave you alone."

"I appreciate it."

"Man, it's cool. If you need me just let me know."

"Hopefully I'll be out of here before that happens," I said as I got up to go back to the phone for my reality break.

Kina and I were getting ready for another visit. It had only been a couple weeks from the previous one, but we were both dying to see each other again. Each day we both grew more dependent on the other. For her it was hearing me tell her about the life we're going to have. For me it was to escape from the madness of the life I was living. We were in this thing together now—for better or for worse. Just when things started looking up, everything started taking a turn for the worse. It started out on a Monday night. I was sitting around watching TV when all of a sudden the channel changed.

"What the fuck?" I said looking around. To change the channel you needed to press the button underneath the TV. People had stolen remotes from education, but none of the white guys did. Then it changed again.

"Man, what the fuck?" I said again looking behind me and seeing Foxy changing the TV with his remote.

"Yeah, I changed it. What?" Foxy waved the remote at me. He was drunk and ready to make a point. "What? What?" he shouted.

Now, Foxy is black and from DC. He's changing a white TV. A TV that he's not allowed to touch under convict rules. It doesn't happen.

"Yo, you fucking serious?" I said in disbelief.

"Yeah, motherfucka, I'll put on what I want."

Is that right?!" I stated while assessing the situation.

Foxy was in the wrong. Changing another race's TV was something that people have gotten killed for, most recently two years prior in the same unit. A race riot started and two dudes got killed. Technically I'm supposed to go to his shot caller and get him taken care of, but I know Foxy is Shady's boy. I also know if my name comes up for anything then I'm getting voted off the island. But I can't let Foxy disrespect me. Allowing another race to switch the TV on me, a white TV at that, could get me voted off too. I was really in a catch twenty-two of penitentiary politics.

"You know what?" I said.

"What?" Foxy shot back.

"You got that," I got up and walked away.

"That's what I thought," Foxy said with a satisfied grin. His eyes were like daggers as I walked over next to James.

"Hey, James, this motherfucker just switched the TV on me."

"Who did?" James asks.

"Foxy."

"Fuck that. It's a white TV. Watch whatever you want."

"I know that, but Yaberz said if my name comes up in anything I'm fucked," I explained.

"Shit, if you want to get him, then get him. You're in the right. Joey can't do shit about you standing up for the white TV."

"Yeah, but Foxy is Shady's butt boy. They'll spin it around some way."

"How? I'm right here. I'll back up what happens."

"Naw, fuck it. I only got another month before my transfer."

Just as I said it, Foxy came shooting over. "Motherfucka, we got a problem we'll deal with it right now," Foxy said.

"Who the fuck are you talking to?" James said, turning around looking at Foxy.

"He's talking to me," I say.

"There's the cell right over there motherfucka." Foxy pointed towards our cells. His cell was right next to mine.

Now he had really pushed me into a corner. Not only did he disrespect me with the TV, but now he was calling me out. I couldn't let it slide.

"Fuck this," I said as I jumped out of the chair and shot towards my cell. Everything was vital in prison. There was a strict "no hands" policy toward other races in the prison since the race riot. Any problems were to go through the shot callers of each race, and they would take care of their own. If I went in his cell, I was in violation. The same with him. I opened my door and headed to the edge of my bunk, with my back towards the wall. My hand was in my pocket clenching my bone crusher.

"Come on," I dared him.

"Go ahead and pull it out," Foxy challenged me with his hand in his pocket grabbing his knife.

He knew he couldn't pull out his piece or come into my cell unless I pulled out first. We both knew whoever pulled out first was in violation and would get voted off the island, if they didn't get killed first.

"Come on in here," I urged him. My mind was made up that if he stepped one foot inside the cell I was pulling out and trying to take his head off. Kina, the kids, my transfer be damned. I wouldn't do them any good if I was dead. This was life or death.

"Pull it out, motherfucka!" Foxy said, making a show outside.

Really he didn't want to come in and have a knife fight. He thought that I'd back down when he challenged me. When I didn't and called him out on it he had to do something. His way of getting out of it was to get loud and draw attention so that dudes would come over to break it up. In prison, the ones that are quiet are the ones you have to worry about. They're the ones that would stick you and you'd never see it coming. The loud ones just want to make you think they'll do something, when in reality they wouldn't bust a grape.

"Stop talking and let's go," I demanded. I knew I had him.

Foxy knew I had him too. He was just hoping that he got saved before he got exposed. Which happened in the form of James and Foxy's shot caller Buck.

"Yo, Foxy, what's the problem," said Buck, a solid six foot, 250 pound gangbanger from DC.

"This motherfucka was talking shit about the TV," said Foxy.

"Which TV?" Buck asked.

"That one." Foxy shakily pointed at the white TV.

"What was he saying?" Buck asked.

"About me changing it!"

"Shit, that's their TV! You ain't supposed to be changing it."

"We watch wrestling here every Monday."

"That don't matter. You can't change it on him."

"Yeah, but—"

"But nothing," Buck interrupted him.

"You in the wrong."

"Man that's fucked up," Foxy replied.

"Yo, we done with this conversation. Let me talk to my man, Hipster," Buck said, waving Foxy off.

"What you trying to do about this Hipster?" Buck and I had been cool for a while. I knew if there's any problems with his people, Buck would take care of it.

"Fuck that dude. I ain't got no rap for him," I said.

"How are you trying to handle this?" Buck was tight with Foxy, but he also knew Foxy was in the wrong

"Fuck it. Just keep him under wraps and we don't have any problems."

"You sure? You cool?"

"Yeah, I'm cool. Just handle your people."

"Without question," Buck said as we slapped hands and he rolled out.

I saw him wave for Foxy to meet him in his cell where no doubt he'd put him in check.

"You're cool then?" James said coming into my cell. He stood outside, posted up ready to roll if it even looked like anything was going to happen.

"Yeah, I just know this shit is going to get to Joey and it's going to get bad."

"Fuck, Joey. You're in the right."

"That don't matter with these dudes, you know that."

"If you want I'll pull him up tomorrow and let him know the deal."

"Yeah, let him know what's up," I said.

"Alright. You know I hate talking to that motherfucker though."

"I know man. I just want to quash this before it gets out of hand."

"I feel you. I'll talk to him in the morning."

"Thanks, man."

"No problem," he said as he gave me a pound and walked out of the cell.

I avoided the yard like the plague in the morning. It wouldn't have mattered if there was a naked Crisco twister competition featuring the Hooters girls outside. Ok, maybe just for that. But for anything else it wasn't going to happen. I sat in my cell armed to the teeth, waiting.

James came in and said that he didn't see Joey, or any of his crew for that matter. Which was definitely not a good sign for me.

I skipped lunch so that I could be at the indoor recreation doors as soon as it opened up. There wouldn't be any walking of the gauntlet for me. I would move in quick, right inside with my knife in its holster. If they wanted me, they knew where to find me. My eyes stayed on the door while I was in the band room. Watching to see who came in on the move. I saw Jason, another AM and Yaberz come inside. They quickly disappeared into another music room with a piano.

I wasn't worried about Jason. He was their heavy hitter. When the shit got really deep, Jason would step up and slaughter whomever. He was a good dude who I was cool with. He wouldn't put himself out there like that over me.

Yaberz and I always had it down that if he came around and wasn't wearing his glasses it was go time. He'd make a good show of it, but all in all I wouldn't get too messed up. He always let it be known to Joey and everyone that if I had to go, it was going to be him to do it. So after an hour of jamming with Sergio, when Jason and Yaberz came around sans glasses, I got a bit nervous.

I just kept playing, looking over at them every couple seconds. Waiting for it to happen. I wasn't going to pull my knife because it was Yaberz. The only thing I could do was bob and weave. Use my guitar as a shield and hope that the CO's saw it quick enough to save me from the slaughter.

If Joey was sending Jason with Yaberz, he meant to seriously fuck me up. My only shot was to make it out of the room before going down. Once you go down it's a wrap. I've literally seen a dude's face get kicked off after going down and getting the boots. No way was I going to let that happen to me. I also couldn't tip my hand. If I made a break for the door they'd get me for sure. That and Yaberz could get exposed for tipping me off. I had to wait for them to make their move.

Tom Petty sang, "*The waiting is the hardest part.*" He hit it right on the head with that. I played a song, and nothing. Then another, and another. Still nothing. I don't know why they were waiting. Hell, they were even requesting songs. I was like the jester, entertainment for the elite and as soon as they got tired of me, I was gone. But fuck it, music was what I loved so why not go down jamming.

I played for over an hour till they left. Just strolled out as nonchalantly as they came in. To say I was perplexed was an understatement. Either I rocked so fucking hard they forgot why they even came in, or—shit—or what?

That night I caught Yaberz out in the yard. He wasn't supposed to be talking to me per Joey's orders. Not that he cared, but he had to make it look good to them. He didn't want them to know his allegiance was toward me.

"What's up, bro?" Yaberz asked.

"I don't know? I was hoping you could tell me," I asked.

"About what?"

"Shit, I thought you came to get me today."

"Why'd you think that?"

"You weren't wearing your glasses!"

"Oh, fuck, I forgot about that." Yaberz shook his head. "They were getting fixed."

"Man, goddamn, kid."

"I was wondering why you kept looking at us." Yaberz laughed.

"Yeah, yeah, real fucking funny." I slapped his hand.

"What'd Joey say about the Foxy thing?"

"I know Shady said shit to him about it, but I don't know what's going on."

"I knew that motherfucker was going to start some shit."

"What happened? I heard it was over the TV," said Yaberz.

I told him the whole story and asked him what he thought.

"Shit, he's in the wrong. You did what you were supposed to do."

"Yeah, but is Joey going to see it like that?"

"Bro, I don't know. They won't even say anything about you around me anymore. I do know that they're looking for a reason to get you."

"Yeah, and this is the reason."

"But it was a white TV and you were in the right."

"He doesn't give a fuck," I explained.

"He does hate your guts, Hipster."

"No, shit." I sunk down low.

"Man, I told you to stay out of the way."

"Shit, I am. I couldn't help that."

"Damn, bro, I'll see what I can find out."

"Let me know," I said, sliding away to head back into my unit.

I didn't need to wait for Yaberz to find out. I felt it coming. It was like being in the eye of a hurricane. It was calm, but I would be a fool to think that I was safe. I started preparing. Catching Bruce to give him all my info. He had instructions to call Kina and let her know what had happened. I told him to call her every couple weeks to make sure she was alright. You would only get 15 minutes a month on the phone back in the hole. I wouldn't be able to call all the time to make sure Kina was ok. It helped that I could trust him not to take her from me. He was too smart to get involved like that.

Bruce was really positive about life in general so I wanted Kina to talk to someone that would keep her spirits up. I could deal with the hole. I'd done over a year in the hole over an eight year period. My main concern was for her. I also went to see Tony. He was a professional knife cutter.

Any type of knife you wanted, Tony could make. What I need was a stainless steel beast. Something that could go through metal detectors. Fuck having to switch my knife from my bag to my holster. I'd have a bad motherfucker on me at all times. They called the stainless steel knives that went through the metal detectors safeties as in they kept you safe at all times. They told me he could do it. But it'd take a couple days. He could cut and sharpen it in no time. The hard part was getting the stainless steel out of the kitchen. I'd have to give a down payment on my monster. He'd have to pay off a cook to get it, then a Mexican gangbanger to bring it out.

"Give me five books now, and ten after it's done," he said.

"Alright, here's ten now. Another ten if you have it tomorrow," I said, hoping to expedite things.

He looked at the stamps and shrugged. "Fuck, I'll try."

"Cool, let me know when it's done."

The next thing I had to do was see Yaberz. He was always out on the yard and easy to find. The main thing was to catch him away from Joey and the AM's. We couldn't be seen together.

"What's up, bro?" I said coming up behind Yaberz as he came out of the bathroom.

"Damn, Hipster. I didn't even see you," Yaberz said, jumping with his hand going into his pocket to grab his knife.

"That's the point. I want you to know I'll get that ass if I want," I backed off laughing.

"Hey . . . I don't want no problems, sir," Yaberz laughed and put his arms up over his head.

"I didn't think so. But what did you find out?" I asked.

"Nothing, but I know Youngster got out of the hole today and he was on the same range as Dom."

Youngster was another AM who just got patched up. I knew what was up. I lived with Dom for over a year and knew damn well all about the lies he'd spin. He'd say and do whatever it took to get me.

"Ah, fuck! I know he told Youngster some bullshit."

"I'm sure he did. You know how he is," said Yaberz.

"They didn't say anything to you."

"Nope, they're all with him right now in church," he explained.

Church was what they called their meetings. They'd talk about whatever was going on with the yard and the gang. They would take votes, pass down orders and plan missions and things for their gang members to accomplish.

"Is it still going to be you if they get me?" I asked.

"I told them if anyone was going to get you, I wanted it to be me."

"They still going to go for it?"

"I said what you did was fucked up and since you were my boy you disrespected me by doing it. Said I was pissed that I didn't fuck you up more."

It was an okay story but would it be enough? I wondered. "I hope they let you. If not I'm pulling out my piece and gutting whoever comes at me."

"You better not fucking gut me," Yaberz teased.

"And I'm getting a new stainless piece from Tony."

"Shit, you really better not hit me when you get that."

"Not 'til tomorrow. I already put down ten books on it though."

"Damn, you aren't fucking around are you, Hipster?"

"Fuck no. I'm taking someone with me when they come."

"Just make sure it's not me," Yaberz said laughing as we slapped hands.

"Make sure it is you so I don't have to."

I thought all my bases were covered. I didn't know when it was going to happen. But I knew it was going down, again. The best I could hope for was Yaberz being the one doing it and it being over quick. I decided to retreat into my comfort zone and call my baby.

"Hey, sexy," I said to Kina after she accepted my call.

"Hey, baby, I missed you," Kina answered.

"I missed you too."

"What took you so long to call me?"

"I was outside getting things together," I said.

"Like what?"

"Well, a lot of things. Listen, everything's going to be ok."

"What's wrong?" Kina could tell by the tone in my voice that something was up.

"A dude got out of the SHU who was back there with Dom."

"Ok, what's that mean?"

"You know how Dom is. I don't put anything past that weasel."

"I thought all of that was over with?"

"Not if he pulls some type of move, which I'm sure he's going to do."

"What about me coming to see you this weekend?"

"Shit, come see me. I'm dying to see you again."

"Will it be behind glass?"

"If I'm back in the hole it is." Anything could happen before then.

"I won't get to kiss you?" Kina asked.

"Not until I make it to another spot," I explained.

"Baby, that's going to kill me being so close and not getting to touch you."

"I know, beautiful, we'll be fine though," I consoled her.

"You're not going to get hurt are you?"

"I'll be fine. You don't have to worry about me."

"How will I know though?"

"Bruce will let you know the deal."

"You're still going to be able to call me though, right?"

"Of course, but only for fifteen minutes a month."

"What? Only fifteen minutes."

"Listen, Kina, I love you to death. You're an amazing woman. You're raising two kids on your own. You're stronger than you know. I can get through this. But only if I know that you're ok."

"I'll be ok."

"I believe in you, Kina. That's why I'm marrying you."

"I love you, baby," Kina said softly to me.

"I love you too. If I don't call you back tonight then you know what's up," I said. "We're going to make it beautiful."

"You promise?" she asked.

"With all my heart."

"*Mwah*," she blew a kiss to me over the phone.

"*Mwah*," I kissed back. Taking that love with me as I went out to the yard to face the unknown. *We're going to make it*, I assured myself.

Before heading outside I pulled up James and told him the deal. Youngster got out and was on the range with Dom.

"If you feel like something's going to pop off then come get me." James said.

"You sure?"

"I told you I got you back. When I roll, my guys have to roll."

"Alright, thanks, man," I said.

I knew that James had been wanting to move on the AM's for a while now. With me, he could do it and make it look justified. This could very easily turn into a mini riot. Fuck it though. If I'm going to go, why not go out in a blaze. Let them tell stories about me while I slide out somewhere else.

I surveyed the landscape before heading outside when they opened up the compound. We had a big soccer game but it was the farthest thing from my mind. There was nothing out of the ordinary. But that made me more wary. In prison everything was set like clockwork. Dudes followed the same routine down to the T. It was easy to spot when something was about to go down. Still I felt uneasy about it.

I headed toward the soccer field with my gray net bag slung over my shoulder. My right hand hidden inside, tightly clenching my knife. I'd easily catch anyone with a vicious stab wound before they could get to me. I had it all planned in my mind but what happened after that was up in the air. But I knew I'd draw first blood.

My team was out on the field warming up. We were in first place at

10-0, playing the second place team. There was a lot of money bet on the game and all the Mexican gangbangers turned out to watch.

"What's up, big, Hipster?" asked Sergio, slapping my hand after coming over from the field. "You ready for this?"

I still had my hand inside my bag. Taking everything in. It was like I was watching a movie. I wasn't about to let my guard down, not at all. With the nagging feeling in my stomach I knew it was going down but I didn't know when. I snapped back to reality. "Yeah, I'm ready," I said. "Let's do this!"

"Well, let's go," he said, heading toward the field.

"Alright, hold up for a minute."

"What's up?"

"Youngster, got out of the SHU today."

"So . . ."

"He was on the same range with Dom."

"Who gives a fuck?" Sergio waved me away.

"I don't put shit past Dom." I cast my eyes over to survey the landscape.

"That shit's dead, homes. They got you already. They can't get you again."

"Says who?" Whatever rules there were Joey didn't seem to care.

"Fuck them dudes. They aren't gonna do shit," said Sergio.

"I hope."

"Look, they aren't gonna do shit while we're playing. They know better than that." Sergio tried to calm me down.

"You'd think."

"They ain't even out here Hipster. I'm telling you, you're cool."

"Man—"

"Put your cleats on. Let's go beat these dudes."

"Alright, fuck it. Let's fuck these dudes up," I said as I pulled out my cleats and changed my shoes. Nevertheless, I still kept my bag on my shoulder until game time. I couldn't let my guard down.

Right before the game started I took one more look around the yard. Nothing was out of place, so I put my bag down on the bleachers and headed out on the field. It proved to be a mistake. We were only playing for about five minutes when all the white guys started popping up. It started with Joey and his cronies. Then all the other different white cars. It was almost like there was an APB calling all crackers to the field. Come one come all to see the soccer slaughter. There were dudes out there that you'd only see at holiday meals in the chow hall. It was a honky fiesta, and I was the piñata.

"Yo, kid, they're going to get me," I said to Bruce, who was playing on the other team.

"What? How do you know?" he asked.

"Look at all the white dudes out here." I nodded my head toward the growing crowd of tatted up spectators.

"So?"

"Have you ever seen any of these dudes at a game?"

"No," he admitted.

"Exactly. They're here to watch me get got."

"Man, I wish it didn't have to end like this."

"Just make sure you call Kina like you're supposed to."

"I will."

"No matter what happens, tell her I'm ok."

"Alright, bro," he said.

"I'll shoot you a kite as soon as I can," I said. "You better make me famous with this music thing" I slapped his hand and gave him a hug.

I kept playing the rest of the first half. Contemplating what my move should be. I knew they wouldn't run out onto the field during the game and get me. They wouldn't disrespect the Mexicans. It would either be at halftime, or after the game. I figured I could make a break as soon as the whistle blew. Run over to the next yard and grab James, who was playing softball. Don't even give them a chance. It would be effective. It would also look like a bitch move, and no matter what you always had to protect your reputation. No matter how bad mine was at that point. The system was small. You'd always see someone from another yard. It was only a matter of time. I had to save face.

They could say, "That's the guy that stole another man's wife." What they couldn't say was that I went out like a bitch. Never that. Grabbing my bag I reached for my shank. The one thing I had to even the odds. My mind was set on sticking the first one that came at me. I was in straight kill mode. Only when I reached in the bag, my knife was gone.

"Fuck," I cursed under my breath.

I started digging through the different folders of music and papers that I always carried around with me to camouflage the knife. Hoping I just hid it really good from myself.

"FUCK," I cursed again tearing through my shit. Praying that it popped into my waiting hand. Then it instantly hit me what happened to my piece. During the first half I noticed a couple of Joey's nut huggers sitting on the bleachers by my bag. They were really the last of my worries at that moment. But now I realized why they were there, to steal my equalizer. I dropped my bag in resignation of what was about to happen. They never come with just one. My plan of gutting the first one was shot. All I could do was try to tap into my inner Chuck Norris and go out swinging.

Looking around the bleachers, I saw Yaberz. It was almost in slow motion. He was walking around the concrete slabs in the opposite direction of everyone else. The glasses were gone from his face. I knew it was going to be him and someone else. But Yaberz would be doing most of the work. That would always be a bad thing since Yaberz was a beast. But he was my brother and he was doing it so I didn't get seriously fucked up. He looked me in the eye and gave me the nod. Letting me know what was up. I gave him the nod back and turned around to face the field. That's when all hell broke loose.

I got tackled from behind by Yaberz. Going down immediately. My body getting beat with fists and feet. It was Yaberz and another kid named BB. BB wasn't shit. He was just one of Joey's flunkies trying to earn some points. I'd have fucked him up in no time if he came by himself. But the two of them, along with whoever else would've jumped in if I started fighting back, kept me down. The blows really weren't that bad. I was covered up mostly, playing defensive. Down on my hands and knees with my head ducked down to my chest. Mostly my back was getting hit. BB I'm sure was trying to hurt me but he failed terribly. Yaberz on the other hand wanted to make sure I didn't get hurt. But he also had to make it look good.

I was waiting for the alarms to get hit and the CO's to come and "save" me but the beating just kept coming. Normally the sirens would be going off in about five seconds. A minute into getting beat on and the only sound was blows landing and the onlookers roaring. That's when Yaberz stepped back and kicked me square in the ribs.

It sounded like a gunshot. The force lifted me off the ground. My ribs instantly cracked as all the wind rushed out of me. My lungs fought for oxygen as my mind recoiled in horror. I couldn't take too much more of the ass whooping. Just as fast as it started, it was finished.

Joey called them off. I guess he felt that they got me good enough and got away with it, so he called off his dogs. Crawling off the ground I grabbed a hold of my right side. My ribs were killing me. The shirt that I was wearing was shredded and barely hanging onto my body.

"Get your ass up top!" I heard someone yell. Because the cops didn't see it, I'd have to go to them and tell them I needed off the compound. That I needed protection. It's called "checking in". Which was something you didn't do. Check-in's were looked at just as bad as rats, and a step above a rapist.

If I went to another compound and produced paperwork that I was a check-in from another spot I'd get jumped immediately. There was no way I was going to check in. I had way too much pride in myself to do that. The system was small and I had eight years left. There was no way I was going to do that wearing a check-in tag around my neck. It might as well be a rope.

No, I'll go find James, I thought as I slowly walked off the field. They were still yelling for me to go up top. Yelling at me, "You're done here." But fuck them, I was done when I said I was done. I would never give them the satisfaction.

The yard was broken down into three different fenced in sections. One was the soccer field. Another was basketball and handball courts. The third was a softball field. If I could make it to the softball field and get James, then I could turn the tables. He always had two knives on him. I could grab one and get to sticking. Since he'd be with me, his car would have to ride with us too. I was still trying to catch my breath when I saw that the gates were locked. It was something that they just started a couple weeks earlier for this exact reason. So that you wouldn't be able to get back up if something happened.

"Fuck!" I yelled as I stopped walking. I turned around to see the enemy trailing me.

"Get your ass up top, Hipster," Pat said. He was a long haired biker that just patched up with the AM's. About six feet tall and 230 lbs. He was who Joey sent to make sure that I went to the lieutenant's office to check in. If I deviated from it, he was supposed to get me.

"I'm not checking in," I said.

"What?" he blurted out, stunned.

"I ain't no fucking check-in," I repeated.

"What?" He said again in shock.

"We're doing this again," I said as I ripped off the rest of my torn shirt and punched Pat square in the jaw.

Both of us were throwing punches when the sirens went off. It all happened fifteen feet from the gun towers. I held my ground with Pat when Mike, another one of Joey's nut huggers, flew in with a running kick to my already busted ribs.

I lost my breath but refused to go down. I was now trading blows with two AM's, and I knew that they were not going to take it easy on me like Yaberz did. The alarm was going off telling everyone to get down on the ground or they'd be shot. CO's were running toward us as the gun tower doors opened and a concussion grenade was thrown. The sound was deafening. Especially when it's going off ten feet away from you. If you weren't down on the ground before it went off, you sure as hell were eating dirt afterwards. That was unless you were fighting for survival against two tat'd out gang members.

They both backed off and got down after the blast. Knowing that the next thing going off was the gun and that would deter even the hardest cons. I backed away from them but refused to lay down. When you had just gotten jumped twice in the belly of the beast, the last thing you wanted to do was lay face down surrounded by the enemy. I staggered a bit and then locked my knees like a prize fighter waiting out the clock.

"Get down and cuff up!" the CO's screamed at me.

"Fuck no," I yelled back at them and put my hands behind my head. "I'm not cuffing up."

"Cuff up!" they yelled again.

"I'll cuff up as soon as I'm off the yard. There's no fucking way until then." I spat blood on the ground.

They cuffed up Pat and Mike then led them off the yard. Two CO's grabbed each of my arms to lead me away.

"What happened?" one of them asked me.

"Shit, you saw what happened."

"What was that all about?"

"Dude, I don't know. Just take me back to the SHU," I said in resignation. Defeated, but still in one piece, I walked across the yard toward the hole. It would be the last time I walked on the yard. I cuffed up once I got inside, but not a second earlier. They took me to medical before going back to the hole. I was having trouble breathing from the cracked ribs, but all and all I was ok. Especially after getting jumped twice, by four different dudes, in the span of about two minutes.

"Who were the guys that jumped you?" asked the lieutenant.

"I don't fucking know."

"Who do they roll with?"

"No clue."

"What are their names?"

"I don't fucking know," I said.

"You know we're going to find out their names. You might as well just tell us who they are," the lieutenant snapped back.

"Listen, I'm not trying to be a dick. Whatever you find out, you find out. I'm just trying to get back to the SHU and get the fuck outta this spot."

"Alright, take him to the SHU," the lieutenant barked and two CO's grabbed me from behind and led me to the box. I was placed into one of the 20 by 20 foot cages in the outdoor recreation part of the SHU. Basically a dog kennel for fully grown men. The hole was always full and you're lucky if you got to a cell right away. I was kept separated from dudes in the other cages that were also waiting for an open cell to call home. Two cages down from me were Pat and Mike. They were talking to each other while walking the ten steps or so back and forth that the cage allowed.

Once the CO that was in charge of watching all of us left, I yelled down to the other prisoners. "Yo, Pat!"

"What's up?" he hollered back.

"So what's your reason for getting me?"

"You know what it was about."

"Yeah, I know. But what's the excuse you're using? I already got it from Yaberz before for that Dom shit."

"What did you tell Yaberz about today?"

"I don't fucking know?" I said.

"You didn't tell him you were getting anything?"

I didn't know what the fuck he was talking about for the life of me. I wasn't going to say something that could get Yaberz in a jam. "What the fuck are you talking about?" I called down.

"You didn't tell him you were getting a piece?" asked Pat.

"What the fuck?" I mumbled to myself. Yaberz told them that? They must've really put a press down on him to get that information.

"Yeah, so what. I'm not allowed to have a piece?" I yelled. Everybody in the pen had some kind of weapon for protection.

"We take that as a threat," he hollered back.

"Really? And you didn't think the other ones I had were a threat?"

"I don't know about any of that. I just know that's the reason."

"Wow, that's the excuse you're going to use to the yard?"

"It is what it is."

"Whatever, man."

"Now that you're back here you and Dom can work out all that shit and then come back out."

"Dude, I'm not talking to that motherfucker," I yelled down.

"I'm just saying, if you guys work it out, maybe you can come back on the yard."

"I'm not coming back on this yard. You know that. Besides, I'm up for a transfer to an FCI in a month. So fuck it," I said.

"Fuck. I was supposed to be going to an FCI too in a few months," said Pat. "Now I'm hit. All I was supposed to do was make sure you left. Then you turn around and start swinging on me."

"Hell, what'd you want me to do? Lay down and get shit stomped."

"No, you did what you did. I respect that. You ain't no bitch."

"I wasn't expecting to get fucking ninja kicked by Mike over there!" I yelled down and we all started laughing.

"Shit, Yaberz kicked the fuck outta you!" Pat laughed.

"No shit. My ribs are fucked up right now."

"It lifted you off the ground!" Mike called out and started laughing.

"Sounded like a shotgun went off when he hit you!" Pat added.

"Yeah, he got me. But I'll tell you this. I fucked up his foot like a motherfucker!" I said and we all laughed again.

My brother always told me, "If you don't laugh about it, you'll cry about it." That was just what we were all doing, knowing that we'd be back in the box for a minute.

After a couple minutes Skip came down and went to talk to the AM's.

"Hipster, what's up?" Skip said to me as he walked past.

Skip was a skinny 25-year-old kid from Texas. He'd been back in the SHU for about six months. He started out in a low security prison and worked his way up to the pen. He was doing all of his 5 year sentence and was looking at a new charge for about his fifteenth knife. He'd been back in the hole so many times and for so long that he was considered now the default shot caller for the whites back in SHU.

The CO's let him get away with a lot of shit because of it. Due to the fact that two of his "homeboys" were back here, they brought him out of his cell to talk to them. They talked for about twenty minutes before the CO's came back to get him. As he walked past me he gave me a nod and shook his head as he smiled. Gesturing, *I can't believe what happened to you.*

I've known Skip for about a year. We were pretty cool with each other and would shoot the shit out on the yard together. Even though he was the number one AM nut hugger on the yard, I still didn't take him as a threat. The fact that he was about 150 pounds soaking wet also played into my perception. But the kid got his respect, I'll give him that

After the CO's left with Skip I yelled down to Pat. "Yo, Pat! What's the deal with Skip?"

"He's taking the knife charge to trial," answered Pat.

"No, what's the deal with me and Skip?"

"You're cool. You didn't go out like no bitch or check in. I told him you're good."

"Cool, I'll tell the lieutenant that this was a mistake. That I turned around real fast and you thought I was coming at you. So you swung and we started fighting because of it."

"Yeah, man. I appreciate it. I'm trying to get to the FCI."

"It's all good," I yelled back.

"Yo, Hipster, you know what time it is, if they put you with a check-in."

"Yeah, I know."

What he meant was it was on me to get them. I couldn't live with a check in. That's just as bad as being a check-in and would follow you wherever you went. Which was the last thing I needed on top of everything else.

They came and got both the AM's about twenty minutes later and gave them a cell. I, on the other hand, wasn't so lucky. I sat down on the hard concrete floor with my back against the chain link fence until 4 a.m. staring up at the full moon and thinking about everything that had happened since I met Kina.

There were no open cells for me to go to, so they stashed me inside the law library. There were no books to keep me company. All that I had was a foam mattress thrown on the floor. They gave me a sheet and blanket to use as I wished. There was no toilet, sink or shower. A CO brought me a bottle of water to drink, and an empty quart bottle to piss in. I folded my blanket up into a pillow and wrapped myself with the sheet. My body throbbed as I laid down and wished for a sleep that wouldn't come.

I could barely get up off the mattress when they brought in breakfast. The meal consisted of bran flakes, cake, and milk. My ribs felt like there was a knife sticking into them. Just breathing was something that brought about agonizing pain. All I could do was hold my right rib cage as I drank the milk and gave the rest of the food back.

Depression always came when you first went back to the SHU. Everything that you did to ease your time stops immediately. Every little comfort that you had was gone. All you're left with was prison in its rawest form. One button up prison jumpsuit, one pair of socks, boxers, and one shirt. One sheet and blanket. Nothing else but your mind to keep you company. The confinement could play hard on a person.

I normally worked out to pass the time in SHU. With broken ribs I could barely even move, let alone do some pushups. I would be back here for a while. How long I didn't know. It was the summer time too. All I knew was that it'd be cold outside before I touched down on my next yard. I just said, "Fuck it." What else can you say?

The lieutenant came a few hours later to give me an incident report. "Here's your shot," The tall black muscular lieutenant said and handed me the paperwork.

"Shit! Shot?" I asked.

"Yeah, for fighting on the yard," he said and lingered as I read the shot.

It stated that Pat and I were throwing punches and Mike jumped in and started kicking me. Basically it said that I got jumped by two gang members.

"You're writing me up for that?" I asked.

"It'll get dismissed at your hearing, but we got to do it like this."

"Man, that's fucked up."

"I know. Do you have a statement?"

I thought about what I could say to try and get Pat off, but not incriminate myself in any way. Plus I wasn't a rat and whatever I said would be used against me, with the cons as well as the cops.

"It was all a misunderstanding. I turned around and he thought I was threatening him. So . . . shit happened."

"What about the other guy?" the lieutenant asked.

"Dude . . . I don't know."

"Alright, well like I said, it was a two-on-one and the DHO should throw this out when you see him."

"Ok."

"Are you going to be coming back to the compound?"

"Shit, I don't know." I said.

"Hey, at least you held your ground with them," he said.

"I guess," I said, holding onto my ribs.

The pain in my ribs and breathing was getting worse. I didn't even try to sit back down. The room was a little bit bigger than a cell. I walked around the square room slowly. Each step was a chore. All I could think about was Kina. I was sure Bruce called her and told her what happened. I was dying to know if she was alright. I would get a call in the next day or so, once I got a cell. But I hoped that she would come down and see me. Take me out of this cage, this misery I was in, for the two hours that I'd be allowed to see her.

"Let's go," came the call from outside my door.

"What's up?" I asked the CO.

"We got you a cell. Cuff up."

"Good," I said as I turned around and crouched down to put my hands into the slot to get handcuffed. Although it was agony doing it, I knew I'd finally get out of this box.

"Don't put me with no rat or check-in," I told the CO.

"Why not?" he asked as he led me down the hallway.

"Dude, don't put me in the spot where I got to do something. I'm already fucked up."

"Well, it's back into the library if you don't want to go in with him."

"Fuck, I guess it's back into the library," I told him with disgust.

He turned around and led me back into the brightly lit dungeon of a room. "Alright, your choice," he said.

It had been over 24 hours since I used the bathroom or taken a shower. My body was beaten and I was running off of only a couple hours of sleep. No matter how bad I felt, I couldn't allow myself to make a bad decision. Everything followed you, broken ribs or not. If I lived with a check-in and didn't do anything, I'd be marked too. I'd be a lot safer living with a check-in instead of someone else.

Who knew if the person they put me in with would have a vendetta against me? It could be a gang member from one of Joey's rival gangs that he wouldn't let on the yard. Someone looking for payback against anyone they could who was out on the compound. Or someone that heard the stories about me, "stealing Dom's wife, money, and kids." who thought I needed to get jumped again. With the condition that I was in, I was prime to lose no matter who it was.

Fuck it, I thought after a couple more hours in the box. *They'll have to let me use a toilet and shower sometime.* I'd just have to keep walking. Try to block out the pain and rank feeling of my body. It *can't get any worse*, I kept telling myself.

A note shot under my door from an orderly right before lunch. It was from Skip. "Hipster, you're good to go in with Jacob (the check-in)," it read. "He didn't do any grimy shit. He's about to go to an FCI and checked in so he didn't get into any trouble."

Since Skip was calling the shots for the whites in the hole, that meant I was clear to live with Jacob. There couldn't be any repercussions against me for living with him. I would finally get out of the box and get to a cell. I'd finally take a shower and use a toilet for the first time in almost two days.

Jacob was a 23-year-old kid from Seattle. He just got to the pen from another spot. As soon as he got here and found out he could get to a medium, he checked in. He said he'd rather spend six months in the hole, then maybe get into some shit on the compound.

When I first got to the cell, I had to tell the CO's there wouldn't be a problem. That was the only way they'd let me in. We both were hand-cuffed behind our backs when they locked us inside the cell. They un-lock each person one at a time through a tiny slot in the door. If you want to get your celly, and win, that's the time to do it. Just make sure that you're the first one to get uncuffed, and proceed to kick the ever loving shit out of your defenseless victim.

Jacob made sure that he was the first one to get unhooked. He was a check-in and I had already refused to live with him because of it. For all he knew it was a set up move to get him. Hell, I'd think it was if I was in his shoes. Now, with broken ribs and my hands cuffed behind my back, I had to hope that he didn't make a preemptive strike.

He moved to the back of the cell while I went to the door to get unhooked. Jacob never turned his back on me. He was in a strike pose ready for action. I crouched down and stuck my hands through the slot keeping my eyes on Jacob. I'd seen someone get kicked straight in the head going down to get unhooked before. If he was going to hit me, now would be the time. Uncuffed, I stood up eyeing Jacob. He didn't know my ribs were broken and I wasn't going to let on that I was disabled.

"What's up? I asked, feeling him out.

"What's up?" he said back.

"I think I remember you," I said.

"Yeah, I came and watched you in the band room."

"Yeah . . . that's right. What happened to you?"

"I came from USP Atwater. As soon as my counselor told me that my points would drop in six months to go to a medium, I checked in. I've been down for five years and seen a lot of shit. I know how easy it is to get pulled into some bullshit and I'm trying to hit a medium. I'm not a cho-mo or a rat. If you got a problem with it, then we might as well deal with it right now."

"No, we're cool. Skip shot me a kite and told me you're straight to live with, we aren't going to have any problems."

"Cool," he said as he came up and shook my hand.

"He shot me a kite too and said you're good to live with. What happened to you?" he asked as he noticed me wincing in pain.

"Well . . ." I proceeded to tell him the whole story about what happened, leaving out how Yaberz was in on it of course.

"I heard about that. Dom is on C Range right now."

"Man, fuck that dude. Do we go out to rec with them?" Dom was the last one I wanted to see.

"No, we only rec with our range. Skip hollers down at him through the vent though if you're trying to pass him a message."

"No, I'm not trying to say shit to that dude. I'm just trying to get the fuck outta this pen and land in a medium," I said as I tried to put the sheets on my bunk.

"I feel the same way."

"Well, we're going to do just fine together then," I said. "Now I'm going to shit, shower and sleep. That law library was fucked up."

"Alright, we'll kick it later," he said, laying down on his bunk.

"Cool." I draped my sheet off of the top bunk making a little cave for Jacob to hide in while I went about my business. This was SHU etiquette, we made do with what he had and tried to live like civilized people and give each other privacy even in a 12 by 6 foot cell.

There really was no such thing as a good night's sleep with broken ribs. Any way that you laid was going to be painful. Especially when you were lying on top of a steel slab with only a foam mattress for support. But after two nights of sleeping on the floor, the steel slab was like a cloud. I could only sleep for about twenty minutes at a time, but those twenty were well needed.

The next morning I felt somewhat refreshed. There was definitely something good about having a toilet to use when you needed it. At breakfast Skip shot me a kite saying it was good to see me again, and asking me if I was going to go outside to rec. I hollered down to him telling him that I was and I'd tell him about everything when I came out.

I laid back down on my bunk and listened to my celly's radio. All I could get was top forty stuff, but it was still a needed distraction from reality. It had been three days since I talked to Kina last, and that felt like an eternity.

When they called rec, I slowly crawled off the top bunk and got dressed. I put on my orange one piece button down jumpsuit, and slipped on some blue canvas shoes.

"Hey, Hipster. You're still going out right?" Skip yelled down.

"Yeah, I'm going."

"Alright, I'll see you out there," he said.

I was the first one that they took to go outside. It was a beautiful cool summer morning in the swamp of Louisiana. The fresh air and sun was something I truly missed. Walking around the rectangular dog cage was the most exercise I was going to get for a while. A far fall from running five miles every morning, but at least it was something.

There were six different cages for outside recreation, with four men in each cage. They keep all the cages separated by race and car. They won't put check-in's in with other dudes. Everything was based on trying to keep the violence down to a minimum. There was also a little cage inside the big cage. This was where you went in, to get cuffed and uncuffed. A little slider closed you in and let you out. This was so that you can't get jumped or jump someone that is still cuffed up. At least you were given somewhat of a chance out here as opposed to going into the cell.

Skip and Timmy came down next. Timmy was a short little AM nut hugger from Ohio. He was cellys with Skip and was back in the hole for getting busted with a knife. Timmy kept catching write ups while he was back in the hole so that he would get transferred to another pen.

"What's going on, Hipster?" Skip asked while they were taking off his and Timmy's cuffs.

"Man, a whole lotta fucking nothing," I shot back to him.

"I heard you got some new tats while I was gone."

"Yeah, got my ribs done. Hurt like a bitch," I said as they both walked into the big rec cage and we all shook hands.

"Let me check it out," Skip said as he was standing in front of me.

I noticed Timmy walking a bit suspiciously around me as I went to lift up my shirt to show off my tat. I could feel that something wasn't right as I started to lift my shirt. That's when I saw Timmy turn around and try to hit me with a right hand.

I ducked his punch and hit him with a quick right to his stomach. Just as I did that, Skip hit me in my jaw with a right. I took a step back and rushed Skip, tackling him to the ground. I sat up on top of him and punched him square in the face. Timmy ran up and kicked me right on my broken ribs.

A blinding pain shot through my whole body as I doubled over. There was no breath entering my body as they both started to punch and kick me. I did my best to cover up and soften the blows as I tried to get up. I was in the worst spot that anyone could be in while in prison. Locked in a cage with broken ribs and getting beat on by wanna be gang members. The CO's wouldn't usually save you in this spot. They would wait until someone gets tired from beating the daylights out of their victim and decide to come and cuff up. Either that or they'd bring the tear gas and pepper ball gun to spray down everyone in the cage.

Neither of these options really boded well for me as I threw a couple punches to back off my aggressors. Just as I was up on one knee they both tackled me into the side of the cage. My back was down on the ground and I was fully exposed to their blows. I rolled onto my side facing the cage so that my back and ribs were taking most of the shots. This was life or death and my body didn't have any more gas left to defend itself. I knew I was done.

Just then the CO's rushed the cage. Maybe ten of them ran in and tackled Skip and Timmy to the ground. Two of them got on top of me and cuffed my hands behind my back. They picked me up by my arms and dragged me out of the cage. I looked back over my shoulder and saw Skip with three CO's hovering over him. They had their knees in his back as they cuffed him up. He looked at me, rolled his eyes, laughed and shook his head. Gesturing, *hey, man, sorry. I had to do it.*

The CO's marched me straight to medical. They must've known I was in bad shape to save me like they did and to bring me here. There was no way I could've lasted in that cage. My ribs were now busted beyond belief. I could hardly even sit down without doubling over in pain. It felt like a dagger was piercing my flesh. Each breath feeling like the knife was being twisted deeper and deeper.

The nurse checked me to see if I had a punctured lung from the assault. Thankfully, I didn't have one. Just a couple broken ribs that could only heal with time. There was nothing they could do for you, but give you a couple Motrins and send you on your way.

"Try to take it easy," the nurse urged me as they led me back to the hole.

"Dude, what the fuck happened to you?" Jacob asked as I uncuffed.

"Skip and Timmy fucking jumped me," I said as I clutched my ribs and tried to sit down on the desk.

"I heard the cops running. I was hoping it wasn't for you."

"Shit, I got lucky they rushed the cage. I was fucking hit."

"How bad they get you?"

"They busted my ribs to shit! Other than that they didn't do shit to me."

"Fuck. How you feel?"

"Like there's a fucking knife in my ribs," I wheezed.

"You don't look so good."

"Dude, I can't fucking breathe right now."

"Here, I'll give you the bottom bunk. Go ahead and lay down." He said as he switched our bunks around.

"Thanks, kid. There's no way I could get up there."

"Shit, you look like you can't make it off the desk," he said laughing.

"Dude, I'm afraid to even fart right now." I laughed and immediately grabbed my side wincing as the pain shot through me.

"Come on, I'll help you up," he said as he eased me off the desk and helped me lay down on the bunk.

"Oh . . . fuck!" I breathlessly said as I eased down onto my back.

If I thought I was bad off when I came back here, now I was fucked. When I woke up in the morning I couldn't even move. I was like Ralphy's little brother in *The Christmas Story* movie, where he fell down in the snow and couldn't get up because of his snow suit. Only it was my busted side keeping me down.

I would roll around a little bit to gain momentum, then swing my left arm up to grab the top bunk. From there I'd pull myself up out of bed. Always keeping my right arm clenched onto my ribs. I'd broken some bones in my day snowboarding and riding bikes, but this far exceeded the pain of any of those injuries.

To make matters worse, the goon squad came in and pepper sprayed some dudes a couple cells away. They refused to cuff up over some bullshit and out came the gas. So here I was, crawling into the corner of my bed with a wet shirt over my face to block out the gas when the CO's came to my door.

"Cuff up," they ordered.

"What?"

"Cuff up," the CO repeated.

"Goddamn," I cursed as I slowly went through the motions of getting up out of my bunk and cuffing up.

The gas was tearing me up. I could already only take shallow breaths, now even that was hard. When I made it down the stairs I was passed off to a young black lieutenant.

"What's going on?" I asked.

"You've got some visitors," he said as lead me to an adjoining room outside of the hole.

Inside the room were two federal agents. A white middle aged man and younger woman sat at a desk in the middle of the room.

"What the fuck is this?" I said, standing in the doorway.

"Please, have a seat," the man in the suit said to me.

"Man, I'm not going in there," I told the lieutenant.

"Sit down!" he forced me into the chair.

"Thank you, Lieutenant," the woman said as the lieutenant left the room.

"How are you feeling, Mr. Judge?" she asked me.

"I've got broken ribs."

"We know."

"So obviously I'm feeling pretty bad."

"Listen, we've got information that there's been money put up for a hit on you," the man said.

"Ok," I said.

"We also have information that Dominick Tisdell placed a hit out on the prosecutor of his case."

"Ok," I said, incredulously.

"Do you know anything about this?" the woman asked.

"This is why you called me in here?"

"Yes, we've got a threat on the life of a United States prosecutor along with you. We already know what happened to you so far and we're taking this seriously," the man said.

"Dude, I don't know shit. Now let me get the fuck outta here before you really get me killed."

"What's that mean?"

"That means that word travels fast around here and I'm not trying to be sitting alone in a room with some feds."

"Can you just tell us if Mr. Tisdell ever talked with you about putting a hit on his AUSA?"

"Listen, I told you I don't know shit. Don't make this any fucking harder on me. Get me the fuck out of this room." I got up out of my chair and the lieutenant came bursting through the door.

"Sit down!" he yelled at me.

"Fuck that. You're not getting me killed," I said as I tried to get past him.

"It's ok," the woman said to him. "You can take him back to his cell."

"Alright. Take him back," the LT said to a couple CO's standing around. They each took an arm and escorted me back to my cell.

"What was that about?" one of them asked me.

"A whole bunch of bullshit," I said to them as I shuffled painfully down the corridor and back into my cell.

"Dude," I said to Jacob after they put me back in the cell.

"That was the fucking feds."

"What?" He said, popping out of bed.

"That motherfucker Dom put a hit on me and his prosecutor."

"What?" He shook his head. Even for prison life it was unusual.

"The feds just came to tell me that they got info that Dom put out a hit on the prosecutor of his case. That and that he put a hit on me."

"Holy shit. That's what they pulled you out for?"

"Yeah, they wanted to know if I knew anything."

"What'd you say?" asked Jacob.

"I told them I didn't know shit and to let me get the fuck out of there," I explained.

"Shit, that's fucking bad, bro." He shook his head.

"No shit. This motherfucker just can't stop fucking shit up."

"Where would they hear that?"

"Dom was writing Kina all types of crazy ass letters from back here."

"What was he saying?"

"All types of shit. That I was gonna get killed and who knows what else."

"He doesn't realize that they read the mail?"

"Fuck yeah, he knows. He just doesn't give a shit."

"Wow," exclaimed Jacob. "what are you going to do?"

"I'm going to shoot a kite down to Skip and tell him the fucking deal."

"Yeah, you damn sure know the CO's are gonna tell him the feds came to see you."

"No shit. These motherfuckers aren't going to get me killed," I said and sat down at the desk.

I wrote out a kite telling Skip what happened. Telling him to get word out to the yard that they better chill cause the feds are investigating everything. When chow came I passed the note with the CO's to give to Skip.

"Yo, Skip!" I yelled.

"I got it!" he yelled back. "I'm sending one back! Hold up!"

About five minutes later a CO slid a kite under my door.

"Hey, Hipster. Sorry about what went down," the note began. "I was told to hit you, and I can't go against the yard. I'll make sure Joey knows what's going on. On another tip, you know your celly is a check-in. I know you're too fucked up to do anything to him. Try to get him outside and we'll do the rest."

"Wow," I murmured.

"What?" Jacob asked.

"This piece of shit wants me to set you up to go outside and get jumped."

"What?" Jacob said, jumping off the bunk to read the kite.

"Those motherfuckers are crazy."

"He knows why I'm back here. Timmy knows me from Atwater. He knows I'm not a scumbag. Here, look at this." Jacob reached under his bunk and pulled out this paperwork.

It explained how he was in for five years for a gun charge and that he didn't cooperate with the feds. He also pulled out paperwork from the prison that showed his points and when they'll drop for him to go to a medium.

"Man, they're just some nut huggers that are trying to suck up to Joey," I said.

"Shit, I'll go take any of them on, one-on-one. But I know I'm not going to get that out there."

"Fuck them dudes. You don't gotta worry about shit. I was at a medium, none of this is going to follow you."

"I know. I'm just pissed off that he said that shit. He told me I was cool when I came back here."

"He told me you were cool too. So as far as I'm concerned you're good."

"Man, fuck that dude!" Jacob said as he crawled back up onto his bunk and started reading a book.

The next day I went to my hearing for the fighting write up. If I got found guilty it would mean I'd have to go to another penitentiary. I'd been in front of the hearing officer before, and he treated me good. He was known for being extremely lenient for a hearing officer. His philosophy was this was a USP and shit was going to happen. I knew that I would be cool going in front of him. There was just one problem, he wasn't my hearing officer.

Ms. White was in her late twenties. She was a petite attractive case manager with blond streaks in her light brown hair. I had noticed her walking on the compound and I'd always do a double take when I saw her. She was in training to become a hearing officer and I was one of her first cases.

"I know you," she said to me as I was led into the hearing room. "You're the one that's always running and doing yoga on the yard."

"That's me," I said as I carefully eased into the chair across from her desk."

"What happened to you?"

"I got jumped and broke some ribs."

"That's why you're here?" She sounded like she couldn't believe it.

"No, I'm here for the first time I got jumped."

"You mean you got attacked twice?"

"Yep."

"What happened?" she asked me.

"Just a little misunderstanding."

She took a look at my battered visage. "Seems like a little more than a misunderstanding," she said.

"Yeah, that's just how things turn out in the pen."

"So I'm learning." She started going through a folder of papers. "Let's read your write up, Mr. Judge. It says that you were engaged in an altercation with two other inmates."

"Yes, ma'am."

"How do you plead?"

"Not guilty."

"It says right here that you were throwing punches."

"Yes, ma'am."

"So you admit that?" she asked.

"Yes, ma'am. I had to protect myself."

"I don't understand. Why did they attack you?"

"Like I said, it was a misunderstanding."

"Well, if you don't have anything else to say I'm going to have to find you guilty."

"What?" I said springing up in my chair.

"I don't have any reason not to find you guilty."

"Listen, Ms. White, if I get found guilty then I'll have to go to another pen and deal with all this political bullshit. I'm a month away from going to a medium."

"So why were you fighting if you were about to get a transfer?"

"Look at me. I'm not some bad motherfucker that goes around picking fights with gang members—two at a time! You've seen me around here. I do my time by myself, which makes me someone that's easy to get. I don't agree with a lot of the politics that go on and that makes me a target. That's it."

"I'm going to check your file. If you really are that close to a transfer then I'm going to expunge this incident report."

"Thank you," I told her gratefully.

"I'd sure like to know what this was all about because you don't seem like a troublemaker."

"I'm not, Ms. White. Just some bullshit that I got caught up in."

"Ok. Good luck," she said, collecting her paperwork.

"We're done here then."

"Thank you," I said again as I was escorted out of the office with two CO's on each arm.

With the incident report out of the way, I was now free to get the hell out of the pen. I'd have to sit in the hole for four or five months, but I'd be done with all the penitentiary bullshit. Back to the safe confines of a medium security prison. No more having to carry knives everywhere I went. But more importantly, I'd be able to start fresh on a compound with Kina being all mine. I went to sleep thinking everything would be all good.

The following day was a visiting day. I knew that Kina would come to see me. We hadn't talked in almost a week and it was killing me. Usually they'd start taking visits around 9 a.m. back in the SHU. They only last for an hour and they're behind glass. You had to talk to each other over the telephones connected to the walls. It sucked but was the best thing in life when you were back in the hole.

Kina drove over eight hours to see me for just one hour. No hugs or kisses. Just the opportunity to see me and hear my voice. Then it was another eight hour drive back home. It put a serious strain on our relationship. It also showed you how much your girl really cared about you.

Nine o'clock came and went. Then it was ten. Then eleven. Still nothing. I was sure she'd come. No way would she leave me back here and not come. Twelve o'clock came and still nothing. I was losing hope.

Maybe she doesn't give a fuck, I thought. I wasn't out there to call her anymore. Maybe I was just someone to comfort her, now that I couldn't do that, she was gone. Come one o'clock I was pissed. I felt duped. Betrayed. Here I was beat to shit because I got with her and she wasn't even coming to see me. Hell, I didn't even get a letter from her. Then the CO yelled down the range that I had a visit.

I was cuffed behind my back when I walked into the little booth and saw her. Everything disappeared at that moment. All the pain and anguish was gone. Seeing her again was like breathing life back into my body. She was life affirming. I had to crouch down to put my hands up to the slot to get uncuffed. When I did, I winced in pain. Kina could see that I was hurt and she started to get tears in her eyes.

"Hey, beautiful," I said to her over the phone.

"Hi baby. I'm so sorry about all this."

"It's ok. Are you alright?"

"I'm a wreck. I don't know what to do. I feel so bad that you're going through this."

"It's nothing. I'm alright. Did Bruce call you?"

"Yeah, he told me they got you but it wasn't that bad."

"No, the first couple times weren't that bad. The third one was what got me," I said.

"The third one?" Her eyes opened wide with shock.

"I got into it with some dudes back here too."

"Dom said it wasn't over with and that you were going to get it worse," she said, wiping tears from her eyes.

"Don't listen to that dude. I'm fine. It's all over with. The feds did come to see me about him saying all types of shit."

"He's been writing and calling, saying all types of different stuff."

"He's been calling? I thought he was back here in the SHU?"

"They let him out after they got you."

"Fucking scumbags," I mumbled to myself.

"That's why I didn't get back here to see you till now. His parents decided they were going to see him because they knew I was coming to see you."

"What? He's out there right now?" I said trying to scan the room from the little view that I had.

"No, I waited till they left before I came in. I told them to leave by twelve so I could get in then, but they didn't leave till one."

"That's not surprising."

"What's going to happen?"

"I'll sit back here for a couple months and then go to a medium."

"Where's that going to be?"

"I'm going to put in for the two closest places to you."

"Will you get it?"

"I'm not getting a disciplinary transfer so I got a good shot at it."

"I hope so, baby. I need to be able to see you."

"We're going to be ok. When I get to where I'm going, we'll get married."

"You still want me?"

"Kina, of course. I love you to death. Nothing is going to stop that."

"And you still want to get married?" She couldn't believe it.

"Officially make you my bitch?" I said smiling.

"You know it!" she said with a sweet smile.

"That's right, baby. I'm all yours," Kina said, her mood picking up after getting to see me.

Before we knew it the short hour was up. We blew kisses to each other through the glass. When I crouched down to get cuffed up and winced, I saw Kina look away. She turned back and said how she couldn't watch me getting cuffed.

We mouthed, "I love you" to each other as I was led back to my cell.

After reflecting on the visit I knew I could do this. After seeing Kina I was sure she was going to ride this out with me. This couple months of hole time was nothing, either was the eight years I had left. With Kina, anything and everything seemed possible. I went to bed that night knowing that life was going to be worth living. I went to sleep dreaming of my woman, all my problems non-existent.

"Judge, cuff up. You're going to medical," yelled a CO outside my door, waking me up.

"Medical?" I questioned out loud. "Alright."

Painstakingly I went through the process of getting myself up out of bed, cuffed up behind my back, and got escorted out of the SHU. I figured they wanted to check and see how my ribs were doing, although they could care less about how I was.

When the SIS lieutenant was waiting for me at the entrance to the SHU, I knew I wasn't going to medical. Lieutenant Crikkel was a black cock diesel, gung ho SIS cop. Meaning, he was the feds inside of the feds. If you were talking with him, well . . . you were in some shit.

"Mr. Judge, a lot of crap has been going on in this yard over you and the girl," Crikkel said as he lead me out of the SHU towards medical.

"Um . . . ok," I stammered.

"We took her off your visiting list."

"What! For what?"

"She lied and said she knew you prior to your incarceration."

"I've known that girl since '99."

"No, you didn't. You know her from your old celly, Dominick."

"The fuck I do. I know her from Phish tour. We just lost touch for a while. We hooked back up through him."

"That's not what the yard has to say."

"What the fuck does that mean?" I snapped at Crikkel.

"It means you'll never be seeing her again," he explained dryly.

"What the fuck! Man, fuck you!" I yelled.

"Hey, it's not on me." Crikkel shrugged his shoulders.

"Who's it on then?"

"The captain."

"Well, let me talk to that motherfucker."

"You'll get a chance. Right now though I suggest that you cooperate with these people."

"What people?" I said as I was led down a hallway in medical.

"They're here to help," Crikkel said as he took me to a room where the two federal agents were sitting down.

I couldn't believe it, not again. "What the fuck are you guys doing trying to get me killed?" I said to them as Crikkel forced me down into a chair and left the room.

"How are you doing?" the man said to me.

"I'm fucked up," I snapped at him. "I got broken fucking ribs, these motherfuckers kicked my girl off my visiting list and said I'll never see her again, and now I got you motherfuckers pulling this shit."

"We just heard about the girl getting taken off your list," the lady said to me. "That's too bad."

"Maybe we can help to get her back on?" the man chimed in and managed a forced smile.

"That'd be pretty fucking cool if you did," I said sarcastically.

"We felt this would be the safest way to talk with you," she said.

"Talk with me? I told you I don't know shit."

"We have copies of all the letters that were sent from Dom to Kina," the man said.

"Ok."

"We also have statements that he paid a thousand dollars for a hit on you," he explained.

"Ok," I repeated. There was no end to Dom's bullshit.

"We need to know about this hit he put out on his prosecutor."

"Dude, I don't know anything." It was all I could say. Claim ignorance. The old, "I know nothing about nothing", song and dance.

"You two never discussed anything about him when you lived together?" she asked me.

"We didn't ever really talk."

"You spent all that time with him and you never talked about anything?" he asked.

"Dude, I wasn't cool with him. Fuck, I stole his girl. Does that tell you enough?" I said agitated.

"You do understand if you go to another penitentiary that you won't last long."

"Whatever."

"With this hit out on you. You'll have to spend the rest of your time in PC. But if you help us, we'll get you sent to a medium security prison close to Kina."

"Are you fucking shitting me right now?" I came unhinged. I couldn't believe the games they were playing. "First off, I don't know shit. Secondly, Kina's kicked off my list. Thirdly, I'm not going to even make it to that point because you motherfuckers are going to get me killed by coming here to see me."

The only one that knows we're here to see you is Lieutenant Crikkel," she said.

"You really fucking believe that?" I said to her. Was she that naive or just leading me on?

"What are you saying?" the man asked.

"I'm saying you two don't know dick about the penitentiary. Everybody knows everything that happens in here, and everybody talks."

"Well, I guess we're done here," the man said, looking at his partner and waving Crikkel into the room.

"Thank fucking god. Get me the fuck out of here," I stood up to be lead back to my cell in pain and not amused.

"Dude, that was the fucking feds again," I said to Jacob after I got back to the cell.

"What?" he said puzzled.

"I thought you just went to medical?"

"Man, fuck no! The feds were down there in medical."

"What do you mean?"

"These motherfuckers set up some shit to see me down at medical."

"That's crazy," he said sitting up in his bed.

"No shit. And these fuckers kicked Kina off my list and said I'll never see her again."

"Why'd they do that?

"SIS said a lot of shit is going down on the yard because of me and he knows I didn't know her from the street."

"So people went to him and ratted you out."

"Yep."

"Wow, this shit is like a soap opera."

"It's fucked up is what it is," I sat down on the desk.

"What'd the feds say?"

"That Dom put a thousand dollar hit on me and that I'm fucked if I don't tell them about the hit on his prosecutor."

"Man, this just gets better and better," said Jacob sarcastically.

"No shit. I told them I didn't know shit and they're going to get me killed by pulling their bullshit."

"Damn right they are. You know the AM's are going to find out about it." That was if they didn't know about it already.

"Yeah, they're going to find out from me first," I said.

I wrote out a kite telling Skip what was all said. Nobody was going to be able to put a snitch label on me about this shit. When the CO's came around for their usual rounds I sent it down to Skip.

"Yo, Skip! You get that?" I yelled down to him.

"Got it! That's crazy, kid. I'll make sure Joey knows what's up."

"Alright," I started to pace the cell. Everything was just so overwhelming. Kina being kicked off my list was my main concern. Whatever happened with all the other shit was something I could deal with. But if I couldn't see Kina then it would be unbearable. She was what kept me going through everything. Since I met her, since seeing her for the first time, I couldn't even imagine her not being in my life. I thought about her all day long. To have that taken away from me was like them taking away my out date. Without her an out date lost all meaning.

"Fucking hell!" I screamed out, losing all composure.

"Dude, it'll be alright. Just have her put in a new form at your next spot," Jacob suggested.

"They said she'll never get to see me again."

"There's ways around all that shit. You just got to get somewhere new."

"Judge, pack up. You're going next door," the CO said outside my door.

"What the fuck?" I said.

"You're getting transferred."

"This shit is fucking ridiculous," I said as I packed up my little bit of belongings and cuffed up to go to the prison next door.

As I was walking past Skip's cell I said, "Make sure you get that out to the yard."

"I will. Keep your head up," Skip said.

"You fucking know it," I replied. I did my best to raise my head and look toward the uncertain future. Beyond reason I held on to fantasies of Kina and the beach and a fresh start.

That was the last I saw of USP Pollack. I was the only one on the van to the medium security prison next door. The fact that I was going over there wasn't that strange. Most of the penitentiary dudes would go over to the SHU of the newly opened medium prison when it was clear they wouldn't be going back onto the yard. The SHU next door was basically empty of medium prisoners whereas the pen was chalk full of dudes who stayed in trouble and broke the rules. So to eliminate all the dudes that were committing stabbings from only doing a couple days in the hole because of overcrowding, they sent us "victims" next door.

What was strange was that as soon as I got next door they placed me in a cell all the way in the back of the SHU. They made sure I didn't have a celly and that I was away from everyone. When I told the lieutenant that I had broken ribs and I was only going to take a celly that I knew because I couldn't really defend myself. He said back to me, "Oh you don't have to worry about that. You won't be getting any cellies while you're here."

"Is that right?" I answered back in amazement. Usually they force you to take a celly. So to hear that was kind of shocking.

"You'll be safe here," he said.

"Um . . . ok," I said as I sat down on my new bunk.

Doing SHU time without a celly was the best way to go. Being crammed in a little cell for twenty four hours a day was bad enough. Having to do it with another person is even worse. Knowing that I would get to do the next couple months back here by myself was calming. I'd have time to heal up and not have to worry about them putting someone in the cell with me that I might have to bang it out with. I wasn't even in the cell for an hour when I was pulled out to see the disciplinary hearing officer again.

"Mr. Judge, how are you feeling?" she said to me.

"I'm alright. What's up?" I asked.

"I'm afraid I've got some bad news for you."

"Yeah, what's that?"

"I tried to dismiss your incident report but I was told I wasn't allowed to," she explained.

"Who told you that?"

"Mr. Smith," she said. Smith was the head disciplinary officer at the pen. He never hit people hard, let alone people that jumped on.

"Why'd he tell you that?"

"He said because you were fighting with them."

"I was defending myself!" I stated.

"It says in the report you were exchanging blows."

"Well, yeah. That's what happens when you're defending yourself."

"Mr. Judge, what is this all about? I've never had a problem dismissing a write up before."

"Just a bunch of bullshit. Bullshit that I'm going to have to deal with at another pen if you find me guilty," I pleaded.

"I've read your file. You don't have a history of violence."

"That's because I'm not violent. I keep to myself and do my own things. Dudes don't like people that won't suck up to them."

"Alright," she said, looking me over. "I'm going to try again to dismiss this again. I can't promise you it'll work. He was pretty adamant that I find you guilty."

"Whatever you can do I'll appreciate it."

"Ok, hopefully you won't see me again," she said smiling and waving the CO in to come get me.

"I hope I never see you again too," I shot back with a smile.

That night I finally got a phone call with Kina. The way it works was you have fifteen minutes to use for the entire month. How you use it was up to you. It cost $3.45 for fifteen minutes. So I'd put $1 on the phone and use that for a call. It'd only give me four minutes to talk. But I'd at least get to hear her voice three times a month.

"Hey, beautiful," I said when she answered the phone.

"Baby, the feds just came with a warrant to search my house," Kina said immediately.

"What? For what?"

"For letters that Dom sent me."

"Did they get them?"

"Yeah, they were in my cabinet."

"What did they say?"

"All types of crazy shit. I told you about all of it."

"Fuck, are you alright?" I asked. Now Dom pulled her into his shit.

"I just can't believe this whole mess."

"I know. They moved me next door to the FCI."

"They did?"

"Yeah, there's also one more thing."

"What's that?"

"They took you off my visiting list."

"What! I can't see you anymore?" Kina said hysterically.

"Listen, it'll be alright. We'll get married and they can't stop you from seeing me."

"Are you sure?" Her voice was shaking.

"I'm positive."

"When can we get married?"

"I'm going to put in the paperwork for it tonight. You still want to get married though, right?"

"Of course I do, baby. I need you. I just hope you don't leave me because of all of this."

"Never, beautiful. I love you. We'll get through this."

"You promise," she asked.

"You know I do," I replied.

"I love you so much, baby," she said.

"I love you—," I said back just as the phone clicked off. We didn't even have a chance to exchange *mwaa's*.

The next day I asked everyone that came around to give me marriage forms. There was always a way around everything. It was only a matter of finding that loophole. They would have to let me see Kina when she was my legal wife. It was only a matter of how long it was going to take before we could do it.

Everyone I asked just kept doing what CO's do best . . . spin you off to the next CO. I couldn't even get an answer about if they did marriages back in the SHU. Let alone get the forms to put in to do it. All I could do was pace my cell. Ten steps from the painted over window to the door. I didn't have any radio or books to use to pass the time. Hell, I didn't even have a pen and paper. I was stuck in a little room with only my thoughts. Normally I would work out all day in the SHU. But the broken ribs made even sleeping hard. I was two days into my new solitary existence when I got pulled out of the cell again.

"Now what?" I said to the CO who was leading me down the hall.

"I don't know what you did, but there's some people here to see you," he said. Sitting inside an office were the two federal agents again. They were accompanied by the head SIS lieutenant of the medium.

"Goddamn, man. What?" I said as the CO sat me down and left the room.

"So, Mr. Judge. Now that you're safe, are you ready to help us?" the man asked. It was the same thing in a new place.

"Dude, I've already told you I don't know shit. What don't you understand about that?"

"Listen, Mr. Judge. I know what goes on over at the pen. That's why we've got you over here where you're safe and nobody will know that you're talking to us," the SIS lieutenant said.

"Look, I don't know shit and I'm not a fucking rat."

"Mr. Judge, we know that your sister received a large amount of money from Mr. Tisdell that was used for drug transactions," he said.

"What the fuck are you talking about?"

"We have our informants."

"Well, they don't know what the fuck they're talking about."

"We know she received $2,300 dollars, Mr. Judge."

"You heard wrong."

"You'd be surprised the people that give us information Mr. Judge. I know everything that goes on here," the SIS lieutenant said sternly.

"Well, they heard wrong," I fired back at him.

"Why do you think I'm over here instead of still at the USP?"

"I don't fucking know," I said.

"Because I'm building cases against everyone. Inmates and officers. You remember ET?"

"Yeah," I said back. ET was a dude that had his own CO on the payroll. He was bringing in everything from pounds of weed to cell phones.

"I'm the one that brought him down." The guy's voice beamed with pride.

"Ok," I said dismissively. Was I supposed to be impressed?

"And I still have my hands around his neck. Anywhere he goes I've got him. You can either do yourself a favor and help these people, or make it hard on yourself and your family."

"What the fuck does that mean?"

"That means we can charge you and your sister federally for committing narcotics violations," the the male fed said to me.

"Yeah, we're fucking done here. You can call my lawyer."

"Mr. Judge. All we want to do is find out if Mr. Tisdell is going to carry out this attack on his prosecutor," the lady explained. "That's it."

"I don't know shit. And now you're threatening my family? Like I said, talk to my lawyer."

"We understand that you'll be going to another penitentiary," the man said. "You won't last long with that hit out on you."

"I've done fine so far," I replied.

"You didn't have a thousand dollar bounty on your head before," he said.

"You know that they're going to get you wherever you go. Especially with information in your file that you cooperated with us," the SIS lieutenant said.

"What?" I was livid. Like Dom would even honor a thousand dollar bounty. It blew my mind that anyone could take him this seriously.

"You know how things go in the penitentiary. All it takes is for me to write down that you cooperated with us and it'll get out on any yard you go to."

"Man, fuck you!" I snapped.

"Or you can tell us what we need to know and we'll get you shipped to a medium right by Kina," the man said.

"I don't know shit, and you can do whatever the fuck you want to do."

"How do you think your family is going to feel about losing another son?" the man said to me.

"What?"

"We know that your brother died last year. How do you think your family will take losing another son?" His voice was grave.

"And their daughter gets put in prison for conspiring to introduce narcotics into a federal institution," the SIS lieutenant chimed in.

"Yo, man, fuck you motherfuckers!"

"There's something else," the lady said.

"What?" I said, pissed off.

"Kina tried to kill herself last night and is now in a mental institution."

"What?"

"We just found out before we came to see you," she said.

"Are you fucking with me?"

"Maybe we can get you a phone call so you can see how she's doing," she said looking at the SIS Lieutenant.

"I think I can make that happen," he said as he left the room.

I didn't say anything to the feds while he was gone. They didn't say anything to me either. I think they knew they weren't going to get anywhere with me from the blank expression on my face as I stared at the floor dumbfounded. I didn't know what kind of games they were playing. At least I hoped they were playing games and that Kina really wasn't in danger.

"Ok, you can get one phone call for five minutes," the SIS LT said as he came back into the room. He uncuffed my hands from behind my back and locked them securely in front.

"What's the number?" he asked. I told him the number for Kina's mom. He dialed the number for me and then handed me the phone. As it was ringing I silently said a little prayer for her to pick up..

"Hello," a voice that wasn't Kina's answered.

"Who's this?" I asked.

"It's Kina's mom, Mary," she replied. "Who's speaking?"

"Hey, this is Hipster. I'm sitting here with the feds. They're giving me a five minute call to see how Kina's doing."

There was a moment of silence until she replied. "She's in the hospital," she said.

"What happened?"

"She got strung out on methadone and got sick because she didn't have it."

"What?" I said in disbelief. I never knew she was even taking any shit. Let alone strung out on it.

"When Robin moved in with her, she gave her methadone to pay her share of the rent."

Kina had mentioned maybe having a friend move in to help with bills. That must have been Robin.

"They told me she tried to kill herself."

"She had a loaded gun on the bed stand and said she was going to kill herself."

"What the fuck? What happened?"

"I took the gun from her and called the police," she answered.

"Holy shit. And they took her to the hospital?"

"Yep, I don't know what was going to happen or how long she was going to be there.

"She'll be there for at least 72 hours. After that it was really on her what she does," I said.

"Yeah, that's what they said. I don't know what she's going to do after this. I'm so upset with her."

"I know you are. So am I. I didn't even know she was on anything. But she's really going to need us right now. I've kicked that shit before and it's terrible."

"How long do you think she's going to be sick for?" her mother asked.

"I only used it for 6 weeks and didn't sleep for a month when I kicked it."

"Oh, God," her voice cracked. "So she's going to have it pretty rough then?"

"Yeah, she's going to have a hard time. How are the kids doing?

"They're at my house right now. They're ok. They didn't see anything. I told them that she's on vacation for a couple days."

"Good. At least they're ok," I said, relieved.

"They can stay with you 'till she's out?"

"Yeah, they're fine. They can stay with me as long as they want."

"Thanks."

"You don't have to thank me. They're my grandkids."

"I know. I appreciate it though." I said. "I've got to go though. Can you tell Kina that I love her and hope she's ok."

"I sure will."

"Thanks. I'll try to call again in a week or so." I didn't know if I could get another call but I hoped so.

"Alright. Take care, Hipster."

I handed the phone back to the SIS lieutenant, comforted Kina was alive.

"How is she doing?" the fed asked me.

"She's alright."

"I'm happy to hear that. It sounds like you're going to need to be as close to her as possible."

"We can make that happen," the male fed interjected.

"Look, I'm done with these fucking games. I don't know shit. I'm not saying shit. Do whatever the fuck you wanna fucking do."

"I can see you're very upset about everything. We're going to leave now. If you change your mind you can have the lieutenant here get a hold of us," the lady said.

"But you better hurry up. This opportunity is going to close fast. If you don't help us, we can't help you," the man added.

"Got ya," I said mockingly as I stood up and the lieutenant grabbed an arm to lead me back to my cell.

On the short walk back the lieutenant kept saying how I better help him out. That if I didn't he was going to make sure that wherever I went word would go with me that I was a snitch. Telling me that I would get shipped as far away from Kina as possible and that I'd never get to see her again.

When I finally made it back into my cell and the cuffs were off I turned around to the window and told the lieutenant, "No matter where the fuck I go, and no matter what you try to do, I'm going to be cool."

"You think so?" he replied.

"Yeah." I had to believe that.

"Well, you'll get to find out," he said with a smirk on his face as he left.

I sat down on my bunk and put my head into my hands. Everything was going through my head all at once. My sister was going for her master's degree and was trying to become a successful lawyer. That would never happen if she received a federal indictment. The only thing she was guilty of was helping out her big brother.

I wouldn't be going to a medium prison. No, they'd send me to the worst fucking penitentiary they could find. Along with the thousand dollar bounty on my head, I'd also have a snitch rap on me. I've seen it before. Shit in a dude's paperwork from another spot that got him brutalized in his new prison. The CO's were the ones that would put the paperwork out there. Kina, the woman that I've come to adore more than life itself was strung out and suicidal. There was really no telling what would happen to her.

Methadone was the queen of all drugs. It was the worst shit, bar none, to kick. It got into your bones and you felt like death for months trying to get off of it. I'd only known one person to successfully kick the habit without getting hooked onto something else. It was a battle that you had to fight for the rest of your life. For real, I didn't know if I'd ever see Kina again. The BOP could make sure of that if they wanted. I would also get shipped far away from her making visits almost impossible even if she was put back on my list.

Every relationship that I had since I was younger was with a drug addict. When I found Kina it was so amazing to be with a woman who had her shit together. A house, kids, car and job. It was something so exciting to me. To have gotten out of prison after all the years and came home to that. It gave me so much hope. To find out what I did just crushed all my dreams of such a beautiful beginning to life after prison. Everything that kept me going through all the madness of life since I got with her was gone.

I have eight years left on my sentence. For those next eight years I would have to be on point at all times. There could never be a point when I allowed myself to become complacent. There could be a crew waiting on me as soon as I hit my new spot and I wouldn't have a chance. If there wasn't, any bus carrying new inmates could have one of Joey's cronies on it and it'd be go time.

If there was something put in my jacket, then at any time a CO could put that paperwork out on the yard about me. That would be an instant slaughtering. At any moment someone could be coming to collect that bounty on my head. When you were surrounded by lifers who already had bodies, one more meant nothing to them.

I laid back gently on my bed. My broken ribs throbbing painfully with each heartbeat. The words Bruce said to me before all this turned crazy rang through my head, "This is going to turn out bad." But never in my wildest dreams did I think that it would turn out like this. It seems I let my lust get the best of me and who knows how this would all turn out. With eight years of hell to go I knew one thing—I was going to need a new drug.

HOMO THUGS

STRAIGHT OUTSIDE, GAY INSDE

You see them in every prison. Homo-thugs creeping on the low, acting like they're gangstas, going hard and then breaking weak, swearing they ain't faggots. But let me tell you. If you let a man suck your dick or you hit one of them gumps, you are a straight queer. Ain't no and's, if's, or but's about it. Well maybe there are some butts about it, but you know what I mean. These dudes up in here are crazy. Closet homos, you heard.

I've seen it all over the feds. And it ain't like some macho movie shit in here, like fuck or get fucked. These dudes are just straight homos. But they' re swearing they're not. I've seen them all up with the gump on the pound, and then they're fronting in the visiting room kissing up on their baby-mama and their kids. These dudes are sick for real.

If you can't get no pussy what would make you wanna let a man suck your dick? I mean if you're straight, that is. If you're a gump, then that's what you are. Don't fight it. Don't deny it. Be who you are. But in here you got a whole bunch of dudes faking it. Like they're tough. Like they're gangstas. Like they're hard. Yeah they're hard alright. Hard for another man to suck their dick.

And these homo-thugs blend in too. All up in the click with their homeboys, but hanging with the gumps on the down low. They're watching the videos on BET, fronting and rapping like they're gangsta, keeping it real and shit, talking about that Lexus they used to have. I keep waiting for the day when another brother will call one of these homo-thugs out. "You ain't no gangsta nigga. You a homo-thug." But it don't happen that often. Dudes are letting shit ride. Don't want no drama, I guess.

These dudes are all up on the court balling and everything. Sweating up on a motherfucker. A lot of these gumps got the package, but that doesn't stop none of these dudes getting theirs. They're digging that gumps back out. Tearing that ass up in the name of what? Getting theirs? That shit's crazy.

And some of these homo-thugs are getting mad love from bitches. Their baby mamas are taking care of them, and they're all up in the feds hitting faggots. And they're thinking these faggots are bitches too. "Prison bitches" they call them. Yo, that's my bitch, you hear them say, referring to the gump. That ain't no bitch motherfucker, that's a motherfucking man, just like you.

And some of these gumps have tits too. The homo-thugs love that shit when a faggot with tits hits the pound. All types of drama will jump off as all the homo-thugs fight over the gump, stabbing each other up and shit like they're fighting over a fine ass broad.

I can see why some of these dudes with life do it. I mean fuck it. They got life. They're trying to get something. But they got homo-thugs in here that are short and they go hard on that gump shit. All up in recreation or education, sweating the gump to meet them in the bathroom or even moving up in the gump's cell for some all night action. I'm like damn, these dudes are short. What are they thinking?

I've heard of dudes that got dilemmas when they hit the street. They got their baby-mama and their prison gump on the street waiting for them, and they're not sure which one they want to go home to when they get out. They're talking about the gump got a good job and their baby-mama is on welfare. Damn, and these dudes swear they're not gay.

I say fuck it, come out the closet. Move to San Francisco. I ain't gonna knock a person for being gay, but don't be no hypocrite. Like, yeah I ain't gay, but I'm fucking with gumps in prison. C'mon man, that shit is retarded. Either you are or you aren't. There's plenty of dudes been in 20 or 30 years that never went that route.

There's a saying in here that after 10 years it's all legal. Meaning that after 10 years in prison it's all good. You can fuck with a faggot and not be queer. But c'mon, that's some bullshit. And some dudes jump right off the boat and into the water. They're like, damn, I'm getting me some, like there ain't no difference between ass and pussy. These dudes are going hard like they're in ancient Greece or something. They think they're Trojan warriors. They go raw dog too. No wonder so many homo-thugs got AIDS, trying to say they were shooting up and shit. All up in the joint going hard on heroin. But motherfucker, you ain't shot no heroin. You're a straight gump.

Going back out to the street and giving their baby-mamas the package, that shit is foul. These dudes are outta control. And it doesn't matter where they're from either. In the prisons a lot of dudes label DC guys as homo-thugs. And to a point it's true. But not all of them are like that. And I even believe the word, gump, came from the DC prisons like Lorton and the like, but for real I've seen homo-thugs from all different places- Carolina, NY, Philly, Jersey, Virginia. It doesn't matter. Some of these dudes get in here and they think they're home free. Like it's ok, I was in prison. It doesn't count. Stop fooling yourself man. That is some bullshit.

I've even seen some Muslim dudes who are supposed to be all righteous and shit on that gump shit. Like they say, it takes all types. But these homo-thugs are a breed of their own. And they stick together too. You see them on the yard all late when it's dark. Walking around the track with their gumps or they're playing ball and their gump up in the stands cheering. And these same dudes, these homo-thugs will swear they're not gay. They'll go home to their woman swearing they never did no shit like that. But in here dudes know. And once you're labeled a homo-thug the label sticks, you can't shake it. Change your ways when you hit the streets. Once a faggot always a faggot.

ONE NIGHT WITH ALANIS
A Meth Fueled "Hook Up"
With A Celebrity Behind Bars

From the moment I cracked my crusty eyes open I knew that it was going to be a good day; the smell of freshly cooked moonshine pouring into my cell pretty-much guaranteed it. And sure enough, before I could even get my morning woody to stand down, I heard a quick knock on the door and in walked my black friend, Samir.

"*As-salaam-u-alaikum*," said the former crack dealer-turned-student of Islam-turned-moonshine manufacturer, pornography dealer, and all around penitentiary hustler. "I got that bomb-ass firewater. What'chu need?" he asked.

I sat up in my bunk. "I'll take both of those," I told him, pointing to the two pints of shine he had in his hand. "And I'm starving. What do you have to eat?"

"Let me see what I got." He sat the booze down on my locker and reached into his kitchen smock. "I got two cheeseburgers and one chicken, egg, and cheese. I'll give you all three for eight stamps."

"Bet. Just put it all on my tab," I said. I mean, why not? I already owed him four-hundred bucks. Another eighty-two wasn't going to make much of a difference.

"What about girls?" he asked, "I got three new *Buttmans* with some fine-ass white girls. You wanna check'em out?"

"I'm good." Call me bias, but I only got my porn from one source, Cockbook Brian.

Samir turned and pushed the door open. "Have a fine day, my friend. Drink responsibly."

I rolled out of bed, grabbed a pint, and guzzled half of it down, just like I do every time that I drink moonshine. I then fixed myself a healthy shot of dope, slammed it in my arm, and ate a cold cheeseburger. I was standing in front of the mirror brushing my teeth when Tommy Rutledge walked in.

"Hey, Tree Top just moved out of cell 263," he said. "If you're trying to move, now's the time to do it."

I was trying to move; I had to get away from my celly, Troy, a weirdo who was hooked on heroin and Jesus. "I'm on it," I said. "Thanks for letting me know."

After guzzling down another half-pint, I lit a smoke, popped a mint in my mouth and headed on over to see Counselor Howard. When I told him that I wanted cell 263, he said, "I'll let you move in right now on one condition, you get that place painted ASAP." I agreed.

Shortly after lunch, I cruised on out to CMS (Construction Maintenance Service) to pick up some supplies. No, I didn't have a pass, and technically I was "out of bounds," but I didn't care—I've never been big on following rules.

As I neared the plumbing shop, a friend of mine named Timmy Holloway motioned for me to come up the stairs. When I got to the top of the loft, he reached into his shirt pocket and pulled out a loaded syringe. "You tryin' to do a shot?" he asked.

"I'm cool," I said. "I just bought a gram yesterday."

"Not of this shit, you didn't," he assured me. "This ain't heroin; it's meth—some real good meth."

I must admit, I was very curious about trying a shot of methamphetamine. I'd smoked it, snorted it, preferred to drink it in my coffee, but I had never injected it before. But still, to just take a loaded syringe right from somebody's hand and stick it in my arm seemed a little junky-ish. Reluctantly, I said no.

Timmy picked up on my vibe. "I ain't got no disease, Robert. You know how I am when it come to my needles. I bleach the piss out of 'em after every shot. So here." He handed me the outfit. "Go on and get'cha some, son."

If you knew Timmy, you'd know that he's not some slime ball. Yeah, he looks like a rough character, with sleeved-out tattoos on his arms, bulging green eyes, and long, brown, stringy hair. And yeah, there was that one little incident in Tennessee when he snuck into his girlfriend's house while she was under police protection and stabbed her to death so that she couldn't testify against him in an up-and-coming drug case. But setting aside his appearance and that one little mishap, he really was a good guy. I trusted him.

"Alright," I said. "Let's do it." I took the syringe, aimed for the fresh puncture wound on my arm that I made earlier, and jabbed the thing into my vein. When the blood registered, I slowly released the stuff into my body . . . and went on one helluva ride.

A bolt of energy shot through me like none that I had ever experienced. My eyes twitched, my knees wobbled, and my heart began to gallop; my mind spun like a slot machine spinning out of control—jackpot! Right before I was able to fully regain my composure, a bubble of gas snaked through my colon and came screaming out of my ass.

"Wow!" I said, still feeling the intense rush. "That was fucking awesome!" I felt like I wanted to tear my clothes off and run right through the window butt-naked; stand on top of the prison and howl at the moon even though it was dead smack in the middle of the day. I wanted to fuck women—lots of women. I wanted to line some whores up and bang my way right through them. I wanted to fight every last CO in the joint, then grab a toothbrush and scrub every crack and crevicef in the chow hall. I was spun-ducky woo-woo.

"I gotta roll, man," I said, eager to get busy. "I got work to do."

"Work? What work?"

I told Timmy about painting the cell.

"Hell, don't just paint the bitch. You gotta hook her up, son," he said. "Come on. Follow me."

We went downstairs, grabbed a push-cart, and went zooming around CMS. We stole boxes of linoleum tiles, glue, and three different kinds of paint, along with enough brushes, rollers, pans, and tape to paint a whole cell block. As soon as I got back to the unit, I wasted no time getting started on the floor; never mind that linoleum was prohibited in cells.

Sometime after 9 p.m., all the tiles were laid. Now, I had to paint the place. After 10p.m. Lockdown I was alone in cell 263 still tweaking. I had my entire night planned accordingly: paint, paint, and paint, some more. Oh, yeah. And use plenty of drugs and alcohol.

I snorted a line of meth off the top of my locker, took a swig of 'shine, and cranked up my baby boom box. In the mood for some good ol' fashioned rock'n roll, I tuned in to Kansas City's leading classic rock station, 101.1 "The Fox." Immediately, I started singing along.

"Busted flat in Baton Rouge, waiting for a train/ When I was feeling nearly as faded as my jeans/Bobby thumbed a diesel down just before it rained/it rode us all the way to New Orleans . . ."

I climbed up on the top bunk and grabbed a roller. With the pan already full of paint, I dipped the thing in and started painting the ceiling, still singing away as I did.

"Freedom's just another word for nothing left to lose/ nothing don't mean nothing honey if it ain't free, now now/and feeling good was easy, Lord, when he sang the blues/you know feeling good was good enough for me/ good enough for me and my Bobby McGee . . ."

I was really jamming now; the whole painting experience was all that I dreamed it would be, and then some. I was especially proud of myself for thinking ahead. I took all of my property out of the cell and put it on the tier so that it wouldn't get covered with paint. And it most definitely would have; there was paint flying everywhere.

When I finished with the ceiling, I next hit the walls. Then right before I started on the bed frame, lockers and desk I decided to take a little break: a drink, a snort, a shot in my arm. I was feeling great. It's not too often that a guy in prison gets to hang out by himself and enjoy the moment, and I most certainly was loving every minute of it. I even took off dancing across the cell as soon as I heard Rod start to sing: *"Who's that knocking on my door/it's gotta be a quarter to four/is it you again, comin' round for more . . ."*

That's right, "Hot Legs." And I was really getting into it. I even started bouncing around on one leg, kicking the other leg in and out as I did, like I had some hot legs. Never mind that my legs (like the rest of my body) are hairy, or that I was dancing around in nothing but a pair of boxers like some big ol' fag, I was having a blast.

"Hot legs/you can scream and shout . . ."

Talk about scream and shout. I wanted to shout at the top of my lungs: "Fuck you, Warden Booker! You and Judge Hendron can both take this life sentence and stick it up your pussies—bitch!" I went from bouncing around, to shaking my ass, to playing the air guitar. In my mind I wasn't in a prison cell, I was live in concert, up on stage with Rod and the boys watching a sea of women go ape-shit over us. Sing it, Rod!

"Hot legs/you can scratch my back/Hot legsssss . . . ."

Out of breath, when the song came to an end I picked up a paint brush and went back to work. I did the locker, the desk, and last but not least, the bed. All I had left to do were the borders, but because I was going to paint them a different color, I had to wait until the base paint dried. So I lit a cigarette and sat down on the toilet. As I sat there puffing away, it occurred to me that the night was young and I had absolutely nothing to do. The cell was wet with paint, all of my property (including my mattress and chair) was just outside the door on the tier, and I didn't have any alcohol left. All I had was some heroin, some meth, paint and paint supplies, and a radio.

If only I would have stopped by Cockbook Brian's, I thought. I could have had myself a nice, private, love fest. When I'm high on meth, like most meth users, I have a tendency to get very horny. And I most certainly was under the influence of meth. When I'm on heroin, such as I was as well, getting off is next to impossible. Hardcore porn could have helped. Fuck it, I thought. I'll just conjure up some memories of those dirty meth whores I use to bang.

I got up, turned down the radio, then washed my hands. As I scanned the room looking for something to dry my hands on, I noticed a magazine peeking out from beneath the bed. I took a few steps, bent down and picked it up.

People Magazine? I must have dropped it when I was moving my property out of the cell. For whatever reason, I opened it up and turned to the celebrity photo section, also known as "Startracks." An array of female stars made my penis perk up. Hmmm, I thought. I guess fully dressed celebrity sluts beats a blank. Magazine in hand, I sat back down on the commode pulled down my underwear, and searched for an imaginary lover. Madonna was the first photo up.

Well, well, well, I thought. If it isn't the Queen of Dirty Whores herself, in the 80's you were ALL THAT, and I even give you kudo's for turning an entire generation of young girls into a bunch of bi-curious little sluts. But I saw that photography book of yours; you, with your legs gapped and that dog's nose all up in your crotch. You're even too skanky for me, M. Next—

The nerve of *People Magazine.* How dare they put a picture of Gwyneth Paltrow next to Madonna? Gwen, I love you. I want to marry you and pump babies into your guts. I just don't have it in me to disrespect you—and trust me, if I mentally hose you down while I'm all perverted out on meth. I will disrespect you.

Mandy Moore. Why, look at you, blossoming into a tasty little treat and stuff. You are a goddess in the making, hon. Please do hurry and grow up.

Britney Spears, you ugly, trollish, overrated tramp you. I don't know why so many guys in here have posters of you hanging on their walls. I mean, your mom's a dog, which means that one day you'll grow up to be a dog as well, and there's nothing even remotely pretty about you now. Pass—

Well, looky here, looky here; Angelina Jolie. Now we're talking . . .

I reached down between my legs, took hold of the general, and closed my eyes. Instantly, me and Angelina popped up in a crowded parking lot—she, bent over the hood of a car, me, right behind her plowing away. She tells me to smack her ass; I oblige. She tells me to pull her hair—I'm on it! Some dude walks up to me and says, "Right on, bro!" and gives me a high-five. Angelina looks back at me, snarls, and tells me to go faster; I speed it up. She cries out, "Don't stop!" I tell her "never." Someone pours a beer over my head, shouts, "You're the man!" I throw up my arms and agree: "Yes! I am the man!"

And then, without warning, my mind went haywire and Billy Bob Thorton appeared right next to us, a vial of his wife's blood dangling around his neck. My fantasy was ruined; I'm just not the type of guy who could fuck another man's wife in front of him. My eyes snapped open. "Fuck!" I said, achingly frustrated. "This is bullshit." Hand still working it, I look once again at the photo of Angelina and try again. "Come on," I pleaded with her. "Help me." But Billy Bob Thorton's wife just wasn't good enough.

"Fuck this." I tossed the magazine on the floor, kicked the underwear off of my ankles, stood up, and put my right foot on the toilet seat, so I could yank away on myself with maximum leverage. I still had enough meth-whores living in my head to last two life sentences, so I decided to put them to use. But just as I was about to close my eyes and take a trip back to 1997, a strange thing happened. I noticed that laying on the floor, captured in between the pages of *People Magazine*, was Alanis Morissette, staring up at me. Wow! Alanis. What happened to you? You're looking kind of smokin' hot, in a strange-little Canadian kind of way. I've never thought of you in this manner. But hey, you must be a freak, right? I mean, you do sing about "going down" on your ex-lover in a theater, not to mention scratching your nails down someone's back. Let's see what kind of girl you can be for me. Concentrating on the photo of Alanis, I easily slip into a sexual fantasy with her:

We're on a bed—not just an ordinary bed, but a real big bed, complete with turned down satin-sheets and lots and lots of rose petals.

"Rose petals?" I say to Alanis in my fantasy. "This is all wrong. Making love is cool and all, and maybe someday we'll get around to it, but I'm all hopped up on drugs right now and I'm trying to fuck. You know, some good old fashioned face-slappin', nail-scratchin', ass-smackin', hair-pullin', teeth-bittin', genitals-chappin', methamphetamine-induced sex." But she acts like she doesn't hear me, just giggles and kisses my neck.

I'd been rubbing myself for so long, I was starting to chafe. Sweat was pouring out of my body, I was feeling a little dizzy, and I was possibly on the verge of an asthma attack. I had to flip Alanis into the appropriate position and pick-up the pace.

"Now we're talking," I tell her in my fantasy. "Keep going just like that." She was on top of me hunched forward, doing justice to a position commonly referred to as the "reverse cowboy." The view from where I laid was awesome, her wet'n fury hole sliding up and down my pole; her starfish winking at me. But still, the war being waged between the drugs in my system was very real, and the heroin was kicking ass. I couldn't cum for nothing.

"Come on, Alanis!" I screamed in my head. "Do something! Turn around and suck it . . . no, bend sideways and—"

And that's when I heard her voice - not an imaginary voice, but a real female's voice. She said, "Are you enjoying yourself, Mr. Rosso?"

My eyes flew open in horror.

Let me stop right here to give you a precise image of what took place. There I was, a 30-year-old man approximately 30 pounds over weight, butt-naked, standing over a toilet. I had one foot on the ground, the other on the toilet seat, and I was looking down at a picture of Alanis. From my neck-line to the tip of my toes I was covered with body hair, not to mention all of the specks of white paint clinging to my fuzz. My skin color had to have been beet-red, with big droplets of sweat raining off of my bald head. And of course, in my hand was a pulsating penis from hell, which, I'm sure from an outsider looking in, would appear that I was very angry at. Then without warning, that's exactly what happened.

A female correctional officer named Ms. Keilione suddenly appeared in my cell-door window and caught me sexually assaulting myself. The only thing I could do was scramble for my boxers, which I did and in the process slammed my head against the steel bunk-bed and in front of me and nearly knocked myself out.

Ms. Keilione laughed, "You having lots of troubles, huh?" she asked. She was a Pacific Islander, probably in her late 30's, and she was known to be cool. But this was anything but cool to me. I covered up my privates with both hands.

"You go ahead and finish," she told me. "I no come back for two hours." And as she walked away, I heard her laughing.

From that day forward, every time that I hear Alanis on the radio, see her on TV, or especially, when I see her in a magazine, I can't help but recall that summer night in cell 263. Yes, it was a very embarrassing experience, yet strangely, I somehow feel connected to her. Alanis Morissette did what Angelina Jolie failed to do.

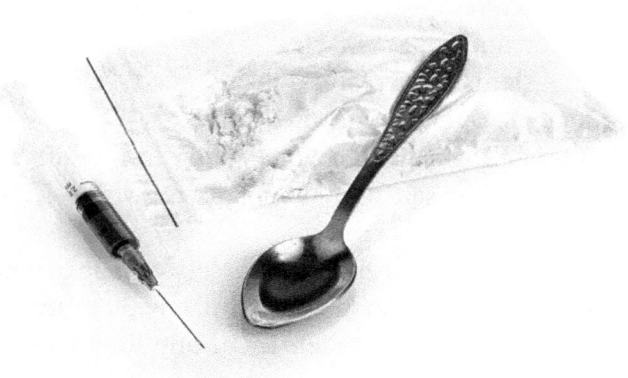

PORN IN PRISON

How Prisoners Get On To Get Off

In many prisons, the most valuable commodity is not tobacco or even hard drugs, but smut. Not everyone gets high or smokes, but every inmate jerks off, out of loneliness or horniness or sheer boredom. During my 21 years of incarceration in America, the one thing that I missed more than anything else was the company of a woman, especially as I had no conjugal visits while in the feds.

The most common form of porn that's circulated in prison is photocopied smut magazines, though modeling magazines that don't have nudity are also popular. Often, actual hardcore porn mags are smuggled in by correctional officers looking to make some extra money. If you have a magazine in its entirety, it can be hawked to other inmates for upwards of $200, depending on what condition it's in. The owners then make copies and resell them in black-and-white for $20 a pop. Copies (e.g. copies of copies) of spreads or certain pin-ups are then sold for a stamp a page, and prisoners often trade when they get bored of "their girls."

The other popular form of sexual entertainment is photos from the web that friends or family on the outside print out in bundles, then send through snail mail. A porn DVD—extremely rare in prison—can bring several hundred dollars to the officer who smuggled it in; phones with downloaded porn videos are sold for upward of $500.

"It's crazy the prices we pay," one prisoner told me. "But then again, it's prison. Checking out a little porn is all a guy really has to look forward to."

Since most prisons nationwide have banned porn, prisoners will go to great lengths to both preserve and conceal their collections. Depending on the individual institution's rules, punishments can range from confiscation or time in solitary confinement to disciplinary transfers to new criminal charges for the introduction or possession of sexually explicit materials. Some prisons have made masturbation, even without porn, an infraction.

To get some insight about how prisoners share smut, we talked to several prisoners doing time around the nation to learn how they get porn in, how it's traded among inmates, and what it's like to hide something that free Americans spend countless hours with each day.

Prisoner One — 31 Years Old
Serving Ten Years at FCI Beckley in West Virginia for Crystal Meth Distribution

There are dudes in prison who live well on the porn trade. They have regular customers, as it's an addiction to some people. I had this old, beat-up issue of *Just 18* magazine from 1999 with about half the pages missing that I used to rent out. The cost to rent was five stamps—approximately $1.50—for a 30-minute rental. That gets a little costly for a serial jacker. Certain dudes who are considered creeps have problems with masturbation, like real addiction problems, and I try to stay away from them. I sold that issue of Just 18 for $100 right before I transferred to another prison.

In another jail, my homeboy had a copy of *Buttman*. This magazine was kept in a pristine plastic protector. He sold it for $200 right before he left. Another guy in here just got shipped from FCI Texarkana to Beckley for getting caught smuggling in a computer. He was renting it out for $5 an hour, and had hundreds of porn videos downloaded. When he got caught, he was taken back to court and received another six month sentence.

Dudes will also sell photos that are sent to jail from their families or homeboys. They'll send a stack of pictures, and the inmates will sell them for three to four stamps a piece. Some inmates, they get tired of the same pictures, so they just rotate and trade them for a new chick. The price of a single photo depends on how fat the girl's ass is. Some guys will even put out special requests or orders for specific girls or porn stars. I've seen inmates become infatuated with them, as if they were literally their chick.

Prisoner Two — 46 Years Old
Serving a Life Sentence at Pickaway Correctional Facility in Ohio for Drug Trafficking

Blacktail, De'Unique, Penthouse, Playboy, Buttman, Freaky Girls, Video Illustrated: These are what we call "fuck books," "fiend mags," and "short eyes" in here. On the streets, the price for a magazine is usually around $10, but in prison a recent issue of *Blacktail* can run you from $200 to $300.

These magazines are contraband and will be confiscated if found. You can even get an incident report, or be put under investigation or in the hole for being caught in possession of porn. To protect your stash, you have to disguise the mag with a smoke cover of an acceptable magazine.

When I was selling magazines, I had to number the pages myself because I swear dudes are so fucking slick at tearing pages out that you might not notice a missing page. And even when you do notice, you might not know who exactly did that shit. I only let a selective few rent the mags I got, and I go through every page before and after so there aren't no misunderstandings.

I got a photo of a nice, exotic-looking chick with silky, curly pussy hair and a dildo in her mouth. The look in her eyes says it all, plus the way she's sitting, inviting me to please her. I paid a bag of Keefe coffee for her, and I don't let no one borrow her. I'm thinking about writing something vague-but-specific like "New York" on the back with a magic marker, just in case police tear my cell up and the photo comes up missing. Putting your actual name on a photo is some sucker shit, but I've seen dudes write their name and register number on their prized possessions.

Prisoner Three — 38 Years Old Serving
18 Years at USP Big Sandy in Kentucky for Bank Robbery

I've been to five different compounds over my 14 years in prison, and I've seen the same black-and-white porn photocopies everywhere. They just get worse and worse, copy-wise, but I still buy them. It's the closest I'll get to pussy in fucking forever. There are different ways of getting them in, such as through special mail. But the main way is the old-fashioned way—through cops and correctional officers. They make fake covers and bring them in with other magazines. The black-and-whites are kept wherever. The guards aren't going to fuck with them because they know you haven't seen pussy since Bush was president, so they'll leave your stash alone.

If a man doing life has an obsession with the porn star Pinky, you don't want to be the one to come in between that. There's no such thing as Internet porn in the big house. We don't have access to anything in here, so that's out. I had the chance to mess around with a screen phone a few years back in another prison. It had so much porn on it, I damn near had a heart attack right there. Dudes were using the phone for nefarious activities, but all I was trying to do was watch porn. They were like, "You can see the security truck driving around the prison on Google Earth!" and I was like, "Dude, fuck that—look at all this porn."

Prisoner Four — 40 Years Old
Serving 35 years at MDC Brooklyn in New York for Racketeering

When you get locked up in this concrete jungle, your girls are *Palmela* and *A-hand-a*; they're right by your side daily and always reliable. When I came in, it was just [PG-13 magazines, without nudity] like *Smooth* and *Straight Stuntin'* that had the jails on smash.

You had models like Buffie the Body, Maliah, CoCo, Rosa Acosta, and Vida Guerra killing it, and dudes was fiending to have some exclusive pics of these women. We would trade mags before lock-in, and release pent-up stress by stroking the mental pain away.

When one homie moved our unit, we had a whole DVD case of porn. We'd put a smuggled DVD player on a crate in the slop sink—like one in a janitor's closet—with a chair, and have dudes lined up waiting to go in to get their shit off. We called it the "Boom Boom Room," and it was right next to where we played poker. It was the best of both worlds and you could pick your poison. It's definitely big business in here, and whenever someone needs to take their mind away from all that's going on, I'd advise them to grab some mags or nude pics, grab some lotion and some tissue, put your towel over your cell window, and get to work. When you finish, I bet you'll feel better until you get home to the real thing.

Prisoner Five — 37 Years Old
Serving 40 years at FCI Gilmer, West Virginia for Money Laundering and Bank Fraud

They took all the girlie magazines, so what's a nigga to do? I mean, fuck, we ain't gumps, you know what I'm saying? We trying to look at some women. We trying to see some female sex acts.

I first came across doll porn in 2002. When I first saw that shit I was like, 'What the fuck is this?' But then, when I looked at a bunch of them joints my homie had, it was all good. Some of them Barbie chicks are vicious. They even got a Vida doll with that big fat ass and everything.

I like the Angelina Jolie one with the big pouty lips. Tomb Raider, son. As long as I gets my nut, I don't give a fuck. I gots my black Barbie photos, my Asian Barbie joints . . . my stable be full. I be renting them joints out. I be selling them for ten stamps a pop. Shit, I be renting them for a stamp a night. Dudes be trying to get theirs.

I traded Barbie and Ken doing their thing for a photo of an original 1960's vintage Barbie. Of course she was butt naked.

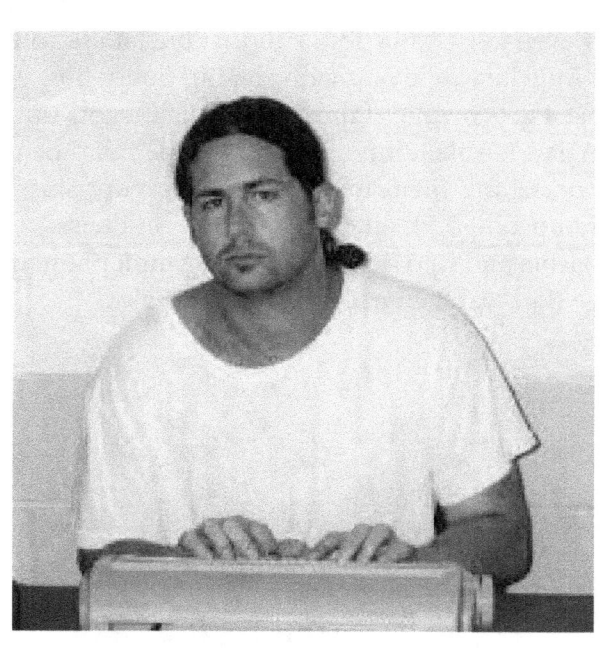

JOURNALISM SENT ME TO THE HOLE

A Conversation with SIS in the Special Housing Unit (SHU) at Federal Correctional Complex Forrest City

Twenty two days I waited in SHU under the pretense of an SIS investigation before I was actually pulled out of my 24 hour lockdown cell and given an explanation for why I was in the hole and under investigation. I was handcuffed and escorted to the interview room where I was joined by SIS Technician Davenport, who I was familiar with, and SIA Meyers, who Davenport told me was his boss. I had never met SIA Meyers before or even seen him on the compound. I guess he spent all his time at the medium-high next door, where all kinds of violence were taking place. The medium-high was a prison infested with gangs and known for being as brutal as a United States Penitentiary (USP), even though it was just a Federal Correctional Institution (FCI). It was a far different environment then the low I resided in. The appearance of the SIA marked the seriousness of my transgressions, since he normally didn't grace the low with his presence.

There was no beating around the bush, I knew why I was in SHU, even if they wouldn't tell me. I don't break any prison rules or regulations, plus I was in the drug program, a unit that was like an honor dorm, where everyone was enrolled in the Bureau of Prison's (BOP) Residential Drug Abuse Program (RDAP), eligible to get up to a year off their sentence. The fact that I was scheduled to start the program and being that I was 20 years in on my sentence meant that I didn't mess around or get involved in all the trivial drama, schemes and hustles that were going on in the prison. I was trying to go home, so I laid low.

I was very surprised to be in the hole, but I should have expected it and considering I wasn't in the mix on the compound or doing anything illegal, there was only one reason for me being in the hole, my writing. So I got right to the point with the SIS gentlemen. It helped that my case manager, Mr. Burns had tipped me off when they first locked me up. He told me it was my writing they were concerned about. He also said that the FBI was monitoring the articles I was getting published for whatever reason.

I didn't understand what the FBI could possibly be interested in, concerning my writing, but with success comes greater scrutiny and like SIA Meyers told me during our conversation, the truth hurts. At this point in my incarceration I had been writing for publication for 14 years, since 1999, when my career in journalism began. After taking some correspondence courses on article writing from the University of Iowa, while working on my bachelor's degree, I embarked on what became my decade plus long battle to shine the light on the life I was living in prison.

I seemed to thrive on exposing the things that were going on inside the BOP. I had no problem offering my insight and opinion on it all. I was very experienced and considered myself an expert on prison life. The best thing about it all was people on the outside were interested in my writing and responded to it. I had established an audience. Plus my writing became therapeutic for me and enabled me to do something constructive with my time. But the BOP didn't see it that way. I have fought fiercely for my right to write, battling the BOP furiously. Technically, under BOP Program Statements, I am allowed to write, but therein lies the paradox. In theory, a prisoner is allowed to write, even encouraged to, but if his writing draws too much attention in the real world, or exposes things prison officials want kept under wraps then there is a problem. Hence, me being locked up in the hole in 24 hour lockdown. I was just too successful with my writing and I managed to gain way too much attention,

I had pieces in *Maxim* magazine on how prisoners make body armor with magazines. I had pieces on the website *The Daily Beast* on how prisoners run tobacco smuggling rings in prison and how the Mexican drug cartels recruit US prisoners that are being released to sell drugs for them. I had pieces on T*he Fix*, a drug addiction and recovery website that outlined my own recovery in the RDAP program and leveled criticisms I found in the program. Plus numerous pieces on how to smuggle drugs into prison, how to make moonshine, hooch, a rig to shoot up heroin and all types of other articles of that type of illicit nature.

I found a niche writing how to articles from the prisoner perspective, explaining how prisoners did all the things they did, right under the noses of prison officials. Who in reality had no clue what was going on in their own prisons. I also had a successful blog *Gorilla Convict* that was promoted as giving the 411 on prison life, street legends, prison gangs, hustling and the Mafia. The blog was getting over 60,000 unique visitors a month and I had six books out, published on my own Gorilla Convict Publications imprint. Two on prison life and four true crime biographies on urban gangsters who were iconic figures out of hip-hop culture's lyrical lore.

I was just doing what I do, trying to stay busy, use my time wisely and prepare for my reentry back into society by establishing myself as a writer and journalist. This was all done so that I would have a future and be able to make a legitimate income to support myself and my wife. I thought I was on the right path, doing all the right things. I was ready to start the program, do the 10 month course, get my year off and go home. Then boom, I found myself in the interview room in the hole at FCC Forrest City- Low with SIA Meyers and SIS Tech Davenport.

Basically I knew and they knew that they had me by the balls. By keeping me in SHU under the pretense of an SIS investigation they were keeping me off the compound and out of the drug program. The time was ticking and if I wanted to be eligible for the whole year off my sentence I had to be in the program. At this point I had 28 months left. That is when they start you in the drug program in the BOP. Ten months in the program, 12 months off and 6 months halfway house.

If I completed the program I was looking at a May 25, 2014 release date to halfway house. Without the program my release date was November 25, 2015. Doing the math was easy. Ten months was way better than 28 months or even 22 months if I got six months halfway house. Of course the SIS gentlemen knew this as they had me in the room to interview me.

They wanted to see where I stood on the subject of my writing for publication. They didn't have to say what they wanted. I knew. They wanted me to stop writing for publication. They wanted me to give up promoting and marketing myself. They wanted me to go on hiatus from my career while I remained in BOP custody. They were in damage control mode. Trying to assess how much more controversy I could cause with my writing. To them it was all about containment of the problem, namely me and my writing. That is why I was in the hole with limited communication. I was effectively being shut down.

I am a fighter at heart, I will battle whoever or whatever relentlessly. I don't like to give in or give up and I am the type of person that doesn't know when to quit. That is just my makeup. That is just what I do. But I realized that this was maybe a fight I didn't want. I have learned in the BOP that in the long term I can usually win and get my way if I am persistent, file enough administrative remedies, have case law on my side and write enough letters of complaint to all the government watchdog agencies like the Inspector General and Office of Professional Responsibility.

Applying pressure was my specialty. I had even started the process of doing all this while I was in SHU. My wife had already contacted those agencies on my behalf and written to her senator, Claire Mckaskill from Missouri outlining what the BOP was doing to me. Plus my wife had complained to the BOP Central Office, South Central Regional Office and the Warden here at FCC Forrest City, letting them all know that I was being retaliated against due to my writing for publication and in essence was being denied the chance to start the drug program and get the year off my sentence. Even bigger than that was the fact that the websites I was writing for publicized what the BOP was subjecting me to.

The Fix ran an article, "Fix Writer Locked up in Solitary" and *The Daily Beast* ran one also, "DB Writer Locked Up in Hole for Practicing Journalism." They even told their readers to write and complain to the BOP, South Central Regional Office and the Warden. The websites listed all the contact info for the government agencies, including their phone numbers and emails. Both of these websites had huge audiences and got a tremendous amount of traffic. The story about me being locked in the hole for my writing generated a buzz on social media as other websites picked up and reran the story. With the exposure I was showing that I could push back. Put me in the hole, cut me off from the world and the world will still respond.

I have found that the only way to get BOP officials to back off is to apply pressure in the public and private forums simultaneously. It is the only thing they understand. The BOP is like a bully, if you let them intimidate you and cower in fear, they will treat you any which way they can. But if you fight back they will eventually leave you alone and move on to an easier target. My writing and the subsequent stories that outlined me being locked up for my writing, put the national spotlight on the BOP and they didn't like the negative PR. So in their minds it was damage control time. They had to do their best to contain what they deemed was the loose cannon and the cause of all their dismay, my writing for publication.

Since I didn't have enough time left for a full on, contracted battle with the BOP over my First Amendment right to write I was ready to cop out. With the time constraints I was facing due to the time I had left to do, and getting into the drug program to get a year off, I knew what time it was. So did the SIS gentlemen I was in the interview room with.

With no outside lawyer or group to advocate on my behalf besides my wife and our letter writing capabilities I was in a bind and the only way out of it was to capitulate. With this attitude foremost in my mind I had a nice conversation with them. It was a conversation where they held all the cards though and I knew this. When you are completely under the power and control of an entity outside yourself it isn't always comfortable but it was a situation I was used to. Twenty years of incarceration conditions you to being on the short end of the stick.

I was familiar with SIS Tech Davenport, he had locked me up when I first arrived at FCC Forrest City in 2011 for a 30 day investigation into my writing. He wrote me a shot for conducting a business and getting paid for my writing. My phone and email privileges were taken for six months each. An outrageous punishment for that type of offense, and on top of that I did 30 days in the hole, but at least I got out. So I counted that as a victory. I appealed the shot and got my phone and email back after a couple of months but I suffered unnecessarily in the meantime.

As I have come to see it, that is just part of the game. That's all it is with these people. No right or wrong, just a power trip. They want to show any and all prisoners who the boss is. As a condition of getting my phone and email back I had to wear the shot, but it was all good. It was just a minor 400 series infraction, the least serious of offenses possible.

After this ordeal I thought my problems at FCC Forrest City were over, but I was wrong. It seems I had pissed someone off again and they were ready to do damage to me. Back in the interview room I was trying to see where this was all going. I was trying to feel them out and see if I had any wiggle room. I am in a constant state of alert because with me it's always a case of waiting for the other shoe to drop. Knowing this I was ready to bargain.

I have mastered the art of diplomacy over the years, and desperately needed a resolution so I could get back on the compound and start the drug class. That was my prime objective. I was straight with them on what I was doing, why I wrote what I did and what my goals were in doing what I did. I have found that truth works best with these types of people and for real I knew I was pushing the envelope with my writing. That is just what I did, but I also stood by the fact that I had a First Amendment right to write, prison officials be damned.

I knew they didn't like what I wrote so I flaunted it in their face using their own Corrlinks email system to write and draft my articles and send them out to editors and websites. That was probably my worst trait, flaunting what I did and a reason I was being handled this way, but so be it. You can't cry over spilt milk. I am a bit of a rebel anyhow. They knew what my agenda was, but I reiterated it to them. I told them I was trying to build up my name and resume with my writing credits and that I found a niche and was exploiting it to my advantage, both monetarily and for exposure and credits.

I didn't deny that I got paid for my writing, that I was conducting a business (at least in their eyes), and that I had an extensive network of prisoners who I used as sources that fed me info and gave me stories on what was going on all over the BOP. In reality I was a prison bureaucrat's worst nightmare. Something could happen in a California or East Coast prison and I would know by the end of the day. All the messages were relayed to me through the Corrlinks email system that the BOP set up. I was using and exploiting their own system to expose things that were happening in their prisons nationwide. I had built an information superhighway that centered on me. I was the hub of the network that made it all go. I was information central.

I figured I would put it all on the table. I didn't know what they knew and what they didn't know, but I was playing it safe. Even if they decided to write me a shot, in my estimation it would only be a 300 series shot. Not the more serious 100 or 200 series shots that prisoners get for assaulting and extorting people or for using and introducing drugs into the institution. I wasn't trying to argue with them or be combative so I said what I had to say and let them respond. But I made it known that I was willing to surrender to their will in the hope I could get back out on the compound and take the drug program. Not the route I usually take in dealing with people infringing on my rights, but at that point I was trying to realize the reality of getting the year off my sentence.

Luckily, they were reasonable men. They didn't seem to be taking the whole episode personally like so many BOP people do. In essence, it seems like they didn't even care what I was doing. Remember these are men who investigate assaults, gang problems and contraband introduction on a daily basis. They deal with prisoners who are hostile to the idea of even talking to them. Who will deny guilt even when presented with clear evidence? I must have been a breath of fresh air to them.

They told me straight out they didn't care about writing me any 300 series shots for what I was doing. Even though SIS Tech Davenport emphasized he could have probably written me a 200 series shot. But I believe that was a bluff, you know they have to hit you with the good cop/bad cop routine. They didn't know what direction I would go with the conversation, so they probably had their strategy in place before they entered. And threats and bluffs are always a big part of it. Their game, that is how they elicit information. We all knew even if he did write me a 200 series shot it wouldn't stick. I could beat it, but putting me through the process of going to DHO and all that would jack off my program, so in reality it was an implied threat. He was letting me know that if I went against them, that was the extent they were willing to go to. It was just his way of letting me know who was in control. Implied threats and casting blame is how they operate.

They seemed to be really annoyed at some of the stuff I was publishing on *The Fix*. I had written a series of how to smuggle drugs into prison articles about a year before they locked me up. The articles explained the different moves and variations that prisoners used to introduce drugs into the institution. It just so happened that the same ways I described in my articles were being used at FCC Forrest City, so they used that as a pretext to lock me up.

I was even in the hole with some of the guys that were locked up for employing the "over the fence maneuver" I chronicled on *The Fix*. The maneuver involves a camper, who resides at the adjacent minimum security prison outside the fence, and has access to the grounds around the prison. The camper uses his access to throw a football, soccer ball or handball over the fence into the prison's recreation yard. The ball is stuffed full of drugs or contraband like cell phones or tobacco and is retrieved by a prisoner on the compound.

The prisoner on the compound is notified by email on the Corrlinks system or by a cell phone he already had smuggled in that the move was completed and the contraband is ready for retrieval. It's a very efficient and low risk maneuver that accounts for a lot of contraband in prisons nationwide. Surprisingly, cell phones were very prevalent on the compound. I had been asked to buy one several times. Even a Smartphone was offered to me one time. Modern technology, including smart watches, are making their way into prisons every day. It was a battle SIS was constantly waging—phones, tobacco, drugs—it was all coming into FCC Forrest City Low.

Several prisoners had just been locked up for doing the same exact move outlined above. Except they used a softball. Since I had previously published articles about it, I was immediately made a suspect. It was all coincidental, but in the eyes of SIS it was a serious breach of etiquette and a threat to the security of the institution. This was the reason they used to justify locking me up. But I found out it went deeper than that.

About two weeks before I got locked up I had gotten an article published on *The Fix* entitled, "What Long Term Recovery Looks Like From Prison". In this article I gave an honest assessment of my recovery and need for it. I included quotes from other RDAP participants and their opinions on the program and their recovery. Finally to wrap up the article I leveled some criticisms at the RDAP program in general. My intent was constructive feedback to make the program better.

I had done shorter pieces on RDAP for *The Fix* before but this was a longer, more in-depth piece that was a featured column on the site. The acting RDAP coordinator, Dr. Boyles, was notified of this article I wrote by someone, I presume in the BOP Central Office, and she and the staff of Drug Treatment Specialists had what they call a team meeting. This is where prisoners in the program are called in and teamed. They asked what my intentions were in writing the article, how I got it published and how did I as a prisoner in recovery get the opportunity to write for a popular drug addiction and recovery website. To say the very least, they were a little flustered at my criticisms. To cover up their outrage they cited privacy concerns that regulated the program and tried to insinuate that I violated them.

But I countered that easily because I told them everybody I interviewed knew they were being interviewed plus I didn't identify anyone by full name, so I knew there were no real privacy concerns. Just concerns that I had the audacity to criticize the program they helped to run, making them look bad in effect. But everyone is allowed an opinion, right? In the free world maybe, but in prison it seems you are not allowed to express your opinion.

They countered that my other writings on urban gangsters, prison gangs and prison life showed that I immersed myself in prison culture and criminality and that they had concerns this would lead me back to prison after I was released. I told them that I didn't consider myself a criminal and that I would never commit a crime again. I had been drug free since 2002 and I stopped of my own free will. Everything I had been doing in prison up to that point was to prepare for my eventual release back into society.

My journey into drug dealing was a youthful indiscretion and mistake that I made in my teenage years. I asked them to remember that I was indicted and given a 25 year sentence for a first-time, non-violent offense when I was 22 years old. Hardly enough time to establish myself as a drug kingpin. Clearly I was a victim as the punishment didn't fit the crime I was convicted and sentenced to. I told them that Martin Scorcese and Francis Ford Coppola make gangster films, but that didn't mean they were gangsters. I pointed out how Ice Cube started out rapping "Fuck tha Police" with NWA and now starred in kids' films and that none of the writers that write violent crime movies like Quentin Tarantino or novelists like John Clancy who create worlds of high espionage, murder and betrayal, live the lives they portray in their creative works. I let them know I had a firm grip on reality and knew the difference between what I wrote about and who I was.

They disagreed but I left it at that and told them that if they wanted to set any parameters or limits on my writing to let me know because I was trying to do what I had to do to complete the drug program and go home. It seemed like a good conversation and I thought I was good. But obviously Dr. Boyles (who was just an acting coordinator), the drug treatment specialists and the person who contacted Dr. Boyles in the first place weren't convinced.   They kept investigating my writing and found the smuggling series I wrote for *The Fix*. I guess that was the last straw. They were likely outraged that I was in prison and had the nerve to write about stuff like that. This was all confirmed in the interview room with the SIS guys. They gave me the rundown of what happened and why.

SIA Meyers told me that the BOP was pumping a lot of money into two things: RDAP and reentry programs. He informed me that my writing put a national spotlight on the situation by criticizing the RDAP program and that my writing and the subsequent coverage was creating a lot of heat in Washington DC for the BOP. It appeared I had really pissed somebody off.

That is something I tend to do a lot. I am used to my words and actions being deemed controversial. I like being a lightning rod for controversy. I pride myself on being a Howard Stern, Charles Barkley, Rush Limbaugh type of personality. It seems I am a controversial person by nature. I have always been the person that can evoke a reaction. The price of being me I guess. The truth of it all is it's either I don't care or I just don't see the implications or fallout from what I do or say or write. SIA Meyers told me that the whole thing of me being locked up in 24 hour lockdown wasn't from them, it wasn't even from the Warden or administrative staff at the institution. He told me it was from the bureaucrats in the BOP's Central office. Supposedly they were the ones who had such an interest in my writing. I didn't know whether to believe him or put it down to a good cop/bad cop routine. I have learned that you can never trust these BOP people. But I did believe what they told me next.

"Shit runs down hill, Ferranti," SIS Tech Davenport said. "If I get a call about you and a mess ends up on my desk then that shit is running downhill and you are at the bottom." I know that is how it works in the BOP from experience. Nobody is really trying to fix a problem, just cover their ass. Like I said before, it's not about right or wrong, only about right now.

I let them know that I wasn't trying to buck the system and that I was looking for a resolution to the problem. I told them I had been in prison 240 months so far and if I got in the drug program it was 10 months and I was gone. I told them I would stop writing for publication for 10 months so I could complete the drug program and go home. They agreed this would be a good course of action for me to pursue. They agreed so quickly I wondered if I overplayed my hand and put it all on the table too soon. You never know with these people.

But they confirmed my worst fears. They told me I could end up in a Communications Management Unit (CMU), which were new experimental lockdown units the BOP had recently opened up to house Muslim radicals, ecoterrorists or anyone they wanted to keep under lock and key. This was where the BOP was now housing what they considered to be problematic prisoners.

CMU's were 24 hour lockdown units. Where prisoners were not allowed normal privileges like phone, email, visitation or programming. Everything was restricted and limited. The emphasis is put on scrutinizing and controlling the prisoners ability to communicate with the outside world.

SIA Meyers told me if I wasn't so short and on the RDAP wait list, already accepted into the program, I would have been whisked away to the CMU, with no way of stepping down or out of the restrictive environment. If this was true or a bluff I had no way of knowing, but I had already considered it as a worst case scenario considering my predicament.

SIS Tech Davenport was also very interested in what I had slated for upcoming publications. This was how I knew they were in serious damage control. I told them what I had written and who I had written it for and I told them I could probably stop any of my work from being published and they jumped on this. They also requested that I get my wife to delete everyone on her Corrlinks list that I was corresponding with. They wanted to put me out of the information business.

This contact list represented my whole network of sources all over the BOP that I had painstakingly built up over numerous years. I agreed to get my wife to delete the list and to not get any of my work published if they put me back on the compound and let me start and complete the drug program. It was a fair trade for me considering the time off I could get.

It was a sit-down and parlay where they held every advantage, but they agreed to put me back on the compound and go talk to the Drug Treatment Specialists and RDAP coordinator to let them know I would be back on the unit the next week so that I could start the program. A resolution that worked for me. Not perfect considering what I was giving up, but it benefitted me enough.

They let me call my wife right there on a speaker phone, so I could stop publication of any pieces that were slated to go up on *The Fix* and *The Daily Beast*. Also so I could tell her to delete her Corrlinks account list. I was making a sacrifice, but it was enabling me to go home in 10 months so it was worth it.

It was nice to talk to my wife and hear her voice after 22 days in the hole with no phone privileges. I told her what to do, told her I loved her and that I would be back on the compound the next week to call her and that I wanted her to come visit also. My wife has rode with me my whole bid and helped me to reach out to the world with my writing, Internet presence and books.

Before taking me back to my cell the SIS guys gave me the obligatory threats and told me they had to run the agreement up the wire to make sure it was all good. They also let me know that if I didn't uphold my end of the bargain they would bury me in SHU and make sure I didn't complete the drug program or get the year off. Just when you start thinking these guys are all right they have to flex their muscles and show you who's the boss.

I remained humble, because in reality what else could I do. Like I said 10 months was much better than 22 and my opportunities in publishing would not be lost, only delayed. And of course I could still write, I just couldn't get my pieces published until I went home. So I would be writing like crazy, getting all my pieces ready so when I finally got out of the halfway house and onto federal probation I could resume my career.

The way I feel right now is that as soon as I get out from under the BOP's jurisdiction, it's war. I am dead serious. I just have to rock these motherfuckers to sleep my last 10 months so I can get the time off for this program and go home. They have already showed me that they fear my pen game and they haven't seen anything yet. They should have just left well enough alone. That's all I have to say.

ABOUT THE AUTHOR

OUTLAW WRITER/FILMMAKER SETH FERRANTI

When Seth Ferranti received a twenty-five year LSD kingpin conviction, after faking his suicide and landing on the US Marshals Top-15 Most Wanted list in 1993, he thought his life was over. As a first time, non-violent offender, the lengthy sentence attracted media attention from *The Washington Post, Rolling Stone, The Washington Times*, and others.

Despair soon turned to drive as Seth embarked to rise above his past and focus on his future. Ferranti started penning prison and gangster stories for *VICE, Don Diva, FEDS, Hoopshype* and others from the cellblock. He went on to get three college degrees, found a publishing house Gorilla Convict, and write 22 books from behind the walls.

Released in 2015, Ferranti continued his writing career as a journalist penning pieces for *VICE, OZY, The Daily Beast, Dazed, MERRY JANE*, and features for *Penthouse* and *Real Crime Magazines*, among others. He also started writing and publishing comic books under his imprint GR1ND Studios and embarked on his true passion, filmmaking with Outlaw Films.

Ferranti wrote and directed a web-series, *Easter Bunny Assassin*, played the antagonist in an indie feature, *Dog Days*, and joined forces with Shawn Rech and Transitions Studios to make *WHITE BOY*, a feature documentary on Richard Wershe Jr. that is now airing on Netflix. Seth also starred in the season one finale of VICE's "*I Was A Teenage Felon*". In 2022 he premiered the award winning documentary *Night Life* has five films in production including *Tangled Roots, The Psychedelic Revolution* and *Dope Men*.

www.sethferranti.com

OTHER WORKS BY SETH FERRANTI

Thug Life: The True Story of Hip-Hop and Organized Crime

Criminal Escapades: A General History of the Most Notorious Gangsters

Street Legends vol. 1

Street Legends vol. 2

Prison Stories vol. 1

The Dope Game — Misadventures of Fat Cat & Pappy Mason

The Supreme Team: The Birth of Crack and Hip-Hop,
Prince's Reign of Terror and the Supreme/50 Cent Beef Exposed

Washington DC Hitman — Wayne "Silk" Perry

Rayful Edmond: Washington DC's Most Notorious Drug Lord

The Ambassador of Chocolate City — Michael "Fray" Salters

Cocaine Tales: Vol 1: The Story of Brian "Waterhead Bo" Bennett

Cocaine Tales: Vol. 2: Iron City Drug Game Tales

Junior Black Mafia — Aaron Jones

Puerto Rican James Bond — George "Boy George" Rivera

Crack, Rap, and Murder: The Cocaine Dreams of Alpho and Rich Porter
(Street Legends Book 6)

B-More Drug Lord — Anthony Jones

Street Kings of Miami - Boobie Boys

The New World of Islam — Muslim Gangsters

B-More Legend — Peanut King

Sex, Money, Murder — Peter "Pistol Pete" Rollock

The Short North Posse - Ohio Gangsters

American Gangster — Kenneth "Supreme" McGriff

The Black Godfather — Frank Matthews

Gorilla Convict: The Prison Writings of Seth Ferranti

Join our e-mail list @
www.gorillaconvict.com